Penniless Brides of Convenience

Four Regency Cinderellas say, "I do"

Orphaned sisters Eloise, Phoebe
and Estelle Brannagh grew up in the shadow of
their parents' tumultuous passion. They are now
making their own way in the world, penniless but
proud. They are looking for freedom and security—
definitely not love!

Inspired by the experience of their close friend
Kate, Lady Elmswood, they have decided
marriages of convenience are the answer. But all
four of them are about to discover that sometimes
love is found where you least expect it...

Read Eloise's story in

The Earl's Countess of Convenience

Read Phoebe's story in

A Wife Worth Investing In

And look out for Estelle's and Kate's stories,
coming soon!

Author Note

This book is my tribute to two of my favorite things: food and the film *An Affair to Remember*. If you've seen the film, my tribute will leap off the page at you in chapter one. If you haven't, why on earth not?!

I love to cook and I love to eat. One of the great things about writing is that you can create characters to live your dreams for you—and in a way, that's what Phoebe, this book's heroine, is doing. I make no apologies for the anachronisms in her culinary journey, which has little to do with the nascent nineteenth-century restaurant scene and everything to do with the twenty-first. Phoebe is initially wowed by Michelin-starred "fancy" cooking, but she's less eager to embrace the more outré side of it, whether it's ingredients that should never in a million years share a plate, or a plate of food that is more work of art than a meal. I can't imagine Phoebe putting micro salad on as a garnish with a pair of tweezers any more than she would serve up lovage ice cream with parsnip doughnuts. Phoebe, like me, prefers her food to look and smell and taste like...well, a delicious plate of food!

Does she get her happy-ever-after as well as her restaurant? Read on to find out! I hope you enjoy this serving of the Penniless Brides of Convenience series as much as I enjoyed cooking it up.

MARGUERITE KAYE

—

A Wife Worth Investing In

HARLEQUIN HISTORICAL

Recycling programs
for this product may
not exist in your area.

ISBN-13: 978-1-335-63516-7

A Wife Worth Investing In

Copyright © 2019 by Marguerite Kaye

HARLEQUIN®
www.Harlequin.com

Printed in U.S.A.

Marguerite Kaye writes hot historical romances from her home in cold and usually rainy Scotland, featuring Regency rakes, Highlanders and sheikhs. She has published over forty books and novellas. When she's not writing, she enjoys walking, cycling (but only on the level), gardening (but only what she can eat) and cooking. She also likes to knit and occasionally drink martinis (though not at the same time). Find out more on her website, margueritekaye.com.

Books by Marguerite Kaye

Harlequin Historical

Scandal at the Midsummer Ball
"The Officer's Temptation"
Scandal at the Christmas Ball
"A Governess for Christmas"

Penniless Brides of Convenience

The Earl's Countess of Convenience
A Wife Worth Investing In

Matches Made in Scandal

From Governess to Countess
From Courtesan to Convenient Wife
His Rags-to-Riches Contessa
A Scandalous Winter Wedding

Hot Arabian Nights

The Widow and the Sheikh
Sheikh's Mail-Order Bride
The Harlot and the Sheikh
Claiming His Desert Princess

Visit the Author Profile page
at Harlequin.com for more titles.

For J. My food hero, and my everything hero.
Always.

Chapter One

Paris—August 1828

Though it was long past midnight, the oppressive heat of the day had not dissipated, having been trapped by the tall, elegant buildings which lined the street down which Owen Harrington wandered aimlessly. He was not exactly lost, but nor was he quite sure where he was. Having crossed to the Rive Gauche at Notre Dame some time ago, the Seine should be somewhere on his right. He thought he'd been walking in a straight line, assumed that he was headed west, but the streets of Paris, as he had discovered to his cost several times in the last week, were not laid out in a neat grid. Instead they veered off straight at an imperceptible angle, often arriving at an unexpected destination. Rather like the locals' conversation.

He had been away from London for less than two weeks, but already felt disconnected from his life there. It had been the right decision. He was not trying to avoid the commitment his late father had made on his behalf, he planned to honour it, but he could not embrace it as his sole role in life. He still had two years' grace, time to be alone to be himself, free to do as he pleased, to discover a sense of purpose that would also accommodate his father's wishes. He had no idea what form this might take, but he was already excited by the endless possibilities waiting to be explored.

Above him the sky was inky, the stars mere pinpoints. The air, redolent of heat and dust, felt heavy, forcing him to slow his pace, encouraging him to dally. A faint beacon of light caught his attention. The lamps from a café tucked down a narrow alleyway flickered. Intrigued, for most establishments had closed their shutters hours ago, thinking a very late *digestif* might be just the thing, Owen decided to investigate.

The main room of the Procope Café was dark-panelled, smoke-filled. Two men were frowning intently over a chessboard cleared of all but five pieces. Around a large table, another group of men were disputing their bill, while a bored waiter looked on, answering Owen's mimed request for a glass of something strong with a shrug, pointing at the ceiling. He returned to the foyer and began to climb the rather elegant staircase. The first floor was silent, the doors of the rooms, presumably private dining salons, all closed, their customers either long departed or wishing to be very private indeed. A burst of laughter lured him to the top floor. The room was built into the eaves and stretched the full length of the café. Black and white tiles covered the floor, the narrow windows were flung open to the Paris night, the red-painted walls lined with banquettes which were crammed with late-night drinkers. Lamps were hung from the rafters, their muted light giving a rosy glow to the café's clientele—though perhaps that was the wine, Owen thought, which was in plentiful supply, with large earthenware jugs jostling for space on the tables.

No one paid him any attention as he stood in the open doorway. It was one of the things he liked about this city, being entirely anonymous and quite alone, lurking on the fringes, listening and watching. The French were so much more garrulous than the English. They conducted conversations at top speed, using their hands expressively, talking over each other, spinning off at tangents, around in circles, but never quite losing the thread.

There were no free seats. Disappointed, he was about to leave when two young men got up from their table. He stepped out of the doorway to let them pass, but they had stopped at another table where a woman sat alone. She had her back to the room, facing one of the open windows, and had been writing in a notebook, head bent, making it clear that she had no wish to be disturbed. Though not clear enough, it seemed. The two late-night revellers were hovering over her. He could see her shaking her head forcibly. Her posture gave the impression of youth, though he couldn't say how. Was she a courtesan? In London, there would be no doubt about it, but in Paris it seemed to be acceptable for women to dine in the cafés, to enjoy a glass of wine or a cup of coffee. Though alone, and late at night? Surely even Paris was not that decadent.

Owen looked around, but the waiter now was engaged in an altercation with one of the bill-hagglers and no one else was taking any notice of the woman's plight. One of the men took a seat beside her. She gesticulated for him to leave her alone. The other caught her arm. She leapt to her feet to try to free herself and was roughly pushed back down on to her chair. Owen was across the room before he was aware he'd made any decision to intervene. It occurred to him that he might well be embroiling himself in a dispute between a *demi-mondaine* and her clients, but it was too late to stop now, and whatever the relationship, it was clear the men's attentions were unwelcome.

Though he didn't doubt his ability to see the pair of them off, he was not particularly inclined to get into a fist fight. Hoping that the fair damsel—exceedingly fair, he noted as he arrived at the table—would instinctively follow his lead, he greeted her with a broad smile.

'I have kept you waiting,' he said in French, 'a thousand apologies, *ma chérie. Messieurs*, I am grateful to you for keeping my little cabbage company, but now I am here, I understand that you are *de trop*?'

He allowed his smile to harden as he stood over them, making sure that they could see his clenched fists but making no other move. There was a moment when the decision could have gone either way but Owen knew to wait it out, and sure enough, the man at the table shrugged and got to his feet, clapping his friend on the back and nudging him toward the door.

'Bon nuit, messieurs,' Owen said, standing his ground, keeping his gaze fixed firmly on the men until they had left, before turning back to the woman at the table. 'Will you allow me, *madame*, to keep you company just for a few moments, in case they return?'

'Please, sit down. Thank you very much, *monsieur*. May I offer you a glass of wine? Unless you prefer to drink alone?'

She smiled up at him tentatively, and Owen found himself gazing down into a face of quite dazzling beauty. Her hair was a rich burnished gold threaded with fire. Her eyes, almond-shaped, thickly lashed, seemed also golden, though he supposed hazel was the more prosaic term. She had a pert nose, a luscious mouth, and the hint of equally luscious curves under the demure neckline of her dress. If he'd had a poetic bone in his body, now would be the moment to spout some verse.

He did not spout poetry and he didn't gawk! 'No,' Owen said, rallying, 'it is merely that I did not wish to intrude, *madame*, since *you* clearly do prefer to be alone.'

'I'm waiting for someone, actually.'

'Then with your permission, I would be delighted to act as your chaperon until they arrive,' he said, taking a seat. 'Allow me to introduce myself. I am Owen Harrington.'

'Ah, you are English?'

'As English as you are, judging by your French,

which is excellent but not without accent,' Owen said, reverting with relief to his native language.

'My name is Phoebe Brannagh, and I'm actually Irish.' She poured him a glass of wine. '*À votre santé*, Mr Harrington.'

'*À la vôtre*, Mrs Brannagh.'

'It's Miss Brannagh.'

'Miss Brannagh.' He touched her glass, taking a sip of the very quaffable wine. Her voice was cultured. Her clothes were expensive, as was the little blue-enamelled watch she was consulting. Miss Phoebe Brannagh was most certainly not a member of the *demi-monde*, which made her presence here rather shocking. 'You are waiting for a friend, a relative?' he hazarded.

She snapped shut the watch, rolling her eyes as she returned it to her reticule. 'He is very late. As always,' she said ruefully. 'I'm waiting for Monsieur Pascal Solignac.'

She enunciated the name with such reverence, Owen was clearly expected to know who the gentleman in question was. 'I'm sorry, I'm afraid...'

'The celebrated chef. Perhaps you've not been in Paris long?'

'A week.'

'And you have not dined at La Grande Taverne de Londres? My goodness, where on earth have you been eating?'

'At places like this, by and large.'

'Oh, the Procope is all very well if you like honest hearty fare, but really, Mr Harrington, one comes to Paris to dine, not to eat. Have you heard of Monsieur

Beauvilliers, the author of *L'art du Cuisinier*, the bible of French gastronomy? My sister bought me one of the first English editions. Monsieur Beauvilliers's restaurant closed some years ago, following his death, but La Grande Taverne de Londres has reopened with Pascal at the helm—Pascal Solignac, I mean. He has elevated cooking to another plane and is the talk of Paris, Mr Harrington, I can't believe that you have not heard of him. Perhaps you prefer to drink rather than eat?'

'I eat to live, I'm afraid I don't live to eat, which probably makes me a culinary philistine in your eyes.'

She gave a burble of laughter. 'I love food with a passion. If it were not for the heat of the kitchen and all the running around, and being on my feet for fourteen or fifteen hours at a stretch, I should be as fat as a pig at Michaelmas.'

'Good lord, are you a chef?'

'Not yet, but I hope to be some day. I've been incredibly fortunate to find work in Pascal's kitchen for the last nine months. I'm on the patisserie station at the moment.'

Owen hardly knew what to make of this. 'I'm no expert, but I'm not aware of any female chef working in a restaurant kitchen in London.'

'It's very unusual, even in Paris. In fact, I am the only female in the brigade.'

'And how do the other staff react to having a beautiful woman in their midst, and English to boot—I beg your pardon, Irish—my point is that you are not French. Do they see you as a interloper?'

Once again, she laughed. 'I have earned my stripes

the hard way, peeling sacks of potatoes and chopping mountains of onions—that is a rite of passage in a professional kitchen, Mr Harrington. Fortunately, my eyes don't water, for I've been chopping onions and peeling potatoes since I was this height,' she said, touching the table top.

'You astonish me. It is obvious from your accent that you are well born.'

She gave a pronounced Gallic shrug. 'Oh, I'm born well enough, I suppose, though what matters to me is not the colour of the blood in my veins but my determination to live life to the full. In that sense, I take after my mother.'

'So she approves of your being here?'

Her face fell. 'I believe she would, if she were alive, but I lost both my parents and my little brother six years ago. I hope she would have been proud of me, for I've already achieved far more than I expected in such a short time. In a restaurant kitchen, you know, a strict hierarchy exists. You have to earn your place, and any promotion. To reach patisserie in just nine months is almost unheard of. To be honest, there are days when I have to pinch myself to make sure I'm not dreaming.'

There was pride in her voice and a gleam in her eye. 'You are obviously passionate about your chosen vocation,' Owen said, a little enviously.

Miss Brannagh beamed. 'It is all I've ever wanted, all I've ever dreamed of—and that's all it was, until last year, a pipedream. Were it not for my sister's generosity, I wouldn't be here, learning from Pascal.'

Pascal. It was not only admiration that he could

hear in her voice, Miss Brannagh was in thrall to her mentor. Lucky man, Owen thought. He hoped Monsieur Solignac, who he had already irrationally and instantly taken a dislike to, appreciated his protégée and did not take advantage of her obvious reverence for him. 'The same sister who gave you the famous recipe book?'

'Yes, Eloise my eldest sister. The Countess of Fearnoch.' Miss Brannagh chuckled. 'Goodness, I still find it quite strange, calling her that. She made a most *excellent* marriage just over a year ago, which allowed her to settle a small fortune on myself and Estelle.'

'Another sister?'

'My twin.' Miss Brannagh's smile softened. 'We were a such a close-knit little group until recently—the Elmswood Coven, Estelle called us—myself, Eloise, Estelle and Aunt Kate—she is Lady Elmswood and our aunt by marriage. She very kindly took us in when we lost our parents and there we lived, cosily and very contentedly for five years, until Eloise's wedding.'

'I presume that the appeal of cosy and contented began to wane?'

Miss Brannagh chuckled. 'Though I love Aunt Kate with all my heart, why on earth would I choose to stay in the wilds of Shropshire when I could come to Paris and chase rainbows?'

Chasing rainbows, wasn't that exactly what he was doing, Owen thought, utterly charmed. 'What pot of gold lies at the end of your rainbow, may I ask? Becoming the top chef in Paris?'

'I aim to become the *second-best* chef and part-owner of the pre-eminent restaurant in Paris, along with Pascal.' Miss Brannagh's smile faded slightly. 'The proprietor of La Grande Taverne de Londres is just a little too traditional in his thinking for Pascal, you see. Our intention is to buy him out, so that Pascal's genius can flourish unhindered, and if he will not sell, then we will buy new premises and start from scratch together.'

'You will not mind playing second fiddle to Monsieur Solignac, then?'

'It will be an honour! I will never supersede Pascal, he is a—a maverick genius and what's more, he enjoys being in the public eye—whether it is chatting to diners or talking about his menus to the press. Estelle, my twin, would excel at that sort of thing, and even Eloise—for she is so confident, and takes after Aunt Kate. But I much prefer to avoid the limelight, and am happiest behind a stove.'

'As a lone female in a kitchen though, you must have to fight to hold your own.'

'Oh, that is a different matter all together, for the kitchen is my milieu. But I have never been confident among strangers.'

'I am a stranger, and you seem—forgive me—perfectly at ease with me.'

She flushed. 'You are my knight errant. Besides, there is something about you—but you're probably thinking I have talked too much. I have. I do beg your pardon.'

'I am very much enjoying our conversation. I have

never met anyone like you, Miss Brannagh, you are quite unique.'

'I'm a twin, so actually one of a pair.'

'Are you identical twins, you and your sister?'

'Oh, no, though we look very alike. Estelle is much more talented than I. As well as being an extremely accomplished musician, she is a bit of an actress—a mimic. I'm not any sort of performer.'

'What does she think of your ambition to become the *second*-best chef in Paris?'

'Estelle—oh, Estelle, I have lately realised, has a much more conventional outlook on life than I, but she'll come round.' She took another sip of wine, frowning slightly. 'Do you have any sisters or brothers, Mr Harrington? No? Well, the thing about sisters is that they think they know you better than you know yourself, and in a way they do, but they can also—they assume things, you see. I am younger than Estelle by twenty minutes, which makes me officially the baby of the family, since we lost our poor little brother. They think, Estelle and Eloise, that I need protecting, that my cooking is just a hobby. They have not said so outright, indeed Eloise never would for she was determined her gift came without strings, but I know they both believe my coming here is a mistake.'

'But you hope to prove them wrong? By the sounds of it, you are already doing so.'

'Do you think so? I tell myself I'm doing well. In fact I know I am doing so extraordinarily well, I've astonished myself. I wish my sisters shared your confidence in me, but in time, they will come to see that I've made the right decision to flee the comfort of the nest.'

'All the same, for one who hasn't been abroad much in the world, to come to Paris on your own must have been a daunting prospect.'

'A baptism of fire—the kitchen was, at any rate. But as for Paris—oh, I fell in love with Paris almost from the first moment. The way of life suits me, it is so very, very different from England. I love my sisters and Aunt Kate, but they are such strong women. I have always lived in the shadow of their low expectations, you know?'

'I do,' Owen agreed wholeheartedly. 'Though I don't have any close family, I have a reputation which I'm rather tired of living down to.'

'My own feelings exactly! I hope that Paris suits you as well as it does me, Mr Harrington. It is the most beautiful city one could ever imagine. I spend every Sunday exploring, following my nose, drinking coffee in cafés, sitting in the parks just watching people stroll by. I play a game with myself,' she said sheepishly. 'I like to guess what their favourite foods are.'

'And what would you guess mine would be?'

'*Rosbif* is what any Frenchman would immediately say, but you are very far from being a typical Englishman.' She studied him, her hazel eyes gleaming like gold, her chin resting on her hand. 'I'd say you prefer breakfast to dinner. Eggs, coddled or perhaps scrambled with cream, delicate but delicious. A ham, boiled in spices and served cold. Fresh rolls and salty butter. Coffee. Am I right?'

'Even if you were wrong, you make it sound so delicious that I would change my preference for a dinner of venison stew immediately'

'Now it's your turn. What do I like to eat?'

He took the opportunity to study her as she had him, struck afresh by her lush beauty, which so perfectly complemented her charm. 'Supper,' he said, smiling, 'definitely supper, at the end of a long day when you have finished serving dinner to your clientele. Asparagus with a hollandaise sauce and perhaps a lightly poached egg, and a glass of champagne. Essentially English, but with a soupçon of French flair—though I know you're Irish. How am I doing?'

She laughed. 'I shall return the compliment, Mr Harrington. Even if you are quite wrong, you make me long to have it. You see, it's a good game, isn't it? I can while away hours playing it and don't mind at all sitting by myself to do so. I love the fact that no one knows who I am, far less cares. In Paris, for the first time in my life, I can be completely myself without having to consider anyone else—on my Sundays off, at any rate.'

'You wander Paris alone?'

'Yes, and I love it. Pascal spends his Sundays either experimenting with dishes or catching up on his sleep. Even if I wanted company, I have no acquaintances outside the kitchen, there's been no time to make friends. But I don't need them. It is—it is *liberating*, being alone after always being Estelle's other, younger half. That sounds terrible, I love my sister—both my sisters—with all my heart and I know they are only being protective but they smother me a little and patronise me just a little too.'

'So you want to cast off the shackles?'

'Yes! Exactly! You do understand.'

'I do indeed. I was thinking something similar just before I stumbled upon this café. And I'm very glad I did stumble upon it. Very glad too—if you will forgive my saying—that Monsieur Solignac is so tardy.'

Monsieur Solignac, who by the sound of it was more than just a friend to the beguiling Miss Brannagh, Owen thought, his animosity towards this *maverick genius* increasing.

'I take it he does not have the wherewithal to set himself up in business?' he asked.

'No,' Miss Brannagh answered sunnily, entirely unaware of his scepticism. 'Pascal has the reputation, I have the financial means. That is what I call serendipity.'

Almost too good to be true from the Frenchman's perspective, Owen thought as she took out her watch again, frowning at the time.

'He has clearly become absorbed while practising a new dish. It is only after service has finished that he can try out his ideas. Though the dishes he serves are exquisite, they are in essence traditional receipts tweaked with his own flourishes. Classic cuisine with a twist, so to speak, but when we have our own establishment, we will serve food such as the world has never imagined, never mind tasted.'

'And while he creates, you must wait here patiently?'

'Genius must be indulged,' she said, bristling slightly. 'And nurtured too.'

To be nurtured by Miss Phoebe Brannagh was an appealing prospect, Owen thought, regretfully. He had not felt so drawn to a woman in a long time. If only they had met under different circumstances, he'd have made a concerted effort to get to know her better. Captivating, that was the word he'd been looking for, not only in her looks, but in her outlook. She had a true *joie de vivre*, as if she was reaching out and embracing life—a feeling he had lost. He felt jaded, and had travelled abroad to rediscover a sense of purpose, a zest for life, a freshness. She was brave and she was bold. He admired her audacious attitude.

'I wish you every success,' Owen said, raising his glass. The words were a hackneyed toast, but he found that he meant them.

'Thank you,' Miss Brannagh touched her glass to his. He noticed her hands for the first time, the nails cut brutally short, the skin work-roughened, scored with tiny cuts and burn marks. Catching his eyes on them, she snatched them away, hiding them under the table. 'Testament to my trade,' she said, clearly embarrassed.

'Testament to my lack of purpose,' Owen said, holding up his own.

'Goodness, you have a sculptor's hands. Such beautifully long fingers.'

'I don't have an artistic bone in my body. I prefer more physical pursuits.'

Miss Brannagh sipped her wine, smiling. 'It is so nice to converse in English, and though I love being in Paris, I do miss chatting with Estelle and Eloise and Aunt Kate. But I have talked far too much about myself. Tell me what brings you to my adopted city, Mr Harrington.'

'Let me see if I can attract the waiter's attention first and order us another *pichet*. The man seems determined to ignore me. Excuse me, but I think it might be quicker if I go and buttonhole him.'

Phoebe watched the Englishman cross the room and accost the waiter. Had she been indiscreet? Had he guessed that she and Pascal were lovers? Her affaire was so very recent, so much part of her new life here in this exciting city, she hadn't thought how it might appear to anyone else. Had she betrayed her feelings for Pascal in her enthusiasm for him? Mr Harrington had said nothing, but now she wondered what he'd thought of her, sitting alone drinking wine in a café in the early hours of the morning. He had treated her with perfect courtesy. He was certainly surprised to discover her reasons for being here, but he seemed intrigued rather than shocked.

Most people would think her affaire was scandalous. It was why she'd been very careful in how she described Pascal in her letters to Eloise and to Aunt Kate. She had been much more frank with Estelle, thinking that her twin would understand, but to her astonishment, Estelle had taken the very same attitude that she'd guessed Eloise would, if she knew the truth. Instead of lauding Phoebe's daring, she had been appalled, drawing some very unflattering parallels with Mama.

Poor Mama. Phoebe had always known that Eloise didn't understand her, and to be fair, their eldest sister had borne the brunt of Mama's rather careless attitude towards her children. But Mama was a free spirit. Eloise couldn't see how trapped she must have been, by the bonds of matrimony and the expectations of society. It was tragic, for the terrible mismatch that was their parents' marriage made both Mama and Papa very unhappy, and it could not be denied that their children suffered too, but Mama was such a very bright and particular star, it was quite wrong to judge her by the usual standards. To keep such a glamorous, wild creature confined was like imprisoning a beautiful butterfly in a bell jar. Eloise had never understood this but Phoebe had, and she'd assumed that Estelle did too though they never discussed it, out of respect for their elder sister's views.

But Estelle's response to Phoebe's shy confession of her affaire with Pascal had made her position very clear. She imagined Phoebe was in thrall to Pascal rather than in love with him, as if she was blind and had no mind of her own. And she had been rather scathing on the subject of Pascal's involvement too, to the point where Phoebe had even begun to doubt whether he could really be in love with her. She had never in a thousand years expected Pascal to notice her, yet from the first he had seemed to rate her in the kitchen, and he'd made it clear that he found her attractive. She had been hugely flattered, had expected his interest to wane with time, but it had increased. Estelle was wrong. The bond between them was special. It hurt, that her twin didn't understand that, but Estelle obviously hadn't inherited any of Mama's free spirit, so there was no point in trying to sway her. When she came to Paris and saw for herself how deliriously happy Phoebe was, and what a success she was making of her life, she would stop trying to persuade her to come home, but until then, they'd have to agree to differ.

In future, she would be a little more careful in her letters to Estelle. She would definitely not be telling her of this encounter for a start, Phoebe thought, smiling back at Mr Harrington as he returned, armed triumphantly with a new *pichet* of wine. Even though she had eyes only for Pascal, she was not blind to the Englishman's attractions. Although his dark blond hair and cornflower-blue eyes made him look more Norse god than English gentleman, an impression initially formed by the way he'd strode across the room to her rescue earlier, heedless of the fact that he was outnumbered. He was dressed with the kind of careless elegance that only the very rich and the supremely confident can carry off, and there was in his smile a kind of devil-may-care recklessness. Was she being fanciful? No, the term dangerously attractive might have been invented for him.

In fact, if it were not for Pascal, she would be very tempted to spend more time in Owen Harrington's company, while he was in Paris. He had none of Pascal's Gallic flamboyance, a characteristic which Phoebe very occasionally and most disloyally felt teetered over into arrogance. She certainly couldn't imagine Mr Harrington waxing lyrical in the middle of a market over the first ceps of the year, or tearing his hair if they had already sold out, but then she couldn't imagine Pascal rescuing her with such finesse from those two men who had accosted her. Pascal would have come charging over waving his fists and shouting, drawing the attention of everyone in the room to her plight. If he actually noticed she was being harassed in the first place, that is. While Mr Harrington had acted with a quiet self-confidence that was far more effective and infinitely more discreet. Though he was very far from being the stuffed shirt that the Parisians imagined all English gentlemen to be, he was clearly very much a gentleman. Paris would take to him, and he to Paris, Phoebe reckoned. It was a shame, she thought, as he sat back down beside her, that she would not be party to it.

'*Santé,*' Phoebe said, touching her fresh glass to his. 'Now, you were going to tell me what it is that brings you to Paris?'

'To quote the dictionary man, Dr Johnson, when a man is tired of London he is tired of life.' He stared down at his wine, swirling his glass. 'I'm here because I'm sick of both London and my life there, but that makes me sound like an over-indulged, arrogant narcissist.'

'What is the truth?'

'That I'm chasing rainbows, like you, though I don't have any particular pot of gold in mind as yet. I want to—not so much discover who I am as who I might become. Lord, that really does sound pompous.'

'No, it sounds exciting.'

He laughed wryly. 'Excitingly vague. I envy you your certainty and your verve. You know what you want, and you don't care if you have to flout convention to achieve it. I can't tell you how refreshing that is, and how much I admire you for it.'

'You make me sound like a rebel.'

'I think you are, even if you don't realise it. I have always thought myself a bit of a rebel, but I simply behave badly in the conventional manner of spoiled, rich young men. You have widened my horizons already, Miss Brannagh. Until now, I've never had any ambition other than to enjoy myself.'

'Goodness, how lucky you are to be able to indulge yourself.'

'I inherited a fortune from my father, who died ten years ago when I was sixteen. Since I came of age, I have been the toast of society, both high and low. If one pays heed to the scandal sheets I am the richest, the wildest, the wittiest, most handsome, most daring, man in London. My presence can make or break a dinner party or a ball. I never refuse a dare and have never suffered anything worse than a broken wrist in doing so. In a nutshell, for all of my twenty-six years, I've lived a charmed existence. Or so my best friend, Jasper, tells me. What I've come to wonder, these last few months, is whether what I'm living is actually a feckless and shallow one.'

'Good heavens,' Phoebe exclaimed, taken aback and extremely intrigued. 'Are you being entirely serious?'

'I am never serious, unless it's regarding something trivial.'

'Estelle, my twin, does that,' Phoebe said. 'Resorts to sarcasm when she's embarrassed, I mean, or when she's talking about something that she cares deeply about.'

'My problem is that I don't care very deeply about anything.'

'That can't be true!'

'No less an authority than *John Bull* magazine described me as "a dedicated hedonist with a penchant for death-defying dares, who cares for naught but funning."'

Was he teasing her? There was an edge to his smile though. 'Save that you are bored with having fun and have come to Paris to—I'm sorry, I still don't know what specifically you hope to gain from your visit?'

'No more do I, Miss Brannagh, save that it is a very different city from London, and I am already glad that I decided to visit, since I have made your acquaintance. If only you lacked the funds for your restaurant, I would offer to go into business with you, but sadly for me, you can already finance your dream.'

'Then fund your own dream. You must have one, Mr Harrington. Everyone has a dream.'

'Do they?' He threw the contents of his glass down his throat in one gulp. 'I am living most people's dream, and it bores me rigid. I am carefree and I couldn't care less. I'm an *ungrateful* over-indulged, arrogant narcissist, for there is a part of me that wishes I had not been so blessed, then I may have had something to live for.'

'You should be careful what you wish for, Mr Harrington,' Phoebe retorted, 'and grateful for what you have.'

'Well said, Miss Brannagh. You are quite right, of course. I need a purpose in life. Though what form that will take, and whether I will discover it in Paris, or Venice, or St Petersburg or Vienna, I have no idea.'

'Why look so close to home? If you are as rich as you claim, you could try the Antipodes, or Brazil, or Argentina.'

'Or China, perhaps? I'll tell you what, why don't we meet here in—say, a year's time, and I shall unveil the new, improved Owen Harrington to you, and you can then invite me to dine at your new restaurant, which by then will be the toast of Paris.'

'I'm not sure that a year will be sufficient for either to have happened.'

'Two years then. Are we agreed?'

His smile was infectious. 'Two years to the day,' Phoebe said, smiling back. 'You have my word, Mr Harrington.'

He took out a gold case, handing her a card from it. 'And you have mine. Take this, in the unlikely event you need to get in touch before then, to break our assignation, which I sincerely hope does not happen. Otherwise I look forward very much to seeing you again.'

She put the card in her reticule, smiling at the absurdity of it. He poured the dregs of the wine. They raised their glasses in a toast, and their eyes met, and the oddest thing happened. It felt as if time stopped. As if the room and the people in it melted away. And there was only the two of them.

'Phoebe!'

She leapt to her feet, spilling her wine. 'Pascal!'

'Who the hell is this?'

Mr Harrington was on his feet, making a bow. 'Owen Harrington. I met Miss Brannagh quite by accident, but it was a happy coincidence, for I was able to bring her news of her sister, the Countess of Fearnoch, with whom I am acquainted. How do you do, Monsieur Solignac.'

Pascal gave a short bow. He was frowning suspiciously at Mr Harrington. 'Mr Harrington didn't like the idea of my sitting alone so late at night,' Phoebe said. 'He was kindly keeping me company until you arrived.'

'I am grateful to him, but I am here now.'

Mortified by his aggressive tone, Phoebe would have remonstrated, but Mr Harrington was already taking his leave. *'Monsieur,'* he said, making a brief bow. 'Miss Brannagh,' he said, pressing her hand briefly. *'Adieu.'*

He threw some notes on to the table, enough to have paid for all the wine for the entire room for the evening, then with a curt nod, he left.

Despite her lover's arrival, Phoebe was suddenly despondent, and disappointed to have her encounter with Mr Harrington cut short in such a brusque manner. 'I am tired,' she said. 'It's very late, I've had more than enough wine and I want to go home.'

Chapter Two

London—October 1830

Phoebe stepped out of the hackney cab that had transported her from the posting house and gazed apprehensively at the imposing town house. The front door was painted a glossy black, the brass knocker and bell pull brightly polished. She shivered, pulling her cloak around her. It had been sunny when she left Paris, but the rain had set in at Calais, and had poured down relentlessly ever since, reflecting her mood.

She checked her watch needlessly. It was just after ten in the morning. Far too early to be calling on anyone. The shutters of the town house were not closed, which meant someone was in residence, but not necessarily the person she sought. So much could have happened in the intervening two years. He might have changed address. He could be married and settled. It was perfectly possible he was still travelling the world.

He could even be dead, for all she knew. After all,

he hadn't turned up at the Procope café in August as arranged. She'd told herself that it was ridiculous of her to expect him to, that their so-called assignation had been light-hearted banter, nothing more, but she'd gone anyway, three nights in a row. When each night ended without him making an appearance she had been bitterly and quite disproportionately disappointed. She had been so eager to hear what he'd made of his life, fervently hoping it would counterbalance the disaster which constituted her own. She had tried hard not to attach undue significance to his failure to turn up, but it had felt like the last straw, a signal to cut and run. Though she had struggled on for another few weeks, in her head, his non-appearance marked the end of her dream.

Which was one of the reasons why she was here, hoping against hope that Mr Harrington had succeeded where she had so signally failed. Though he probably wouldn't even remember their brief encounter in Paris, she thought despondently. If by some miracle he was in residence and did agree to see her, there was every chance that he'd look straight through her, as if confronted by a complete stranger. Which, in essence, she was.

A footman was eyeing her cagily from the steps of a house across the street. She probably looked suspicious loitering in this genteel locale unaccompanied. Phoebe climbed the first step. If Mr Harrington was not here—oh, God, no, she couldn't bear to think of the alternative. *Please let him be here*, she whispered to herself. *Please.*

The footman was making his way across the street to accost her. Phoebe climbed the remainder of the shallow steps and rang the bell.

The door was opened just a crack by a stern, elderly servant. 'May I help you?' he asked, making it clear that he thought it very unlikely that he could.

She held out the worn card which had lain in the recesses of her reticule for over two years. 'Does Mr Harrington still live here?'

'Yes, but I'm afraid he does not receive visitors.'

Startled, she was about to ask why ever not, when the man made to close the door in her face. 'Please, will you ask him if he will make an exception for me?' Phoebe said urgently. 'My name is Miss Phoebe Brannagh. From Paris, tell him, the young lady from the Procope Café.'

'Phoebe Brannagh,' Owen repeated.

'The young lady wasn't sure if you would remember her,' his butler informed him, careful to keep his expression bland. 'You met in Paris, apparently.'

Not long before his life had changed for ever, in fact. 'Our paths did cross,' Owen said, 'but I can't possibly see her.'

Propped up in bed, his hands hidden under the sheets, he rubbed the extensive scarring on the backs of them compulsively. Phoebe Brannagh! His thoughts often drifted back to their encounter in the Procope. Beautiful, passionate, ambitious and determined, she was unforgettable. He had left the café that night inspired, invigorated, full of optimism for the future, not

exactly full of plans but certainly full of determination. He had recalled, many times since, her words of
caution when he had so foolishly bemoaned his privileged lifestyle. *'You should be careful what you wish
for, Mr Harrington,'* she had said, *'and grateful for
what you have.'*

Such prescient words. In the months which followed, in the aftermath, how often he had wished he'd
heeded them earlier, returned to London, satisfied with
his lot. He might have remained feckless and shallow,
but at least he'd have still been himself.

'No,' he repeated, 'I can't possibly see her, it is out
of the question.'

'Very well, sir. Shall I convey the usual message?'

The usual message. That Mr Harrington was not at
home to callers under any circumstances. Owen hesitated on the brink of assent. What on earth was she
doing here, in London? He had wondered, back in August, if she had honoured their assignation. Though it
was impossible for him to make the journey he'd still
felt guilty, picturing her sitting on her own up in that
top room of the Procope sipping wine and waiting for
him, just as she had waited patiently, night after night,
for Solignac. Had she realised her dream of opening
her own restaurant? Were she and the chef who had her
under his spell still sharing both a kitchen and a bed?
For his part, he fervently hoped not the latter. The little
he'd seen and heard of the man had made him certain
Miss Brannagh deserved a great deal better.

Why was she here now? It was ludicrous to imagine her concern for him, sparked by his failure to turn

up in August as agreed, had brought her all the way to England, though if the boot had been on the other foot, he might well have done just that, for he had imagined their second meeting countless times. During the darkest days, when the memory of her zest for life had been a small beacon of light, he had imagined himself well, fit, successful. Happy. He had dreamed up endless versions of how his life had turned out, picturing himself recounting them to her in the cosy light of the Procope, a *pichet* of wine and two half-empty glasses on the table.

What had she achieved in the last two years? Now he had the opportunity to find out, was he really going to pass it up? He was genuinely curious, which was a refreshing change from his increasing indifference to the world and its inhabitants. *Miss* Phoebe Brannagh, she had declared herself, though that didn't necessarily mean she wasn't married, merely that it was the name he would recognise. The chances that she had abandoned the kitchens for an easier, more prosaic life were high, but Owen hoped Phoebe had remained true to her highly individual self, and beaten the odds. The more abjectly he felt he had failed, the more fervently he had hoped that she had found success in Paris.

Though if she had, then why was she here? Her family lived in England, he recalled. It could be that she was visiting, and on a whim had decided to look him up. But why hadn't she written to ask if she could call, if that was the case? And why call at such an early hour? In the old days, he'd have been up since dawn, would have gone for a ride or a run with Jasper while the roads were quiet, or he'd have had a fencing lesson, a shooting lesson, put in some time sparring or at the gymnasium. He could barely recall those days now. When he did, it was as if it was a dream, as if it had all happened to a different person.

Which it had. He was utterly changed in every way. His accident had destroyed him physically. He had battled back for a while, regaining some measure of mobility, but the slough of despond he was sinking into of late was like a pool of black tar, slowly smothering him. His world was muffled, devoid of any feeling, and not even on his best days, when he could just about recognise the importance of not throwing in the towel, did he feel any inclination to take action. He couldn't possibly let Miss Brannagh see him in this sorry and broken state.

Though he wanted to see her. Hearing about her success might just act as a balm for his malaise. It was a ridiculous notion, to imagine that her triumph could offset his disaster, but it might, it just might make him feel a tiny bit better, even give him the kick up the backside he required. And if he didn't see her, he'd always wonder, wouldn't he, what had become of her?

'Wait,' he called to Bremner, who hadn't in fact moved. 'Have her shown to the breakfast parlour. Light the fire there, and in the morning room. Offer her tea. Food. She likes food. Offer her breakfast. Tell her I will join her presently. I need a bath.'

His butler rushed to do his bidding, failing to hide his astonishment, for visitors, Miss Braidwood's du-

tiful calls aside, were unheard of these days. Owen
slumped back on his pillows, already having to fight
the urge to change his mind. It hadn't been one of his
better weeks. He'd barely crawled out of bed since that
last depressing visit from Olivia. He rubbed his jaw,
averting his eyes from his un-gloved hands. He needed
a shave. He was going to have to work a minor miracle to make himself look even halfway respectable.

Pushing back the bedclothes, Owen placed his feet
gingerly on the ground, gritting his teeth as the familiar searing pain shot through his right leg. He had
abandoned the exercises prescribed by his doctors. The
regime had succeeded to a point, but he'd long ago hit
a plateau. He'd been an athlete once. Those simple, tedious stretches, which were the limit of what his doctors thought he could manage, reminded him that he
never would be again.

Dammit, he was not using his stick. It was always
worst first thing, he simply had to endure it. He took
a faltering step, cursing the grinding pain in his hip,
forcing another step and another, slowly making his
way to the new bathing room he'd had installed, locking the door securely behind him. It was an unneces-
sary act, as he had no valet, and all the household knew
not to intrude on him on pain of death, but it made him
feel better all the same.

The breakfast served to her was good plain fare, but
though she had not eaten properly for days, Phoebe
could only manage a few desultory forkfuls of eggs
and ham. She drank an entire pot of tea though. Tea

didn't taste the same in Paris, somehow. The different water probably accounted for it. She was gratefully accepting a boiling kettle to brew a fresh pot and wondering what could be keeping Mr Harrington, and why on earth he did not receive visitors, when the door to the breakfast parlour opened and he finally appeared.

She was so shocked that for a moment she couldn't move from her place at the table. He looked as if he had aged ten years. His hair had darkened, he wore it considerably longer than before, and he had lost a good deal of weight. Lines were etched between his nose and his mouth, and more lines fanned out from the corners of his eyes, which were darkly shadowed. Nature had given him excellent bones, and the loss of weight, instead of making him look gaunt, drew attention to his razor-sharp cheekbones, and to the clean lines of his jaw. He was still a very handsome man, but missing the ready smile and easy charm that had previously complemented his looks, the impression he now gave was forbidding, almost intimidating.

Belatedly, Phoebe got to her feet, making her way to the door where Mr Harrington remained stationery. 'Good morning. I'm so sorry to intrude on you so early.' Her smile faltered. 'I wasn't even sure that you'd remember me, until your butler offered me breakfast, which he wouldn't have done if I was a complete stranger.'

'Miss Brannagh, I have never forgotten that night, or you.' Her host sketched a bow. 'Please, finish eating.'

'I have done, thank you, but I am happy to sit while you partake.'

'I have ordered coffee, that will suffice for me.'

She had preceded him back to the table. Only as she resumed her seat did she notice his pronounced limp and the spasm of pain that crossed his face as he put his right foot down. 'You're hurt. Here, let me…'

He yanked a chair out and sat down heavily. 'Thank you, but I prefer to manage for myself.'

The stern butler arrived bearing a silver pot of coffee, which he poured immediately before leaving them alone, and which Mr Harrington drank back in a single gulp, without bothering to add either sugar or cream. He was wearing gloves. Tan gloves, tightly fitted, so she hadn't noticed them at first.

'Would you like some ham? Eggs?' Phoebe said, making a conscious effort not to stare.

He poured himself a second cup, this time taking a smaller sip. 'Thank you, no. I find I do not have much of an appetite these days.' He eyed her half-empty plate. 'Not up to your exacting standards, Miss Brannagh?'

'I'm not very hungry either.'

His complexion was pale. The man she remembered had been glowing with health. This man looked careworn, the lines on his face, she deduced, carved by pain.

'You look shocked. Aren't you going to ask what happened to me?'

'I get the strong impression you'd much prefer that I didn't.'

He drained his cup. 'I had an accident. My recuperation has been prolonged. As you can see for yourself, I am not the man I once was. And that is all there is to be said.'

Or at least, all that he *would* say. He wanted neither
pity nor curiosity, that much was clear. Phoebe bit back
her questions, opting instead for frankness. 'As you
have no doubt deduced from my appearance at your
door at this most unfashionable hour Mr Harrington,
my circumstances have also changed since we last met.'

'Really?' He pushed his saucer to one side, wincing
as he shifted in his chair to stretch his leg out, before
turning his attention back to her, his frown deepening as he did so. 'Actually,' he said, 'I can see that you
are different. It is as if the light has gone out of you.
You can have no idea how sorry I am to see that. I had
hoped that at least one of us would have been toasting
their success in August.'

'You remembered!'

'Of course I did, and would have been there if it
had been humanly possible, but as you can see, I'm
in no condition to travel to the other side of the street,
far less Paris.'

'I went,' Phoebe admitted sheepishly. 'To the Procope. I hoped—' She broke off, colouring.

'You hoped as I did, that at least one of us would
have something to toast. I take it then, that you do not?'

'No.'

'What happened?'

The sheer magnitude of recent events threatened
to overwhelm her. She could not possibly ask him for
help, not when he was so obviously enduring his own
private hell. Phoebe got to her feet. 'I wish you well
with your recovery, but I really shouldn't intrude any
longer.'

'Miss Brannagh, please wait.'

She was at the door, about to open it when a crash and a shouted oath made her whirl around. Mr Harrington was on his feet, but only just, clutching the edge of the table. His cup and saucer and the coffee pot were on the floor.

'Spare me the indignity of having to call my butler to prevent you leaving.'

'You have troubles of your own. I have no wish to further burden you with my tale of woe.'

He held out his hand, his voice softening marginally. 'Then distract me from mine by recounting yours. If you can bear to.'

Miss Brannagh stepped reluctantly back into the room. Stooping to pick up the shattered fragments of crockery and the coffee pot, she paused, cast him an enquiring look, then completed the task when Owen reluctantly assented. His servants would see yet more evidence of his clumsiness, albeit neatly stacked on the table and not abandoned on the floor, but they were used to it by now. At least the coffee pot had been empty. 'Thank you,' he said as she sat back down across the table from him.

'You haven't eaten anything. It's not good to start the day on an empty stómach.'

'The food won't go to waste, the kitchen staff get any leftovers.'

'I am pleased to hear that, but it wasn't my point.'

'I am not a child who needs cajoled into eating, Miss Brannagh. You cannot fix me with coddled eggs.' He regretted the words as soon as they were out, but it was too late to take them back. Owen sighed, exasperated. 'Very well, I will take some of the damned— dashed eggs.'

She smiled at him encouragingly. 'And perhaps just a sliver of this lovely ham?'

Lacking the will or energy to deny her, he shrugged, studying her as she set about creating a plate of breakfast for him that he had no appetite for. Her smile had momentarily lit up her face, reminding him of the glowing beauty he'd met in Paris, and making the changes in her so much more stark by comparison. She was dressed simply and elegantly in a grey travelling gown, but it hung loosely on her slender frame. He remembered her laughingly telling him how much she loved to eat. He remembered her figure as generous, like her smile. She had lost weight, and he was, unfortunately, willing to bet that it had not been down to working in the heat of the kitchen. As she handed him his plate—like an offering, he thought—smiling at him tentatively, pleadingly, it struck him that what she'd lost most was her confidence. Exactly as he'd said, the light had gone out in her. Ironically, since their paths had parted they had arrived at the same destination, not success but despair.

He eyed the dish she presented him with, the wafer-thin slices of ham curled elegantly into rosettes, the eggs topped with a knob of melting butter, two slices of bread, the crusts removed, cut into delicate triangles. He really didn't want it, but he didn't want to seem churlish by refusing. 'Thank you, Miss Brannagh, this looks most appetising,' Owen said, awkwardly picking up his knife and fork.

'They say we eat with our eyes. Presentation is much underrated by most cooks. It is one of the first things I learned from—shall I have your butler bring fresh coffee?'

He shook his head.

'In Paris, the juice of freshly squeezed oranges is often served in the morning, but the French don't really take breakfast seriously as a meal the way we do. Are you sure you don't want some fresh coffee with that? Or perhaps—perhaps I should simply be quiet and allow you to eat. I talk too much when I'm nervous.'

Her mouth trembled. When she poured herself some more tea, her hand shook. What the devil had happened to her! He'd wager her revered Solignac had some hand in it. He had already taken against the man before he'd finally turned up late at the Procope, and his appearance in the flesh had simply confirmed Owen's dislike. An ill-mannered bully with an inflated sense of his own importance who took his lover for granted.

He forced the last mouthful of breakfast down, and was rewarded with a smile.

'You see, you were hungry after all.'

'Apparently,' he said drily.

'The eggs were a little over. It is very difficult to keep eggs from spoiling, but the simple solution is to add a little knob of butter, I don't know why more people don't realise it. Forgive me, the last thing you need is a culinary lecture.'

Owen pushed his plate away and eased himself carefully to his feet, biting the inside of his cheek as the anticipated fierce stab of pain shot through his damaged hip. 'We'll retire to the morning room, if you are finished with your tea. It is the second door on your left.'

Ushering her ahead of him, he followed her slowly, resisting the urge to use the wall for support, mortified by how vulnerable he felt without his stick. He would not fall over. He bloody well would *not* fall over.

Lowering himself into the wing-back chair by the fireside, he felt as if he'd completed an epic journey, closing his eyes, taking a moment to get his breathing under control, wondering if the doctors had been right after all, and that the pathetic and rudimentary exercise regime at least served to prevent his health from deteriorating further. The footstool was just out of reach, but as Miss Brannagh made to help, he nudged it towards himself with his good leg.

'Thank you, but I'm not entirely helpless.'

He waved her to the chair opposite, where she sat, hands clasped tightly, on the edge of the seat. 'I'm sorry.'

'Stop apologising. Please.' Adjusting his foot on the stool, he tried to force a smile, but it felt strained, and probably looked more like a grimace. 'Now, Miss Brannagh, that we are more comfortable, to what do I owe the pleasure of your company?'

'Well first of all—I know it's silly—but when you didn't show up at the Procope I wondered why. I hoped that whatever your reason for not being there, that you had fared better than me.'

'Then you have been sorely disappointed, I'm

afraid. I assume you are on your way to visit one of your sisters or—did you say you had an aunt?'

'Aunt Kate. Lady Elmswood. She lives in Shropshire.' She gazed down at her hands, which were white at the knuckles, she was clasping them so tightly together. 'I'm not planning on visiting family just at the moment.'

'Then may I ask what has brought you to England—assuming that your concern for my non-appearance at the Procope in August is not the main reason.'

She took a visible breath. 'The truth is that I have lost absolutely everything, including almost every penny of the settlement Eloise made on me. I could not have failed more abjectly and I can't—I simply cannot face my family until I've found my feet again.'

'Good lord! What on earth happened?'

'Exactly what my sister Estelle predicted.'

'Monsieur Solignac,' Owen said, fatalistically.

'You don't sound very surprised.'

'I wish I had misjudged him, Miss Brannagh.'

'You cannot wish that more fervently than I.'

'Tell me.'

She winced. 'It sounds as if you have already guessed. I was dazzled by him. Everyone was, who came into contact with him—everyone that is, save Estelle and by the sounds of it, yourself. I thought myself the luckiest woman in the world to have been taken under his wing as his protégée, to be allowed to train under him, and I thought that I was progressing well.'

'I remember,' Owen said, 'you had reached the

dizzy heights of patisserie. I had no idea what that meant, but it seemed to mean a good deal to you.'

'Yes, it did. And I kept progressing, or so I thought. Pascal even permitted me to introduce a few of my own dishes to the menu. The rest of the kitchen brigade treated me as a fellow chef, not a woman. I thought I was earning their respect too. Perhaps I was, but it was more likely they knew me for Pascal's—Pascal's lover.' She coloured violently. 'I expect you will think that a shocking admission—my sisters were both shocked to the core.'

'Miss Brannagh, I guessed when we met that your— your heart was engaged.'

'You did? I thought at the time that I had been discreet, but I should have known better. I'm not very good at disguising my feelings.' She stared at him, her face set defiantly. 'I'm not ashamed of them, or what I did. They view affaires of the heart very differently in Paris.'

'And you were very much in love with Paris.'

'And with Pascal—or so I thought,' Miss Brannagh replied, looking mortified. 'It is probably difficult for you to understand, but in the kitchen, passions run so very high, and Pascal—he was—he is—the most passionate of all.'

'But your feelings were not reciprocated?'

'I thought they were. Perhaps they were a little bit, for a time. Or perhaps I'm just fooling myself. You've guessed what happened, haven't you? I don't suppose it's difficult. Anyone but me would have seen it coming. That's what Estelle said.'

'You were living your dream,' Owen said. 'That stayed with me, your sheer determination, the way you embraced it all, the way you defied convention to do so. Living life to the full, that's what you said you were doing.'

'Did I? That was what Mama used to say. She was rather more successful at it than me.'

'What happened?'

'Oh, it turned out that Pascal didn't covet me at all, only my money. From the first, when Monsieur Salois—he is the Duke of Brockmore's chef—recommended me to his kitchens at Eloise's behest, Pascal knew I was rich. He was so—so—I couldn't quite believe that I was actually there, in La Grande Taverne, working for Pascal Solignac. Not only working for him, but—he singled me out. He admired my work. He admired me—he seemed as fascinated by me as I was by him. Even at the time, I thought, why would a man so famous, so charismatic, with all of Paris at his feet would fall in love with me. I was enormously flattered, and I suppose it went to my head. I should have known better.'

'Miss Brannagh, you do yourself an enormous injustice. If anyone had Paris at their feet, I'd have thought it would have been you.'

She shook her head vehemently. 'Only because I gave you that impression, because when we met, I was still deluded enough to think that I was what I imagined myself to be. Living life to the full,' she said sardonically. 'I don't have what it takes to make a success of that. I should have known better. I was simply basking in Pascal's reflected glory.'

'I think you underestimate yourself. When I saw you...'

'As I said, when you saw me, I was deluded. We shared a common dream, Pascal and I, but only one of us would achieve it, and the other one would pay dearly. You can guess which was which. We spent hours after service talking of our restaurant, planning the menus. Pascal felt his genius was wasted, having to conform to the dictates of La Grande Taverne's owner. Only in our own place would he be free to unleash his true artistry. And I would be there at his side, Paris's best and most inventive *sous-chef.* That is what we agreed. That is what he promised me.'

'But when he had your money, his promises proved to be empty?'

She shuddered. 'The premises were purchased in his name. As a foreigner, I could not own property. As a woman I was apparently not permitted a bank account in France. I don't even know how much of what he told me was true, I never thought to check. I trusted him implicitly. The new restaurant opened in June this year. What should have been the best night of my life turned into the worst. I had always admired Pascal's burning ambition but it hid a ruthless streak, as I found out to my cost. He didn't even wait until the staff had gone home. When the doors closed and the opening-night party began, he took me to one side and told me that he didn't need me any more. I had served my purpose, and he cast me off like a dirty dish rag.'

She curled her lip. 'I had been incredibly naïve not to realise that all he had ever wanted from me was my money, but I didn't take it lying down. I didn't fight for his affections, though I thought my heart broken, but I fought for what was mine. It was futile. Pascal can do no wrong in Paris's eyes, and he wields a great deal of influence. No one would believe the word of a deluded, scorned Englishwoman, against Paris's new culinary king. He made sure of that.'

Her eyes sparked with anger. 'According to Pascal, he took me in as a favour to Monsieur Salois and tolerated me for far too long because as everyone knows, who has ever met Pascal, he is such a soft-hearted fool, beguiled by a pretty face and a well-turned ankle! Also according to Pascal, he covered up my many mistakes in the kitchen, and took me into his bed because I made it so difficult for him to refuse. The fact that it was my bed in my apartment—but that too, he claimed was my idea. Then when my inflated opinion of my own abilities caused me to demand that I had a place in his new venture, he had no option but to disillusion me. And to ensure that every other restaurant in Paris was similarly disillusioned.

'So there you have it, my full, sorry and pathetic tale. I tried, heaven knows I have tried to secure gainful employment in another kitchen since. But no one would take me on, and the only offers I received were of a—a very different nature. Paris is a wonderful city when you are happy, when you feel that nothing is impossible, that the future is bright. But when your dreams are shattered, when you dare not look into the future for fear of what you might see, then Paris feels like living in a nightmare. I could hardly bring myself to stay in that apartment when he moved out, but I had nowhere else to go. Now the lease has run out, and I am quite penniless. If I started as a kitchen maid, perhaps I could scramble my way back up, but not in Paris. I love that city so much, but it is tarnished for ever for me now.'

Though her eyes were over-bright, she had not shed a single tear in the telling of this appalling tale. Owen would have given a great deal to throttle Solignac's scrawny, arrogant neck, but Miss Brannagh was determined to take the blame for the man's ruthless ambition and callous, abominable treatment of her. In fact she seemed to think she deserved it. Not content with stealing her money and her heart, Solignac had also stripped Miss Brannagh of her self-confidence. 'And was he right,' Owen asked tentatively, 'about your culinary ability—or lack of it?'

Her shoulders slumped. 'That is the hardest thing of all for me—he's made me question just that. All I've ever wanted to do is to cook, and it's the only thing I've ever thought I was good at. I was astounded by how well I did under Pascal's tutelage, but I truly believed it was because I was learning fast, that my promotions were all merited. When he told me that I hadn't earned any of it, that he wouldn't ever have promoted me beyond peeling potatoes—I don't know, Mr Harrington, perhaps I was out of my depth. Perhaps I am simply a competent domestic cook. I'd like to think not. I'd like to think that I can cook to a professional standard, but all I know for certain is that I still want to cook.'

'Bravo, Miss Brannagh, you are bowed but unbroken,' Owen said, though he was furious, for it was clearly far from the truth. As he suspected, Solignac had knocked the stuffing out of her.

'I thought I was broken. I hope that I can put myself back together.'

'I am very glad to hear that. You have taken some appalling and undeserved knocks, but your spirit has not been completely extinguished.'

'We'll see. I'm absolutely determined to try again, which is why I'm here. I got myself into this mess and I am determined to get myself out of it without falling back on my family.' She paused to take a visible breath. 'When I met you in Paris, you told me that you were the toast of society.'

'Once upon a time, but I'm afraid I no longer go out in society, Miss Brannagh, and I'm not quite sure—'

'You still have contacts, influence?' she interrupted. 'You see, I need a job, Mr Harrington. I need work. If I have to start at the bottom I will, though I would prefer—but I know I am not in a position to make demands. Only a request. Does anyone of your acquaintance need a cook?'

'You want me to find you a position in domestic service?' he exclaimed, astounded.

'I would be for ever in your debt if you could.'

Undoubtedly he could. His influence was such that he could find her a position in any of the best households in London, if he chose to exert it. 'Why not ask your sister for a recommendation? The Countess of Fearnoch...'

'No! No, no, no. It's not that I can't, Mr Harrington, it's that I won't. I won't be pitied. Eloise would never say I told you so, but it would be worse than that, she'd blame herself for letting me go abroad in the first place. She was very shocked, when she and her husband came to Paris back in April last year, and discovered—I'm still not sure how—my affaire with Pascal. She did not tell me that I was making a mistake in investing the money she had given me in the restaurant, she promised both Estelle and I that we could spend our settlement as we pleased, but I could see she was very concerned. I tried to persuade her she need not worry, but she obviously did, for she sent Estelle to talk sense into me at the end of last year. My twin had no compunction in making *her* feelings known. We parted on very bad terms.'

'And Estelle would say I told you so, if you went to her now?'

'Probably, and she'd have every right to, but she'd reserve her vitriol for Pascal. It may be perverse of me, but I don't relish the idea of being seen as a witless victim. It was my decision to go to Paris, a gamble that didn't pay off. Pascal exploited my passion and ambition, but I—oh, I was easily duped, let's face it. He told me what I wanted to hear.'

For the first time, a tear escaped her eye, though she wiped it hurriedly away. 'I can't get in touch with Estelle. She'll be furious with me for keeping her in ignorance, but she'd drop everything and come running regardless, if she knew I was in such dire straits, and I don't want her to do that. I've never been at odds with her like this before. We have been out of touch ever since our arguement. I miss her so desperately, but I can't—I absolutely *cannot* make up with her until I've redeemed myself. Do you think you can assist me to do that?'

'Mr Harrington?'

Owen blinked. Judging by the concern on her face he'd had one of his episodes, where his mind froze and went blank. But for how long?

'Mr Harrington, are you in pain?'

Not too long, by the sounds of it, or she'd have rung for help. 'I've been sitting still for too long, that's all,' he said brusquely, removing his leg cautiously from the footstool. Pins and needles made it numb. He had no option but to wait until they passed before standing up. 'You were saying?'

'Are you sure you are—can I get you anything?'

'No, I thank you,' he said, hauling himself upright. 'I need to think about what you have told me.'

'Oh. Yes. Indeed.' Miss Brannagh got to her feet. 'I expect I'll stay at the posting house tonight, until I can make other arrangements. You could send a note to me there, if you think of a suitable position.'

She held out her hand, and he took it in his gloved one. Though he had lost some of the feeling in his fingers, her touch still sent a jolt through him, conjuring the fleeting memory of the last time they had held hands like this, and the way time had seemed to stop. He looked down at her work-roughened hands, the tiny healed cuts, the result of constant chopping, the outline of old blisters from cooking on a hot stove. A permanent reminder, as his scars were, in a very different way, of her broken dreams. He no longer dreamed, but if he could help Miss Phoebe Brannagh to pick up the pieces of her life, then he would have rescued something, for her if not for him. It was scant consolation but it was better than nothing.

The kernel of an idea began to form in his mind. It was an outrageous idea. No, he couldn't possibly—or could he? 'You can't stay in a posting house. I'll have Bremner organise a hotel for you.'

'Mr Harrington, I'm afraid I don't have the funds...'

'You can pay me back.'

'I can't possibly...'

'What you need is a good dinner and a night's rest in a comfortable bed,' Owen said firmly, ringing the bell to summon his butler. 'You'll wake up refreshed, and much more prepared to face whatever the day may bring. I will brook no argument.'

'Very well, if you insist, but I will refund you as soon as I can.'

'Fine. Now, I'm going to hand you over to Bremner. Eat well, Miss Brannagh, and sleep well. I will send my carriage for you in the morning.'

She smiled tremulously. 'I don't know how to thank you. You are very kind.'

Not kind, determined, Owen thought, and already feeling a hundred times better than when he'd woken up this morning. 'Until tomorrow,' he said, releasing her hand as Bremner appeared, his man listening with well-disguised surprise to his clipped instructions.

The door closed on the pair of them, and Owen

dropped heavily into the nearest chair. It was only just noon but the day, which usually stretched like a vast empty desert in front of him, seemed too short. He had a great deal of thinking to do.

Chapter Three

Confounding her expectations, Phoebe slept soundly in the hotel's huge, extremely comfortable bed. It was delightful to be able to stretch out her limbs, find a cool spot when she was too hot, without worrying she would disturb anyone. *Anyone* being Pascal, a light and fitful sleeper who thought that beds were primarily intended for lovemaking.

She couldn't really remember exactly when and why Pascal had come to move into her apartment. She dimly recalled him mentioning a dispute with his landlady, who wished to charge him for laundering sheets. He had refused to pay, and as a consequence found himself homeless. Why waste time looking for new lodgings which could be more usefully be spent in the kitchen, he'd said, especially as Phoebe's rented apartment was so large it was wasted on just her. Since there was no landlady on the premises to object to their scandalous domestic arrangements, and as the other occupants of the building kept themselves to themselves, Phoebe had come to view their living together as perfectly acceptable. Until Estelle found out.

Estelle had been shocked and furious when Phoebe had finally confessed that she and Pascal were living under one roof—and that Pascal was not paying a *sou* for the privilege. Nothing Phoebe said could convince her sister that such arrangements were acceptable in Paris, nor that the situation could end in anything other than disaster. And Estelle had been proved right.

Right about Pascal, and right about Phoebe's ambition too? Estelle simply couldn't understand why Phoebe was putting herself through the rigorous training and unrelenting hard work of a restaurant kitchen. She couldn't understand why Phoebe wasn't content to cook for her loved ones, why she would put herself through all the effort of serving up food to an unknown public who would have no compunction in deriding it, if it didn't please them. Estelle thought that Phoebe would be much happier spending her settlement on building her dream kitchen in her own home, rather than cooking in someone else's kitchen for complete strangers. Estelle simply didn't understand Phoebe's passion, and this was very difficult to bear, especially since Phoebe completely understood her twin's love of music.

Estelle had a very special gift that elevated her playing above the ordinary. Phoebe had hoped that she had such a gift too, for cooking. Estelle didn't understand that, but she'd hoped Pascal, a culinary genius, would. He'd seemed to, at first, but ultimately she'd either failed to prove herself or he'd been lying to her from the first. Either way, the net result was the same. She had set her sights too high, and she had—predictably—failed. All that was to be done now was to try again, with her sights set lower, to make her own way. Though her heart ached at the wedge which the argument had driven between herself and her twin, she was determined to find a way to re-establish herself before the rift between them could be healed.

What would she do if Mr Harrington could not recommend a suitable post? If he could, she would work night and day to prove herself. *Please*, she said to herself, crossing her fingers, *please let him know of someone*.

Her tummy clenched with nerves. She should enjoy the luxury of having her tea and bread served in bed, ask the maid to have a bath made ready, and make the most of her time in this fabulously indulgent and expensive hotel, not waste it fretting.

She had succeeded in this small ambition, but when a message arrived informing her that Mr Harrington's town coach awaited her convenience, Phoebe was immediately assailed by anxiety. Even if he could not help her, she was glad of the opportunity to see him again. The conversation yesterday had been focused on her plight. She had learned little of his own travails save the sketchy details he had told her. His accident seemed to have made a recluse of him. When had it happened? How far had he got on his travels after he left Paris? Pain had changed him, but she found it difficult to believe that the charismatic man she had met two years ago would have given up on the world so completely. He appeared, on reflection, to be a man without hope. Though perhaps she had simply caught him on a bad day.

'Miss Brannagh, how do you do today?' Owen asked, indicating the chair at the fireside she had occupied yesterday. 'You slept well?'

'Very well, thank you.'

She sat down, making a fuss over the arranging of her skirts, thoughtfully allowing him time to settle gingerly in his own chair before looking over at him expectantly, and Owen was immediately assailed by doubts. What right had he to ask so much of one so young and so utterly beautiful? She was unhappy now, her pride and her confidence had both taken a severe blow, but she would recover in time. What had seemed so clear in the early hours of the morning, was now clouding in his mind. The enthusiasm which had kept his pain at bay all morning waned, and he became aware once more of the dull, dragging ache in his hip. One step at a time, he reminded himself, as he had so often in the last two years, though this time the steps were metaphorical and not physical.

'If you had the chance to open your own restaurant here in London, would you take it?' he asked.

Miss Brannagh's eyes lit up. 'My very own establishment, with my own menus, my own dishes. A place where men and women can dine together, as they can in Paris. Just imagine!'

'That would certainly be unique in London.'

'Exactly. Aside from private dining rooms, which are the province of the rich and titled, there is nothing like it at present.'

It was a strange thing, but while his accident had left Owen almost completely numb emotionally, he had discovered that something akin to excitement took hold of him when he sensed a good business deal, a sort of tingling in his belly like an attack of nerves. He felt it now. 'Combine that idea with a female head chef, and you have, if you'll forgive the pun, a mouthwatering opportunity,' he said.

Miss Brannagh's face fell. 'If only, but that will never happen. It's probably just as well too, for I'm not at all sure I am good enough to preside over such an establishment.'

'Not good enough? What happened to being bowed but unbroken?'

'Nothing happened, I'm simply being realistic. It makes much more sense to aim for what I know I can achieve than to even dream of the impossible. I've failed once, I don't want to fail again.'

'Solignac seems to have done an excellent job of cutting you down to size, that's for sure. What if he's wrong?'

'He didn't *cut me down to size*. I was too big for my boots. And it wasn't only Pascal who thought so, it was…'

'Your sister, the musician.'

'Yes.'

Clearly the twin was a very painful subject, Owen,

thought to himself. 'She too could be wrong,' he offered gently.

'I've already wasted all my money and two years of my life trying to prove that, and look where it's got me.'

The same two years he had wasted, trying and failing to recover what he had lost. Owen was now utterly determined to help her, if only to prove her superior twin wrong, never mind Solignac, regardless of whether or not in doing so she could help him. 'Am I right in assuming you would not consider applying to your elder sister for the necessary capital? The Earl of Fearnoch, her husband, is a very rich man...'

'No! Absolutely not. I would not dream of it. I would rather peel potatoes for the rest of my life than do that. I thought you understood, Mr Harrington.'

'Owen. Please, call me Owen.'

'Owen.' She leaned forward earnestly. 'Although my sister is wildly in love with her husband, in fact her marriage was arranged. Eloise never wished to marry, she did so in large part to provide Estelle and I with the means to make anything we wanted of our own lives. The fact that she is so happy is wonderful, but it could easily have been otherwise. Though she swore she would not have married Alexander if she had disliked him, to be perfectly frank, I believe it would have taken a great deal to dissuade her. Eloise has done more than enough for me already. I would never ask her under any circumstances, even if our relationship was not at present strained.'

Owen shifted uncomfortably on his chair. The footstool eased the pain in his hip, but if he sat still too long, his damned foot went to sleep. 'So what you really need is an investor.'

She laughed bitterly. 'The chances of my finding one are about as high as Pascal begging me to come back to Paris. I may not be a *maverick genius*, but I still think I can cook. But Pascal, who *is* undoubtedly a maverick genius, says otherwise, and which one of us would the world believe, do you think? I am about as risky a business proposition as you are likely to encounter. I have no references, I've been sacked from my one and only position, and I'm a woman. Would you invest in me, Mr Harr—Owen? I don't think so.'

'I believe I told you, the first time we met in Paris, that I would and happily.'

'In jest, when you knew that there was no possibility of my accepting.'

'I'm not jesting now, I'm perfectly serious.'

Her eyes widened. Her cheeks flushed and then paled. 'Thank you, you are very kind, very generous, but no, absolutely not.'

'I'm offering to be your backer, Miss Brannagh, not your protector. Believe me, the last thing I'm in the market for is a mistress. I am not Solignac, beguiled by your *pretty face and well-turned ankle.*'

'Forgive me, but no one in their right mind would take such a risk with me, and you know nothing about food—in fact I recall you told me that you are a culinary philistine. If you are not offering me a *carte blanche*, then I can only assume that you must feel sorry for me. The answer in either case is the same. I can't take your money.'

Her refusal didn't surprise him, but his conscience insisted that he press his point. He had to be sure that she believed his final proposition was her best and not her only option. 'Miss Brannagh…'

'Phoebe. Please, call me Phoebe.'

'Phoebe. Just over two years ago, I realised that I was bored with my feckless existence. As fate would have it, my travels were cut short, but my desire for some sort of occupation is one of the few things I didn't lose. Circumstances left me with a lot of time on my hands. I don't sleep well, I rarely go out and I fill a great many of the empty hours with reading. I subscribe to countless periodicals, I read every newspaper, and all the Parliamentary reports. The net effect is that I know what's going on the world I no longer inhabit, and I have discovered that I have an instinct for investment opportunities. It's like a sixth sense. I have a nose for making money. My father left me very wealthy. By investing that money wisely I've made myself rich beyond most people's wildest imaginings. Which is a long-winded way of saying that I have a hunch that you are worth investing in.'

'But you have no evidence to support that,' Phoebe said, becoming agitated. 'I could have a completely inflated opinion of my own abilities. And even if I don't, you are underestimating how *radical* my venture would be. Eating in a restaurant is a much more established tradition in Paris than it is in London—in restaurants such as Le Grand Véfour for example, the clientele is mixed. But as far as I know, the only similar place here is Crockford's and that is for gentlemen only. Imagine the scandal, Owen, if a restaurant were to open in London which served food to both sexes, and had a woman running the kitchen.'

'What you call scandal, I would call priceless free publicity.'

'No, no, no. I want my food to speak for itself, I don't want people to come to gawk at me.'

'Phoebe, your idea is as you said, revolutionary. I hope that your customers would return for the food, but initially, you are going to have to accept that many of them will want, as you put it, to gawk at you.'

'Then it's as well that it's all just a pipe dream,' she said, once again becoming dejected. 'I need to earn my living, not accept charity, no matter how well intentioned.'

Here was a gilt-edged opening. Owen braced himself, taken aback to discover that his heart was hammering, though perhaps it wasn't so surprising, with no less than three lives at stake. 'There is another way,' he said carefully. 'An arrangement which would allow me to invest in you, and for you to legitimately earn my backing.'

'What arrangement could that possibly be?'

Get on with it, Owen urged himself, but now it came to the crux, he was loathe to reveal the true extent of his suffering, and not at all sure he could even explain it without sounding like the madman he had for a while imagined himself to be. His instinct was to get to his feet, to pace, to *move*, but moving entailed pain, and pain interfered with his concentration and induced those lost moments.

'Bear with me,' he said, for Phoebe was starting to look concerned. 'What I have to say is—it is difficult.'

'More difficult than confessing that you are penniless, heartbroken and humiliated, as I yesterday?'

'Are you heartbroken?'

She shook her head. 'I thought I was at first, but I think my pride and my self-esteem were far more damaged than my heart. It's not possible to be in love with a man who loves only himself. If I loved Pascal, truly loved him, I'd want him back, wouldn't I? And I don't.'

'I'm glad to hear it. Wouldn't you like to prove him wrong though, Phoebe? Wouldn't you like the chance to prove yourself right?'

'I don't know. Yes, of course I would, but—'

'Let me help you,' he interrupted before she could once again denigrate her abilities. 'There is a way to secure the funds you need to open your restaurant in an entirely respectable and above-board manner.'

'How?'

'Marry me. As my wife the marriage settlement I would make would be legitimately yours to do with as you saw fit.'

Her mouth fell open. 'You are not serious.'

'I am, deadly serious.'

She looked utterly taken aback. 'You can't be.'

'Hear me out,' Owen said urgently. There was no time for dissembling any more, for Phoebe was making moves to leave. 'It would not be charity, you would be doing both Olivia and myself a huge service. Olivia Braidwood,' he added in response to her blank look. 'The woman I'm going to be obliged to marry, unless I can find a way out of it.'

'You are engaged to be married!'

'I *have* to find a way out of it Phoebe,' Owen said fervently. 'I've already destroyed my own life, I won't destroy hers.'

'You are engaged to be married,' Phoebe repeated, sounding stunned. 'Yet you made no mention of it yesterday. I did wonder if you might have married. That was one of the many possible reasons why you missed our assignation. You are a very attractive man. You are extremely wealthy, you have—I remember when we met in Paris, thinking if it were not for Pascal, because there was something between us, wasn't there? I wasn't imagining it?'

Her words brought such a pang of yearning that it took Owen's breath away. Talk about impossible dreams!

'I am so sorry,' Phoebe said, jerking him back to the present. 'I have embarrassed you. I was simply surprised that you had omitted to mention something of such import.'

'I am not betrothed, not formally,' Owen said, regaining his focus. 'There has been no announcement, though it is well known that Olivia and I have an understanding.'

'An understanding that you think would destroy this Miss Braidwood's life? Why on earth would you think such a thing?'

* * *

'Owen?' Phoebe eyed him with some concern. This was the second time it had happened, this odd blank stare. 'Is there something wrong?'

He started, blinked. 'It's nothing. Nothing serious. I lose concentration, drift off for a few moments now and then.'

'Because of your accident?'

'My doctor told me when I first came back to England that such episodes would pass, given time. I see no point in disillusioning him.'

'Have you also led him to believe that the pain in your leg has passed?'

He shrugged. 'I've tried everything the doctors have to offer. They can't do any more for me.'

His words stirred her compassion. 'Is that why you've shut yourself away from the world, because you believe you won't get any better?'

'I did not make a conscious decision to *shut myself away*. I have a world of my own now, this one, right here, and I'm perfectly content with that.'

'Forgive me, but you don't look very happy.'

'I am not unhappy,' he responded testily. 'I have simply accepted that this is how I am and how I will be. Which is why my proposal requires you to be my wife in name only.'

'Good grief!' Phoebe exclaimed. 'My aunt's marriage is just such an arrangement. My sister Eloise's marriage was also intended to be another such. It seems to run in the family.'

'And are they happy, your aunt and your sister?'

'Yes, though Eloise fell in love with her husband after they married. Their marriage has turned out very differently from the one they intended.'

'But they were happy to sign up to the original agreement?' Owen persisted.

She pursed her lips, recalling the weeks before Eloise was married and the excitement with which she had embraced her changed circumstances. 'Yes, even if they had not subsequently fallen in love—yes, I believe it would still have been a successful match.'

'So are you willing to consider my offer?'

'I still don't understand what it is you are offering and why.'

'But you'll listen? And you'll consider what I have to say? I am, as I said, deadly serious.'

Phoebe hesitated. His words sounded sincere but his demeanour was strangely unemotional, almost detached. His accident had changed him radically, that much was certain, and their entire acquaintance consisted of two brief encounters more than two years apart. But it surely couldn't have changed the essence of him. He was still the honourable man who had come to her rescue at the Procope. A man she could trust. A man now under extreme duress. What on earth had she to lose by listening to him? In fact she'd be a fool not to.

'I remember,' she said, 'when my sister Eloise was considering her now husband's proposal, we talked about it endlessly. We felt, all of us, including Aunt Kate—and she ought to know—that it was extremely important that Eloise went into the marriage with her eyes wide open.'

'You mean you want to know exactly what you'd be getting yourself into?'

'And why. Why do think you would be destroying Miss Braidwood's life if you did marry her? Why must you marry someone else in order to avoid marrying her? And why me?'

'These are big questions.'

'It's a very big decision.'

'It's an outrageous idea, I know, but it is—I truly believe that it could be the answer to both our problems.' Owen shifted on his chair, wincing as he moved his injured leg from the footstool to the floor. 'My accident occurred a little over two years ago,' he said. 'In Marseilles. Not long after we met in Paris, as a matter of fact.'

'Just when you were setting out on your travels! Oh, Owen, how awful. What happened?'

He went quite rigid, staring down at his gloves. 'There was a fire. That's all I know. I remember almost nothing of it and don't want to either. My hands were badly burned. Something heavy, a beam I think, fell on top of me. My hip was shattered. I was unconscious for some weeks afterwards. It was three months before I was well enough to face the journey back to London. Six months before I could walk again.'

Though she could see from the way he held himself, completely still, that saying even this much was an immense effort, his tone was oddly cold, as if he was recounting something that had happened to someone else. Phoebe yearned to comfort him, but she couldn't hug him, and in any case, it was clear the last thing he wanted was sympathy.

'But you can walk now. You must have worked extremely hard,' she said, cringing inwardly at the mundanity of her words. She couldn't imagine how it must have been for him, or how it was even now, to be one moment at the peak of his physical powers, a man who took his athletic prowess for granted, if what he'd told her in Paris of his derring-do was true, and then the next, to be like a baby, learning to walk. But he *could* walk now. So why did he no longer leave his house? And why, more pertinently, was he so certain that he would make his fiancée miserable? 'Does Miss Braidwood...?' Phoebe stopped, floundering. 'I'm sorry, I don't understand how your accident should affect your betrothal.'

'It is a long-standing arrangement made by our respective fathers when we were young. My father and Olivia's father were boyhood friends, so I suppose you could say I've known her all my life,' Owen said. 'The intention was always that we would marry when she reached her twenty-first birthday, which is in January next year. I'm not in love with her, never have been, any more than she is with me, though I had, as she had, always taken it for granted that we would marry when the time came. But I wanted more than that, Phoebe, more from my life than becoming a husband and possibly a father. When you and I first met, I had been living from day to day, enjoying every moment, thinking that the future would take care of itself. It finally dawned on me that I was in danger of frittering my life away. So I decided to go to Europe.'

'And what did you say to Miss Braidwood of your plans?'

Owen shrugged. 'As far as she was concerned, my life was my own until we married, and at that point, our marriage was more than two years away.'

'And then your accident changed everything at a stroke,' Phoebe said, her heart aching with the poignancy of this.

'When I returned to England,' Owen said flatly, 'I told Olivia that she must consider herself free of any obligation. I had all but given up on any hope of walking, but she refused point blank to abandon me in my pitiful state.'

'Well, and so I should hope,' Phoebe said indignantly. 'She would be a shallow person indeed, to do so.'

'Which is almost exactly what she said, and so I suppose you could say, she inspired my recovery, for I determined to walk again.'

'And you did.'

'And Olivia still refused to abandon me.'

Phoebe's nascent smile faltered. 'You learned to walk in order to...'

'Make it easier for Olivia to end our engagement. It is not as ridiculous an idea as it sounds. Everyone knows we have an understanding. She couldn't possibly jilt me when I was confined to my bed, but when I regained the use of my legs...'

'But that makes even less sense,' Phoebe exclaimed,

wondering if Owen was, despite appearances, just a little deranged. 'She had always intended to marry you, and you had always intended to marry her. You didn't wish to tie her to you when you couldn't walk, but now you can—what is to stop you doing what both of you had always expected to do?'

'I can walk, Phoebe, but I lost more than the use of my legs. I am not the man I once was.'

'Oh.' She could feel her cheeks burning as she realised what he must be implying. 'I am so sorry.'

'I don't want your pity. I don't want anyone's pity. You said you wished me to be candid with you, then I will be as plain as I can be. I am not physically incapacitated beyond what you see, but I am—I am much changed by the experience. I have no desire, no passion for anything.'

Such heart-wrenching words, yet they were spoken in that same odd tone, as if he were referring to someone else. 'Nothing?' Phoebe said, struggling to understand.

'And no one. You could say I have lost my appetite for life. Mostly, I'm indifferent.'

'Is it an illness? Did it happen as a result of your accident? Did you—I don't know, did you hit your head?'

'I don't know how it happened. I didn't wake up one morning and think, "I don't give a damn about the world", it just settled over me and I cannot shift it.'

'So you detached yourself from the world?'

'But I have signally failed to detach myself from

Olivia. The more reclusive I've become, the more determined she has become not to be seen by that world as a callous jilt. But she can see I am changed for the worse. The privileged and exciting life she imagined for herself as my wife and the dutiful penance of a life she would have to endure if she married me now could not be more different. I'm a stranger to her these days, I can see her looking at me and wondering who I am. But she can't contemplate *not* going through with it, because she is at heart a deeply conventional and dutiful young woman who would do anything to avoid the scandalous label of jilt, even if it means being trapped in a miserable marriage.'

'So you intend to take the decision out of her hands by marrying someone else?'

'Then she can be the wronged party and free, with a clear conscience, to get on with her life.'

'That is a very noble thing to do.'

'No, it's not. I don't want to marry a woman who feels obliged to stand by me. And her parents,' Owen said, his lip curling, 'are doing their damnedest to ensure that the poor girl does just that. I am a very rich man, and the marriage settlement my father agreed is extremely generous. Olivia doesn't consider it material, but her parents most certainly do, and apply their own particular pressure on her to strengthen her resolve any time it might seem that I have weakened it.'

'Are her family poor?'

'Not at all. Merely avaricious.'

'I don't know what to say. I can't imagine how you must feel.'

'Desperate,' Owen said. 'But determined. Olivia deserves a man who cares for her, who will give her the family she wants. I can't provide that, but I can give her the freedom to find someone who can. That aspect of my life is over, I am reconciled to that. All I ask of you is that you go through with the ceremony. Once I have made it impossible for Olivia to marry me, she will be free of all obligation towards me. In return, I will provide you with the funds to make your dream a reality, and in addition put my business acumen at your disposal.'

'I am not sure what to say,' Phoebe said, her head whirling.

'Then say yes.'

'It's an outrageous idea.'

'That should be no barrier. You are not exactly convention personified, are you?'

'No, but—do you really think Miss Braidwood will think she's had a lucky escape?'

'I am absolutely certain of the fact, and society's sympathy will be entirely with her too.'

'I am not a respectable woman, Owen. If the details of my life in Paris were ever discovered, it would cause a huge scandal for you.'

'I personally don't give a damn about that. Aside from the fact that my own former reputation was colourful to say the least, I no longer go out in society.'

'But if I launch my restaurant, I'll need society to sit at my tables, to eat my food.'

'Phoebe, in my experience notoriety whets the appetite.'

'But what about your family—I know your parents are both dead, but do you have any brothers or sisters?'

'No, I don't. But you do. What will they say if you marry me?'

'That with my reputation—or lack of it—I am fortunate to find any man to marry me.' Phoebe wrinkled her nose. 'No, that's not fair. I don't know. If they felt I had done so out of desperation rather than going to one of them with my tail between my legs, they would be very upset.'

'I don't want you to marry me because you're desperate. I want you to marry me only because you think it's an excellent idea.'

'A excellent idea!' She laughed nervously. 'It is the most preposterous notion, though no more preposterous than my own, to open a restaurant when I have absolutely no idea how to go about such a thing, I suppose.'

'You know all about food. I have the business sense. We will make an excellent team.'

'Dare we? No, no, it's impossible.'

'We have both already lost everything. We quite literally have nothing more to lose.'

'When you put it like that! I can't believe this—are you sure you're not teasing me?'

'I would not be so cruel.'

'No, no, of course you wouldn't.' She stared at him, quite dazed. 'You are offering me my dream. Yet you are asking so little in return.'

'You're mistaken. By setting Olivia free, you'll be

giving me a peace of mind that I've not had in a very long time. One thing I'm not asking of you, Phoebe. It's a delicate matter, but you wanted to know precisely what you'd be letting yourself in for, so I'm obliged to mention it. With regard to your private life.'

She blushed violently. 'I have not—I would not—'

'My interest in such things is over,' he interrupted her, 'but you are a beautiful, and sensual young woman. You were badly hurt by Solignac, but you'll get over that and when you do, all I ask is that you are discreet. It has always seemed to me one of the great hypocrisies of so-called respectable society, that an unattached woman is expected to remain chaste and you will, in that sense at least, be unattached.'

'Owen, my only and overriding attachment would be to my restaurant, my only desire to repay your faith in me by making a success of it.'

'At present, but time, they say is a great healer. As I said, all I ask of you is discretion.'

'You don't think time will heal you?'

'If I can be the catalyst to your success, then there will have been a positive outcome, after all, to our encounter at the Procope. Then I might feel better.'

His words and the memory of him, so full of vitality and hopes and dreams brought a lump to her throat. 'My heart is telling me to say yes, but I followed my heart once before, and look where it got me.'

'I, on the other hand, think only with my head. Being quite literally heartless,' Owen said with a small, mocking smile, 'has made me an excellent businessman. But I won't push you. Take your time, think about it.'

Phoebe thought about it for all of thirty seconds before her smile burst through. 'Let's do it,' she said. 'How quickly do you think we can get married?'

Chapter Four

One week later

Phoebe looked on, slightly stunned, as Owen shook hands with the clergyman before he and Bremner, who had been pressed into service as one of the witnesses to their marriage, left the room to show him out. The other witness, Owen's friend Jasper Forsythe, was in the process of opening a bottle of champagne. Black-haired and with striking hazel eyes, Mr Forsythe was immaculately turned out and rather haughtily handsome, but the warmth of his smile, the genuine pleasure he seemed to be taking from the occasion, had gone a long way towards putting Phoebe at her ease.

'Thank you, Mr Forsythe, that's most welcome,' she said, accepting a brimming glass from him, 'I confess I found that more nerve-racking than I had anticipated.'

'May I be the first to offer my congratulations, Mrs Harrington. And please call me Jasper. I can't tell you how delighted I was when Owen told me he was about to tie the knot. You may just be exactly what he needs.'

'Thank you. I hope our union will prove to be mutually beneficial.'

Jasper smiled. 'He told me that you met in Paris just over two years ago, and he'd never forgotten you. He kept that one under his hat! Having made your acquaintance, I can understand why you made such an impression on him. I've not seen him so—so animated since he returned to England.'

'You are his oldest friend, I gather.'

'And the only one of our circle he remains in contact with,' Jasper said, his smile fading slightly, 'though I'm hoping that now you have entered his life, things will change.'

'Oh, we have no plans to launch ourselves into society.' Not in the manner you might expect, at any rate, Phoebe added to herself for Owen had not, she knew, confided their plans to Jasper.

'That's a shame. I had hoped—before his accident, Mrs Harrington, Owen was…'

'Phoebe, please. Tell me what he was like in those days.'

'Oh, brimming with life. He never stood still for more than five minutes. From the crack of dawn he'd be up and about. Most mornings we'd meet up to go riding, long before anyone else was around, you know, so that we could actually get some proper exercise, but sometimes we'd go running instead.' Jasper grinned. 'You should have seen the looks on the faces of anyone we did come across then, the pair of us dressed in just shirts and breeches, running full tilt around St James's. We'd start at the park there, then into Green Park and round Hyde Park and back again—though some days Owen insisted we took in Regent's Park too. *"Clears the tubes, old man, sets one up for the day,"* he used to say. I was in awe of his boundless energy.'

'Do you still run, Mr—Jasper?'

He shook his head. 'I was never really that keen on the actual running, to be honest, though it certainly helped work off the effects of overindulgence the night before. It's not the same without Owen. I still box and fence, but it's all such a serious business with the younger set these days. That's the thing I miss most about Owen—he never took anything seriously.'

'You must see a very great change in him, then?'

'I hardly recognise him, to be perfectly honest. He's still in there somewhere, my old friend, but it's as if—you'll think me fanciful, as if there's a glass wall between us. It's the pain, I suppose. He doesn't complain, but it must be constant. Has he told you what happened?'

'Not in any detail.'

'No, he never refers to it.' Jasper gave himself a shake. 'Anyway, enough of that. This is a fresh start for you both, and I'm honoured to have been able to witness the dawn of it.'

He smiled as the door opened and Owen came back in. 'Good timing, I was just about to raise a toast,' he said, handing his friend a glass of champagne. 'To my best friend and his lovely new wife. Wishing you good health and happiness. Cheers.'

* * *

Phoebe's meagre wardrobe did not run to evening gowns. She'd had no time in Paris for shopping and scant opportunity to dress up. The dress she wore tonight dated from her one and only visit to Eloise and Alexander in London in the first year of their marriage. Eloise had designed it, and Madame LeClerc, the famous modiste had made it up. Copper-coloured organza silk was embellished with full sleeves of chiffon, puffed at the shoulders, tied tight with satin ribbons at the wrists. The décolleté was plunging, and Phoebe's curves were generous, but Madame LeClerc had cleverly satisfied both current fashion and modesty by using chiffon to create the illusion of a high neckline. A wide sash drew attention to Phoebe's waist, and a broad-hemmed border of ruched ribbon that reminded Phoebe of waves, weighted the gown, giving it a satisfying swish when she walked.

She sat down at her dressing table to tackle her coiffure. The prevailing fashion for regimented ringlets suited neither her hair nor her temperament. She gathered her rebellious tangle of curls into a loose knot, fixing it in place with a satin ribbon and allowing a few stray curls to soften the effect, knowing that many more would follow soon enough.

She had been married—she checked her watch—for the grand total of four hours, and resident in this town house for just over five. It had taken less than half an hour for the simple ceremony to transform her life. Not that she felt transformed, precisely. She felt, frankly, terrified. She had the means to achieve her dream now, but precisely *how* she was to set about achieving it, she had absolutely no idea. She hoped that Owen would know where to start, though how a man who didn't leave the house could help, she was at a loss to understand.

Jasper assumed that marriage would change Owen. Phoebe sincerely hoped so too though not in the manner Jasper suggested. She wished for Owen's sake that he hadn't become such a recluse, but she was grateful for her own sake that he was, since the idea of playing any sort of role as a London society hostess was anathema to her. As to what London society would make of such a hostess, if they discovered how she had lived in Paris—Phoebe shuddered at the very thought.

She studied the plain band of gold that Owen had placed on her finger. She was no longer Phoebe Brannagh, she was Mrs Owen Harrington and her husband was a virtual stranger whom she had met a total of four times before today. Once in Paris. Twice a week ago, when her arrival at his door prompted his proposal. And then yesterday, briefly, to agree the final arrangements.

The drawing room where the ceremony had taken place, thanks to the special licence Owen had obtained, had been cold, and though it was perfectly clean, it smelled musty, with the slightly forlorn air of a room only just brought out of hibernation. Now his town house was her home. His servants were hers to command. Tonight, she would sleep in this bedchamber, which had clearly not been in use for just as long as the drawing room. But before that, she was about to have dinner with her husband.

Gloves! She rummaged in her trunk, which she had not had time to unpack yet. The household appeared to be bereft of female staff, she had discovered with surprise when Bremner, clearly embarrassed, had arrived in response to her ringing her bedchamber bell. Did one wear gloves to dine at home? Owen certainly would be wearing gloves. He had even kept them on when signing their marriage certificate. Did he wear them when he was alone? When he slept?

What would their life together be like? She had absolutely no idea, and that, Phoebe realised, was actually a very liberating thought. Owen had no expectations of her as a wife, but he believed wholeheartedly in her as a chef, even though he had never tasted her food.

Her new husband's confidence in her was a huge antidote to the damage Pascal had inflicted. Though it made her toes curl in her evening slippers to think of him, she forced herself to do so, just to test how well the scars had healed. On reflection, her falling in love with the man was inevitable. He had from the moment she stepped into his kitchen been the very centre of her world, a bright, blinding sun for her to worship, whose attention she craved, whose admiration she would do almost anything to win. She had handed him her heart on a plate. And it had been a dish, she thought whimsically, that Pascal had found distinctly unpalatable, though he'd put up a good show of pretending otherwise! She had been from the first his most fervent admirer. One word of praise from him would keep her going for hours, days on end. One word of censure would set her back for much longer. When he paid no heed to her at all it was, quite literally, as if the sun had departed from her world, and she never doubted that it had been her own fault for failing to hold his attention.

Was it her fault? Was she simply not very interesting? Phoebe gave herself a shake. This morbid musing was serving no purpose. Pascal was in the past. Owen was her future, and her future started today. A future happily, as far as she was concerned, free of the messy complications of love and passion which, albeit for very different reasons, both she and her husband had forsworn. She twisted the wedding ring around on her finger. She wouldn't let him down, she vowed to herself. She would be a brilliant success, and all of London would vie for a table at her restaurant. Then finally Estelle would be forced to eat her words.

The thought of her twin brought a familiar pain to her heart, but tomorrow, Phoebe reminded herself, she would be able to share her news with both her sisters and with Aunt Kate too. They'd be shocked, but she hoped they'd be pleased for her too. She would tell them—what? The truth would bring at least one of them hotfoot to London, sure that she'd leapt out of the frying pan—ha, how apt!—and into the fire. No, she couldn't tell them the truth—but a version of it, such as the one Owen had evidently told Jasper? Smiling, Phoebe recalled the story that Eloise and Alexander had concocted to explain their marriage to the world. Why shouldn't she take a leaf out of her sister's very successful book and spare herself and Owen too, from her family's overly protective enquiries? She resolved to discuss it with him over dinner.

Talking of which, she was in danger of being late. With a sigh of relief she finally found a pair of long evening gloves and quickly pulled them on before giving her hair a final check. Heart thudding, she blew out the candles and headed down the stairs in search of her husband.

The dining room was far too grand for two people, Owen thought as he opened the double doors to inspect the room, but it was too late to change the arrangements now, and Bremner, unable to disguise his delight at having a mistress to breathe new life into the household, had gone to great efforts to make it welcoming. The leaves of the table had been removed to make it smaller, the curtains drawn against the dank October day, and the places set nearest the fire, though it was still screened. The crystal glasses gleamed, the wine Owen had carefully selected was decanted, and there were flowers on the table.

He made his way through to the morning room, which he'd decided to use for *aperitifs* instead of the vast acreage of the drawing room. It had been a mistake to have their ceremony there, for the room had a sad air of neglect, its cavernous nature emphasising the paltriness of their wedding party. Poor Phoebe, without either of her sisters or even her aunt by her side, had looked quite overwhelmed, though the decision not to have them there had been her own. He hoped fervently that she wasn't crying her eyes out in her bedchamber, already regretting her decision. While he was still slightly stunned by the speed at which his circumstances had changed, his overwhelming emotion was one of relief. And gratitude. Something else he'd not expressed nearly enough.

He would try to make amends tonight. He would wine her and dine her. He would do what he could to put her at ease, to make her forget that she was in a strange house married to a virtual stranger. Tonight he would forget the man he had become, the self-pitying hermit, and try to remember the man he had once been, the man she had met in Paris, charming and excellent company. Surely he could manage that, for a few hours? He certainly owed it to his new wife to try his damnedest.

He really was married! The proof was currently upstairs and about to join him for dinner, putting an end to his not-so-splendid isolation. This house was no longer a male bastion, but the implications of that hadn't even occurred to him until this moment. There wasn't a single female servant, so that would have to change. He'd assumed that life would go on as it had for the last two years, his world bounded by his own suite of rooms, while Phoebe did—what? He had no idea. He knew next to nothing about her. And vice versa. Yet here they were, starting out as a married couple and—and he had no idea what that meant.

Whatever happened, it meant change, and any alteration to the stifled, oppressive life he'd been living could only be a good thing. He'd been thinking of himself as the catalyst for Phoebe's success, but could his wife be the unwitting catalyst for changes in him? He wouldn't be able to hide away in his rooms any more. He wouldn't be able to take to his bed for no other reason than that he couldn't bear to get up. He would have to put on more of a show. They'd work together on the plans for the restaurant. They'd eat together—dinner at the very least. He'd not be spending his entire day in a chair or at his desk any more. He'd have to find a way to manage his pain. Return to those wretched exercises? The very idea made him want to scream with boredom, but when he pictured himself limping about the house in Phoebe's wake—damned if he would! So a return to the exercise regime it must be, he resolved, starting tomorrow morning.

He had the oddest feeling. Thinking at first it was hunger pangs, for he'd eaten next to nothing all day, as Bremner arrived, hovering in the doorway with a tray, Owen realised it was nervous anticipation.

'The champagne you ordered, sir.'

'Thank you. If you will set the tray down there. No need to open it, I will do that, but please put a few more bottles on ice for the staff,' Owen said, smiling.

His butler blinked, returning the smile with a watery one of his own. 'Thank you, Mr Harrington, that is most kind of you. We will be pleased to toast this most auspicious day.' Bremner permitted himself a wider smile. 'We were hoping—that is I expect there will be changes in the household, now that the house has a mistress.'

'I expect there will be,' Owen said. 'In fact I'm sure of it.'

* * *

Owen had dressed up for dinner, in a fashionable black tailcoat with a broad shawl collar and deep cuffs, and fitted grey trousers. His waistcoat was double-breasted, dark grey silk with silver buttons, his neck-cloth white, his only adornment a plain gold fob watch. His coat was not quite so tight-fitting as fashion de-creed, but it was clearly new, presumably made by his tailor to previous measurements. Though her heart was now and for ever well and truly her own, her passion reserved for cooking, Phoebe was not blind. What-ever Owen thought of himself, however he might have changed since she had first encountered him, at an el-emental level he was still a dangerously attractive man.

'I'm so sorry,' she said, 'did I keep you waiting?'

'You did not, but even if you had, the wait would have been worth it. You look ravishing.'

She blushed at the unexpected compliment. 'Elo-ise designed this gown. She has an excellent eye. I've only worn it a couple of times. I wasn't sure whether it was too much for tonight, but I am glad I put it on now, for you are all dressed up—I mean, you also look very well.'

'Like you, I don't have much call for evening dress these days. Will you take another glass of champagne?'

'Yes, please. I was too nervous to enjoy the one I had earlier.'

She watched Owen from under her lashes as he set about expertly opening the bottle, turning the cork carefully so that it came off with a quiet hiss and not a showy pop that spoilt the bubbles.

'To new beginnings,' he said, handing her a frothing glass.

'New beginnings.' She clinked her glass to his and took a sip.

'I was very remiss earlier,' Owen said, indicating that she take a seat on the sofa by the fire, easing himself into a chair opposite. 'I didn't tell you how very grateful I am.'

'That implies that I am doing you a favour. I thought we had agreed that our marriage benefitted both of us. Don't be grateful, be—I don't know, relieved?'

'I am very relieved. Jasper has offered to hand-deliver my letters to Olivia and her parents.'

'Is he acquainted with Miss Braidwood?'

'His sister was at school with her, but if you're worried that Jasper thinks that I've done Olivia anything other than an enormously good turn, you're quite wrong. He knows better than anyone other than Olivia herself, how miserable I'd make her. He took to you, I could tell.'

'He doesn't know me, Owen. What he'll think of me when he finds out about our plans…'

Owen gave a bark of laughter. 'I'll make sure to have a large brandy on hand when I tell him. For all he likes to kick over the traces, Jasper's a bit of a traditionalist.'

Phoebe's eyes widened. 'His approval of me is going to be very short-lived.'

'Oh, he'll come round. All you have to do is offer him a table at the opening night. Jasper likes to be at the forefront of fashion. You don't regret what we've done, do you, Phoebe?'

'Already! Hardly. I've no real idea what it entails—I mean aside from the restaurant—but I'm excited by the uncertainty, if that makes any sense? I don't suppose it does.'

'You can't imagine what the future holds, but anything is possible?'

'Yes, that's it.' She beamed. 'By marrying you, I've wiped the slate clean. Now I can start again. And no doubt make a whole lot of brand new mistakes,' she added, wincing. 'But I will have you to advise me on the financial and business aspects, to ensure that I don't make a disaster of the whole enterprise, won't I? There is little point in a restaurant that serves lovely food but doesn't make a profit. I'm a chef, I know nothing of commerce. I think—I hope our skills will complement one another. But let's not talk business tonight.'

'Very well. Tell me instead, if your room is comfortable?'

'Yes, thank you.'

Owen raised his brows. 'You're not a very good liar.'

'It is rather cold from being unused, that is all.'

'You are free to make whatever changes you see fit to the house, provided you leave my rooms as they are—I have my own suite on the ground floor. Bremner will be delighted to help, I am sure.'

Owen finished his champagne and made to rise, but Phoebe pre-empted him, jumping to her feet and topping up both glasses. 'Force of habit,' she said apologetically. 'I like to feed and water people. I don't just mean professionally, I mean it's what I've done all my life—but you don't want to hear about that.'

'But I do. We're married, and I know almost nothing about you.'

'Nor I you. It's very strange, isn't it?'

'Then in the interests of becoming better acquainted, tell me where your passion for cooking stems from.'

'Necessity, in the first instance. I cooked for my sisters—but you know, I don't really want to look back on those days, Owen. My parents had what you might call a tempestuous relationship, which meant we didn't see much of them. Eloise said that Mama was a social butterfly, trailing my father in her wake. I don't agree, I don't think she understood Mama, but I can see why she thought it and even I would admit that we were—oh, it doesn't matter. Today is about the future, not the past.'

'You're quite right. We have just toasted new beginnings. Let us live up to that and consign the past to ancient history, where it belongs. I am more than happy to look forward, but I think we should do so over dinner. Shall we?'

Phoebe preceded Owen, intuiting that he preferred his impaired gait to go unobserved, along the hall to the double doors where the eponymous Mr Bremner stood waiting for them. She took her seat at the table as her husband made his way into the room. Like the drawing room it was cold, but it was also very beautiful in precisely the kind of understated way she preferred, with pale green walls and white cornicing unadorned by gilt or gold leaf. The table had a highly polished walnut veneer, a matching sideboard where their dinner was set out on heated trays, and long curtains of dark green velvet drawn against the winter evening. Bremner poured the wine and served the soup, before retiring.

'Chestnut soup,' Phoebe said, savouring the delicious smell, then taking a spoonful. 'It is quite delicious. In Paris, they set up braziers on all the street corners and roast the chestnuts. I love the taste of them, piping hot and fresh out of their shells.'

'They have such vendors in London too. I take it that you are not well acquainted with the capital?'

'I have spent very little time here. I shall have to buy a guide book to help me find my way around.'

'Are you keen to see the sights?'

Phoebe chuckled. 'Not the kind which most people come to London to see. I want to explore the markets, to see the range and quality of fresh produce available. In Paris, we were very spoiled.'

'London has Smithfield for meat, Billingsgate for fish and Covent Garden for fruit and vegetables, so I don't think you'll lack for ingredients.'

'Good, then I can start to think about compiling my menus. Though before that I'll need to decide what kind of food our restaurant is going to serve. And after that—or perhaps at the same time—I'll need to think about who I'm going to serve it to. And where. That is one of my biggest worries, because I don't know London, and I don't even know who I'll be competing with—if anyone at all. You can probably understand now, why I would never in a thousand years have found anyone to invest in me. You are probably already thinking you have thrown your money away.'

'*Your* money, not mine. Stop thinking about how much you have to do, Phoebe, the prospect is bound to be overwhelming. It's not one big leap you have to take, it's a whole series of small steps.'

'That is a much more sensible way to approach it.'

'Although that's easier said than done, when you are desperate to achieve your objective.'

He was staring down at his almost untouched soup, a grim look on his face. Phoebe set her own spoon down, tentatively putting her hand over his. 'But you've kept going,' she said. 'If I falter, then I'll have you as an example to follow.'

'I don't think I'm a particularly good role model. I certainly haven't been lately.' Owen slipped his hand from under hers and picked up his wine glass, taking a large sip. 'But that's something else I plan to change. Is the wine to your liking?'

'White burgundy,' Phoebe said, taking a sip. 'It is excellent.'

'It is from the Chateau Montendre, the Duc de Montendre's estate.'

'You know the Duke?'

'No, but my father did, back when he was plain Monsieur Bauduin, wine merchant. These days, he spends most of his time on his estates, where he produces his own vintages, but he continues to supply to a select few customers, including myself. I consume very little of it,' Owen added with a wry smile. 'I have a very full, and probably very valuable cellar as a result.'

'Perhaps I'll appropriate it and populate the restaurant wine list with it,' Phoebe teased.

Bremner arrived to clear the plates, making no comment on his master's lack of appetite, but granting her one of his grimacing smiles when she asked him to pass on her compliments to the chef.

'Oysters grilled with parsley and shallots,' she said appreciatively, picking up her fork for the next course, hoping to set an example with her own appetite. 'I adore oysters.'

Owen shuddered. 'I'm afraid I don't share your enthusiasm for them. I am ashamed to say that I once, for reasons I cannot now fathom, took part in an oyster-eating competition for a wager. It was more than ten years ago, but I haven't been able to face one since.'

'I assume you won?'

'Of course, but it all but did for me!'

'The ones you ate were most likely brined. These are very different. Won't you try one? They really are quite delicious.'

'I thank you, but no. Is there any food you don't enjoy?'

'I'm not particularly fond of turnip or parsnip. They are not even improved by being made into a cake.'

'You are teasing me, surely. I may be a philistine when it comes to food but that sounds just plain wrong.'

Phoebe giggled. 'Oh, no, I've made cakes with almost every vegetable you can name. I even once made one with grass.'

'Now I know you're joking.'

'I like to experiment with unusual flavours. I make

excellent lavender biscuits—though Aunt Kate says they taste a little too much of furniture polish for her liking. And I've made ices flavoured with herbs— thyme, rosemary, camomile.'

'And will your customers be able to taste any of these delights?'

'Who knows? I do know these oysters are delight- ful. And the vol-au-vent look delicious. They are called *bouchée à la reine* in France. The filling in these is chicken and mushroom, though you can put anything you like in them.'

'Including grass?'

'Perhaps not quite anything. Would you like one?'

'I'll save myself for the main course. And while I remember, I'll have a word with Bremner about hiring some female staff. I should have thought of it earlier.'

'Thank you. What about our—our domestic ar- rangements, Owen? Shall we dine together? I would like to, but I don't want to disrupt your—your routine.'

He laughed shortly. 'You will be a very welcome interruption. My *routine* has become quite tedious.'

'When I was working gruelling shifts in the kitch- ens, I used to long for a few days of idleness, but these last few months, doing nothing—save for the fruitless task of trying to find new employment—has been chas- tening. And very lonely. To be perfectly honest, Pascal wasn't exactly riveting company. He could be fascinat- ing when he talked about cooking, but he wasn't inter- ested in much else, and he certainly wasn't interested in me.' Looking up, she smiled. 'In fact, I have been quite starved of conversation since our Elmswood Coven broke up. Let that be a warning to you—you'll be sick and tired of my endless chatter before the week is out.'

'I doubt it.' Owen surprised her by touching her hand. 'Perhaps it's because you don't know me and have no expectations of me, but I find I'm enjoying your company.'

'Thank you. The feeling is mutual.'

Bremner appeared once more, and Owen released her hand while the braised beef and spinach ragout was served. He took a small bite before setting his cutlery down. 'You must speak to Murray, my—our cook about menus, he'll be delighted to be consulted.'

'Shall I be expected to—will there be callers, Owen? I don't even know if our marriage will be formally announced.'

'I'll put a notice in the press, but I thought you'd want to inform your family first.'

'I do. I was thinking though, I am not sure that I want to tell them the truth. Not yet.'

'You think they'll disapprove?'

'I think they'll worry, and I don't want that.'

'So what will you tell them?'

'What did you tell Jasper? Not the truth, I don't think. He was far too—enthusiastic,' Phoebe said. 'He seems to be under the impression that I will launch you back into society.'

Owen laughed harshly. 'Jasper thinks that a few nights on the town will cure me of my doldrums. Not that he put it quite like that.'

'He obviously cares about you a great deal.'

'I told him that we'd met in Paris, which is the truth.

I implied that my accident had prevented me from wooing you, and you had come in search of me,' Owen said. 'I hope you don't mind, but he does care, and I am tired of disappointing him. He thought it very romantic.'

'You mean he thinks that we are in love?'

'I didn't say that, but he leapt to that conclusion, obviously. I'm sorry if I've embarrassed you.'

'You haven't. In fact the same story might suffice for my sisters,' Phoebe said. 'If you don't mind?'

'Why should I? Do you think they'll believe you?'

'Owen, despite what you think, you are a very attractive man. And more importantly, you have faith in me, which I shall be sure to tell my sisters. I'll reassure them that you are rich enough to invest in a dozen failed restaurants and not even notice the losses.'

'I'm only investing in one, and what is more I know that it won't fail.' Owen picked up his glass of burgundy. 'They will be toasting our future health and happiness below stairs as we speak. I'd like to propose a toast too. To Phoebe. For being brave enough to take me on, and for continuing to dream her dream. I thank you, and I wish you every success.'

Touched, she had to swallow a lump in her throat. 'I will need all your best wishes and more.' She lifted her glass. 'To Owen. For being brave enough to take me on, and for allowing me to dare to hope that I might one day realise my dream. Here's to making a success of this—this convenient marriage of ours.'

'Fortuitous,' Owen said. 'I prefer to think of it as fortuitous.'

'Very well then, here is to our fortuitous marriage.'

They touched glasses, their eyes meeting as they each took a sip, remaining locked as they set their glasses down. Owen took her hand in his. He lifted it to his mouth, pressing a kiss to her gloved fingertips. Something crackled between them, an awareness of themselves as husband and wife on their wedding night, and the ghost of themselves in Paris over two years ago, looking into each other's eyes in just this way. Then like now, knowing that nothing could come of it. Experiencing again that brief moment of inexplicable, but unmistakable sense of longing. Owen's fingers tightened on hers. And then he let her go.

'I'm afraid I keep early hours these days,' he said.

'No, of course, I mean please don't let me—I'm very tired, anyway.'

Phoebe got to her feet at the same time as he did, and then they both stood, hesitating, as if unwilling to part after all. 'Goodnight, Owen.'

He reached out, as if he would touch her cheek, then dropped his hand. 'Goodnight, Phoebe.' He opened the door, and she brushed past him into the hallway, picking up her candle from the table and lighting it. She was aware of him watching her as she climbed the stairs, and it was only as she turned to climb the second flight that she heard the dining-room door close softly, and the slight dragging sound of her husband's footstep as he made his way slowly to the opposite end of the house and his own bed.

Chapter Five

Owen jerked back into consciousness with a start, his sheets a tangled knot around his legs, his body clammy, a sheen of sweat making his nightshirt cling to him. The room was pitch black. The muscles in his shoulders and his arms ached, which meant he'd been having what he called his reaching dream. He had no memory of what it was he was reaching for, no idea how he came to be reaching for it in the first place, but he always woke at the same point, when it became hopelessly clear that he would not succeed, no matter how hard he strove, and the high-pitched wailing which accompanied his desperate attempts to stretch those vital inches further came to an abrupt halt.

Hands shaking, heart pounding, Owen struggled to sit up, fighting the overwhelming sense of despair and terrible sorrow, the enormous weight of guilt at his failure, which made his chest heave as he suppressed a violent sob. Forcing himself to breathe deeply, he counted each breath in, held it, breathed out, several times before his hands had stopped trembling enough to light his candle and check the time on his watch. Three minutes past three. The night was only half-way through, but he couldn't face yet another failed attempt at sleep, knowing from bitter experience that the nightmare was lurking like a lone wolf tracking its prey, waiting to claim him again.

Shivering, he pulled on his dressing gown and headed for his workroom where, unlike the cold ashes in the grate of his bedroom, the fire would still be smouldering behind the screen, ready to be rekindled. He threw on a few coals before replacing the screen, settling himself in his chair with his leg on the foot-stool. His violent tossing and turning had caused him to wrench his damaged hip. The constant, grating ache which he sometimes thought was his shattered body's way of punishing him for the trauma he had put it through, was now a sharp stabbing pain. In the past, he had turned to opium to help him endure such torrid nights. Only when he caught himself deliberately in-ducing oblivion to prevent such nights occurring, had he realised how reliant he had become on the drug. He couldn't give in to that temptation even if he wanted to now, for he had had the presence of mind to ensure his resolve was not tested by the simple expedient of refusing to give it house room.

Why had it happened on this night of all nights? His wedding night! The first night in a very long time when he was not burdened with thoughts of Olivia, when he had surely earned a peaceful night's sleep. And yet here he was, shivering, aching, the hazy memory of his nightmare taunting him, the details as always just tantalisingly out of reach.

Closing his eyes and resting his head against the chair-back, Owen sighed with frustration. He was heartily sick of himself, of the front he was forced to put on for the benefit of his staff and now his wife, of being inured to his injuries, of accepting that his recuperation had gone as far as it could go.

He was far from content with his lot. Seeing his stern butler begin to thaw, basking in the warmth of Phoebe's smile over the course of the day, made Owen realise, guiltily, how much his own mood had affected the household, how dour he had become. And in Jasper's eyes there had been hope that perhaps Owen was finally on the road to recovery.

Was there hope? Tonight, he had made conversation, he'd even laughed, over dinner with Phoebe. He had forgotten what it felt like to enjoy the simple pleasure of being in another person's company. He had been reminded tonight, but the memory was bittersweet because although there had been moments that could be mistaken for spontaneity on his part, looking back over the evening, maintaining his side of the conversation had been an effort. He'd had to imagine how the old Owen would have responded, taking his previous self as his role model. He had pulled it off, by and large, although there had been a couple of occasions when Phoebe's smile froze as she studied him carefully. They had passed, and she had probably put it down to the strangeness of the situation.

But there had been a moment when he had stopped

being self-conscious. Saying goodnight to his beautiful wife, taking her hand in his, he had fleetingly remembered what desire felt like. He screwed his eyes shut, trying to recapture that elusive moment, the simple pleasure of proximity, the sweet, dragging tug of attraction, the anticipation as their eyes met, and the possibility of a kiss hung between them. He ached with the bittersweet delight of it, yearned to experience it again, longed to be able to touch her, skin on skin, wanting that even more than the kiss they had not shared.

Owen dropped his head into his hands. What was he doing, torturing himself like this, imagining what he knew to be simple fantasy? Just a few hours ago, he had toasted new beginnings. So why not turn his mind to actually thinking about a fresh start instead of looking over his shoulder regretfully at the past and what he had lost for ever. He could not be the man he had once been, but he could try to make the best of the one he was now.

For a start, he could do a damned sight better than blithely wave Phoebe off to explore London's fresh produce markets unaccompanied. London was not Paris. The areas around Smithfield and Billingsgate were not safe, especially in the early hours when market trading was at its peak. He wasn't fit enough to wander around on foot with her, but he could get Jasper to purchase some fresh horses on his behalf since his stables had lain empty for years. He'd have his town coach or the barouche cleaned up, and he could give her the grand tour of London himself.

The heavy, black cloud that permanently hung over him began to lift. Something like a flicker of excitement kindled in his belly. What's more, if he did resume his exercises as he'd planned, he could conceivably escort her to one of those damned markets she was so keen on. It wasn't as if he'd need to worry about meeting anyone he knew there. All he had to do was work on his strength and his stamina—and if he worked hard, he could be ready in as little as a few weeks.

Almost immediately, his enthusiasm flagged. He had followed the prescribed exercise regime diligently for a while, but he'd reached the point where it made no difference, he reminded himself. His doctors, who already thought Owen had worked a small miracle by getting back on to his feet, told him to lower his expectations. But his doctors had only ever known him after his accident. Owen had been an athlete. The rush of pleasure came not from besting anyone, but from challenging himself to run faster and longer to push himself to new limits, the more taxing the better, because what was the point in achieving an easy victory! That was what he'd loved so much about gymnastics. He smiled, remembering the Russian acrobat who had sparked his interest telling him, in that condescending way of his, that it took dedication to master even the most basic of moves. He'd been right, it had taken months, but he'd been wrong in imagining that Owen would give up. He never had, managing to practice even when he was on his travels, rarely missing a day. Until that day.

He missed it. He missed the complete control he'd had over his body. It was bloody hard work, but worth it, when he finally held a position, when his muscles, which had resisted and resisted a particular move, suddenly found the knack. God, he missed that. Once, and only once, a tentative enquiry of his doctors had produced astonished looks followed by vehement admonitions that he must never attempt anything so taxing. He must accept that there were some things he would never do again.

But what if they were wrong? Instead of focusing on what he couldn't do, why not try to explore what might be possible? Owen got to his feet, rolling back his shoulders. He could not control his sick mind, but he could try to reclaim his damaged body. It was an appealing idea. It would at least give him a purpose, and a goal. But he mustn't look too far ahead, nor expect the impossible of himself. Small steps, as he'd said to Phoebe. Though not too small. He'd had his fill of the tedious exercises his physician had prescribed, he needed to do something he enjoyed. He couldn't contemplate going back to the public gymnasium in his condition, but it might be possible to have a small gymnasium constructed here.

To hell with the doctor's regime, he was going to try his own. Casting off his dressing gown, he cleared a space in the middle of the floor and began the slow process of warming up his neglected muscles.

'Are you sure you want to do this?' Phoebe asked.

'We are going for a carriage ride, I'm not setting

out to scale Ben Nevis,' Owen retorted, making for the front door.

'Oh, you've had the hood put up,' she said, disappointed, thinking it would spoil the view, then realising almost immediately why. 'Excellent idea,' she amended.

'It is, because I think it might rain at some point,' Owen said testily, 'not because I am not worried someone might recognise me. Now, shall we go?'

'Please.' She preceded him down the front steps into the dank October air. She had not been outside in the six days since they had been married, occupying herself with putting the few rooms in the town house which she wished to use to rights, and establishing herself with Mr Murray, the cook. Owen was carefully making his way down the steps, wearing a greatcoat, a hat and a look of grim determination. She eyed the waiting barouche, wondering how on earth he was going to get up the steep steps and into the carriage, sick with nerves lest he fall and deciding the best course of action would be to accept the coachman's invitation to climb in first. But Owen, as she observed while pretending very hard not to, got in with surprising ease.

'I would normally have taken the reins myself,' he said, sitting down beside her, 'but since this is my first outing in some time, I decided discretion was the better part of valour.' Owen nodded to the coachman to drive on. 'I thought we'd take a drive along the river, and if the rain holds off, round Richmond Park. Seeing the city from the outskirts gives you a better sense of it, and the air is a lot fresher.'

'I miss the countryside, though I love the excitement of the city—not that I know any city save Paris, mind you.'

'You'll get to know London soon enough.'

'Don't you miss enjoying what it has to offer, Owen?,' Phoebe asked impulsively. 'Owen?'

He blinked, and her heart contracted, for he looked for a moment utterly lost. The enormity of what he was doing struck her afresh. The last thing he'd want would be for her to draw attention to the strain it was putting him under. 'I had a letter from Eloise this morning,' she said. 'I think there were more exclamation marks than words. To say that my news came as an enormous surprise is something of an understatement.'

She was rewarded with a faint smile. 'I hope a not-altogether-unpleasant surprise?'

'It appears Alexander, her husband, seems to have put in a good word for you. "A most enterprising and well-respected investor" was how he described you to my sister, though how he knows that, I've no idea.'

'I have a certain reputation in the financial world,' Owen replied.

'I didn't realise. I thought—oh, it doesn't matter, I know nothing of such things.'

'You thought that because I see no one, no one is aware of my success? My success speaks for itself, unfortunately—I am a "name" in the city.'

'Do people seek your advice, then?'

'Often, and offer to pay me handsomely for it, but the whole point of the game I play is risk, a question of odds. I can easily afford to lose. Others can't.'

'But you don't lose.'

'Not often, but I have done, quite spectacularly too.'

'Really? But then why don't you stop, keep what you have safe?'

Owen shrugged. 'Because I enjoy the game.'

'Something for which I am extremely grateful, though I hope I won't be one of your spectacular failures.'

'I wish that you'd have a bit more faith in yourself. Stop looking over your shoulder at what happened in Paris. I thought you were determined to prove Solignac wrong?'

'And my sisters too. Though I didn't tell Eloise about my plans. I'm afraid I allowed her to think that we had fallen in love. She's so besotted herself, to be honest, I think that even if I had told her the truth she'd have persuaded herself that we fell in love at first sight but—well anyway, I thought I'd better let you know.'

'Why? Is she planning to visit?'

'Oh, goodness, no.' Phoebe beamed. 'I quite forgot, Eloise is expecting a baby. I'm going to be an aunt! I think I forgot because I can't quite believe it. She never wished for children, but I think she has revised her opinion given that piece of news garnered the most exclamations marks in her letter. So she won't be coming to London any time soon, though she has invited us to visit her in Lancashire.'

'When will you tell her about the restaurant?'

'When there is something to tell.'

'Fair enough. And has Estelle replied to your letter?'

'Briefly, to offer her congratulations. I can't tell whether or not she meant it.'

'Did you tell *her* the truth about the terms of our marriage?'

Phoebe shook her head. 'I will when the time is right.'

'Are you fretting about her?'

Phoebe considered this. 'I don't like being on bad terms with her but we will resolve our differences. We always do. Anyway, she's probably enjoying being on her own. Being a twin is lovely, but it can be quite suffocating, you know? No, how could you. I can't imagine being without my sisters.'

'Even though they suffocate you?' Owen teased.

Phoebe shook her head. 'It's not exactly that, but they are over-protective. No one knows you as well as a sister. They know all your foibles, they remember all the embarrassing moments one endures while growing up. And when you have a twin especially, they know your thoughts, sometimes, even before you have a chance to voice them.'

'Your dinner conversations were conducted in silence, then?'

'Our dinner conversations were a noisy rabble! Living in a house with three very opinionated women— well, it was a case of she who shouts the loudest.'

'And I'm willing to bet that your voice was often the quietest. It's obvious that you hold your aunt and your sisters in a great deal of awe.'

'Respect,' she corrected him, frowning. 'And rightly

so. Aunt Kate took the three of us in when she was the same age as I am now.'

'I had no idea. I imagined someone much older.'

Phoebe giggled. 'If you meet her—when you meet her—you'll be astonished. She is extremely pretty and she's quite petite, one of those women you think would struggle to lift her fork to eat, until she turns those eyes on you, and you realise there's a core of steel running right through her. She and Eloise are very alike. My eldest sister was forced to grow up far too quickly—I'm afraid Mama was not a very maternal kind of mother.'

'People who are determined to enjoy life to the full, as I remember you said your mother did, tend to be rather selfish creatures, I'm afraid.'

'Mama was not selfish! Although that is what Eloise believes.'

Owen held up his hands. 'I only meant—'

'There are some people who simply break the mould,' Phoebe interrupted him, glowering. 'One shouldn't judge them by conventional standards.'

Clearly not, he thought, taken aback by her vehemence. 'The little I recall of my own mother,' he said, in an effort to mollify her, 'leads me to believe she wasn't particularly maternal either. I remember being brought down from the nursery to be cooed over before dinner, and when I was at school, she would occasionally accompany my father to sports days. "All that mud, and sweaty, smelly little boys,"' Owen mimicked. 'She was very beautiful, and as I recall, delighted when those sweaty, smelly little boys gazed upon her as if she was an angel descended from heaven to the playing fields of Eton.'

To his relief, Phoebe relaxed. 'How proud you must have been when she did visit you. All the other boys must have been so envious.'

Owen, who recalled simply being mortified, shrugged.

'What age were you when you lost her?'

'Ten, I think, perhaps nine.'

'As young as that? Oh, Owen, you must have been devastated.'

Once again he shrugged. She was drawing parallels that did not exist but he didn't want to disillusion her with the truth. 'I was away at school. It's not the done thing to be upset at school, one must take it like a man.'

'Our little brother, Diarmuid, was on his way to Eton with my parents when their boat sank in a storm in the Irish sea, and we lost all three of them.'

'All at once! That's dreadful. *You* must have been devastated.'

'We all were, though Eloise as usual put a brave face on. That's when Aunt Kate took us in. I don't like to remember those days. We felt as if our world was turned upside down.'

'It was. Poor Phoebe.'

'And poor Estelle and Eloise too. But we had each other, and Aunt Kate too. And though no one could ever replace Mama, even I can see that Aunt Kate gave us a much more stable home. And a happy one too.'

'The Elmswood Coven?'

Phoebe laughed. 'You remember.' Her smile became

whimsical. 'Only to think that my little brother was headed for the same school you attended—though your time wouldn't have overlapped, for Diarmuid was four years younger than Estelle and I. Mama didn't want him to go, but Papa said it would be the making of him. Diarmuid was adorable, but he was terribly spoilt and dreadfully lazy, which I don't think would have been in his favour at school.'

'They do rate brawn considerably higher than brain. I was fortunate enough to excel at all sports.'

Owen, Phoebe thought, would have been popular however good or bad he was at sports, a charismatic little boy, just like the man he had become. And an athlete. Jasper had told her so, but she'd not realised how much a part of Owen's life it had been. No wonder his accident had brought him so low.

'So your brother was the favourite, I gather?'

Phoebe started, wondering if her thoughts had been written on her face, as they so often were. Owen did not like anyone to feel sorry for him. 'Diarmuid,' she said, trying to recall the thread of their conversation. 'Yes, indeed. The only son, and much longed for. I think they had all but given up hope, and I do know Mama dreaded having another girl. I remember her telling us so.'

'How very thoughtful of her.'

'Oh, she didn't mean to be unkind,' Phoebe said. 'But children are not good for a woman's figure, she said, and Mama's figure was—she was quite simply the most beautiful woman I've ever seen. When she entered a room, she drew everyone's attention—you simply couldn't take your eyes off her. She was the toast of Dublin, and would have been the toast of London too, if Papa had taken her there.'

'But Papa was rightly cautious.'

Phoebe frowned at his tone. 'It wasn't Mama's fault that she was so beautiful, or that so many people sought her attention. That was why she had so little time for us girls—there simply wasn't enough of her to satisfy everyone.'

'And she chose to satisfy herself. No, don't leap to her defence, Phoebe, my mother was the same, content to hand me into the care of my nurse or my tutor or my school.'

'Well then, you do understand,' Phoebe said, though she didn't really think he did, any more than Eloise understood their mother. 'Though actually,' she felt obliged to add in defence of her eldest sister, 'it was mostly Eloise who took care of us. We lived in the wilds of the Irish countryside. Our constantly changing governesses didn't much enjoy the isolation.'

'Any more than your mother did, I presume.'

She shrugged uncomfortably. 'Anyway, that is how Eloise comes to be such a strong person.'

'With a dominant voice at the dinner table?'

'Exactly.' She smiled at him, relieved.

'And Estelle too?'

'Estelle is the family comic. She is so funny, Owen, she used to have us in fits of laughter. She could easily take the London stage by storm, if she does not choose to lead an orchestra instead.'

'Which leaves Phoebe to be the quiet one—or are you the peacemaker?'

'No, I simply make sure the rest of them are well fed. They are very appreciative, I assure you.'

'But they think you are overreaching yourself in wishing to make a career of it?'

'What if they're right? They think I need protecting.'

'And in doing so they inadvertently stifle you,' Owen said. 'You don't need protecting. If you did, you'd have run to Eloise, instead of which...'

'I ran to you.'

'You asked me to help you to help yourself. There's a big difference.'

Phoebe considered this. It sounded very feasible. 'Perhaps.'

'Definitely,' Owen said firmly. 'You're perfectly capable of standing on your own two feet, and of springing back from adversity.'

She smiled. 'I like that. I shall spring up from the depths of failure and surprise them all with my success, like a jack-in-the-box.'

'A very beautiful jack-in-the-box.'

'Oh. Thank you. I'm nowhere near as lovely as Mama though.'

'I won't argue with you because it would be futile.'

'Well it would.' Which sounded rather defensive, Phoebe realised, even though it was true. 'I've talked far too much, and likely bored you to death. You'll have to learn to do what my sisters do, and talk over me.'

'I happen to enjoy your conversation. I happen to

find you interesting. All that complicated sibling rivalry, to an only child, is fascinating.'

'It's not rivalry. You don't understand.'

'Oh, I rather think I do, but we won't argue. Tell me, has your aunt added her congratulations to those of your sisters'? We've been married nearly a week, we really should put a notice in the press.'

'I haven't heard directly from Aunt Kate. Eloise told me that she was away somewhere on urgent business. I can't imagine where, Aunt Kate never goes anywhere. But anyway—if you must tell the world, then you can safely do so now.'

'I must. I doubt the world will be much interested, but Olivia is eager to have the announcement made, according to Jasper.'

'He's spoken to Miss Braidwood? And how is she?'

'As I hoped, quietly relieved. She will make a belated formal debut next Season.'

'And her parents?'

'Owen shrugged. Their congratulations read like condolences, but frankly I've never given much of a damn about what they thought.'

They were crossing the Thames, and Owen turned to look out at the river. One of his hands still covered hers. Phoebe wondered if he had forgotten, and decided not to draw attention to the fact. What was he thinking? How did it feel, to be out in the open air like this after—how long? He had admitted at dinner one night that his 'disconnection' from the world, as he called it, had been a gradual thing, not a sudden decision. Why? she longed to ask him. Why had he lost his appetite for life? And what had killed it? It didn't take a genius to work out that his accident had involved a fire. He certainly displayed an unnatural wariness of it, for every fire in the town house was screened and meagre. To have come so close to losing everything, she thought, should surely have made him more determined to embrace life rather than abdicate from it. She couldn't understand it, but she did know that this trip he was making for her, with her, marked a significant step forward. And she also knew better than to say so.

So she held his hand, and she inched a little closer to him on the seat of the barouche, and she watched his profile, trying not to let him see that she was watching him, and at some point her concern for him and her gratitude and her admiration for his courage changed into awareness of him. Of the length of his leg against hers. Of his booted foot against hers. And of his hands, covering hers.

The clouds had scudded away on the breeze, leaving a sky that was bright blue, and a weak sun that was almost lemon in colour. As they turned into Richmond Park, a small herd of grazing deer lifted their heads to watch them pass, a stag, two fully-grown hinds and four youngers, gazing haughtily and quite unafraid. Russet leaves still clung tenaciously to the trees. The air was sharp as she inhaled the fresh grassy scent of the countryside. Phoebe lifted her face, closing her eyes, suddenly, for the first time in an age, relaxed and content. Opening them again, she found Owen gazing down at her, and smiled. 'This is so lovely,' she said.

'It is,' he agreed, raising his free hand to smooth

back a curl which had escaped from her bonnet and clung to her cheek. The brush of his fingers on her skin, even in his gloves, sent a frisson shivering down her spine. She smoothed her cheek into his hand, turning her face so that her lips brushed his palm. She heard the sharp intake of his breath. Saw the flare of awareness in his eyes. Then the barouche drew to a halt, and the coachman turned to enquire which direction they should take home, and Owen dropped her hand. The moment was gone, over so quickly Phoebe persuaded herself that she had imagined it.

The weather turned wet and miserable over the next few weeks as November settled in. The announcement of their nuptials had brought a surprising number of letters and cards of invitation, considering that most of London society would have retired to the country by now. Owen, reading names he had confined to his past, did what he always did with such communications and left them unanswered. Beside him at the breakfast table, Phoebe was sipping her tea and frowning over the latest sheaf of commercial properties available for lease which his lawyer had sent for their consideration. There had been three trips over the last ten days in the town coach to visit a selection of them, but she had been surprisingly unenthusiastic about all of them.

'What's wrong?' Owen asked. 'Don't you like any of these?'

'They all have merit.'

'But?'

'There are too many unanswered questions to be

able to make a decision. I don't know what would be the best location because I don't know who the clientele will be. I don't know how big it should be because I don't know how many covers I'll be serving. I don't know what I want the interior to look like. I don't know—I don't know anything,' she finished, her lip trembling. 'I think you've made a big mistake.'

Owen pushed aside his coffee and his empty plate to reach over for her hand. 'It's not like you to sound so defeatist.'

'I'm not. Only a little. You've found all these properties and personally taken me to view them. Don't think I don't know what an effort that has been for you, and I feel dreadful, Owen, offering so little in return.'

'It's not an effort. I have enjoyed our little expeditions.'

'Have you?'

'Why would you think otherwise?'

'I can't tell, sometimes, whether you really are enjoying something or simply acting as if you are. You're very adept at it.'

He released her hand, taken aback by this. He knew that it had been an act that he put on every moment of the day, but it had become so easy for him to be with her that he didn't have to think, most of the time, about how to behave. When he disappeared into himself as he did occasionally, Phoebe rarely remarked upon it, allowing him to pretend she hadn't noticed. And then there were the moments when he became so caught up in the act that he fooled himself into thinking that what he was feeling was real. Wanting to kiss her. To touch her. To hold her. Imagining that her touch could bring him back to life.

It seemed to him that he paid for such foolishness with his nightmares which, though less frequent, had taken a new turning. His usual reaching dream had ceded precedence to another, more sinister scenario in which he wandered the corridors of some sort of hospital or asylum opening door after door on to empty rooms. He was as desperate in this nightmare as in his other dream to find something, as overwhelmed with grief and guilt when he awoke. And there was the same high-pitched wailing too, which jolted him awake when it stopped. He had always assumed that his reaching dream had something to do with his mind's distorted memory of his accident, but this dream, which he'd had again last night, made no sense at all.

Phoebe folded up the stack of papers and wandered off to the window to gaze out at the rain-drenched street. She thought he was having another blank moment, Owen realised, and was giving him time to recover. He joined her at the window, where she was tracing the path of a particularly plump raindrop with her finger. She wore her hair in a simple knot on top of her head, her copper curls trailing down over her shoulder. Her gown of dark blue wool was trimmed with a ruffle of white lace leaving the long line of her nape exposed. She didn't wear perfume, but smelled of lemon soap. Before his accident, he'd have put his arm around her waist and drawn her back against him. Her hair would have tickled his chin. Or he'd have buried his nose in the warm, soft skin of her nape, his hands sliding up from her waist to cup her breasts. She'd press the soft rump of her bottom against him, and she'd feel that he was hard, and then she'd twist around in his arms, her mouth curved into a sensual smile, and she'd kiss him.

Phoebe turned around, bumping into him, and Owen instinctively caught her.

'I didn't realise you were so close,' she said.

'I'm sorry.'

She smiled up at him, shaking her head. 'What for?'

He made to let her go, but she caught his hand. 'Do you ever take these off?'

Completely thrown, still half-caught up in their imagined embrace, he shook his head. 'Only when I go to bed.'

'Wouldn't they benefit from a little air now and then?'

'The scars are healed.' He snatched his hand away.

'Alexander, Eloise's husband, calls her painfully observant, and she is, but it's a trait we all three sisters have to a degree. We notice everything.' She coloured. 'I have no right to comment on your behaviour. You are coping admirably with something which would defeat most people, including me.'

'Am I? By acting out a part?'

Phoebe sighed. 'To be honest, I feel like a bit of a fraud myself. Maybe Estelle was right after all when she said that I should stick to cooking for friends and family. The last time in Paris—when we argued—that's what she told me. She finds the idea of me cooking for complete strangers incomprehensible.'

'She aspires to be a musician. Surely that involves playing for complete strangers?'

'It's not the same thing. That would be a performance, my cooking...'

'Is also a sort of performance,' Owen said, 'with you taking the roles of both the conductor and the composer. Think of the entire meal as a symphony or an opera.'

'With the *amuse-bouche* as the overture, and the dessert as the finale.'

'And as many acts or courses in between as you care to compose. You are as much an artiste as your twin, Phoebe.'

'You are very good at making me feel better. But Estelle is the genuinely talented one, I'm merely well practised.'

'You are certainly well practised at denigrating yourself,' Owen exclaimed, exasperated. 'You readily admit that you were stifled by your sisters' over-protectiveness. So much so, that you fled all the way to Paris.'

'I did not say that!'

'Not in so many words, but it's what you did, Phoebe. Yet despite the fact that you don't want to wear the label they've attached to you, you never question their rather humble opinion of your considerable talents.'

'Every time we discuss my family, I feel as if you are undermining all I know about them.'

'I am questioning your assumption that you were at the end of the queue when it came to handing out talent.' Owen sighed. 'All I want is for you to start be-

lieving in yourself. It pains me, how easily you fall
prey to self-doubt.'

'But it's hardly surprising is it, after what Pascal
said and did?'

'If your family hadn't already eroded your fragile
confidence, it wouldn't have been so easy for him. I
know you won't hear a bad word said about your sisters, especially not your twin, but please, Phoebe, just
think about what I've said. You underestimate yourself. As to your restaurant—do you remember what I
said, about taking a step at a time? Never mind what
it will look like, who will frequent it or where it will
be. Think about the most important element.'

'The food?'

'Precisely. What food do you want to cook? And in
order to establish that, you need to know what ingredients are to hand, don't you, what is available, what
the quality is like?'

'Yes. You're right.'

'Which means a visit to London's markets is long
overdue, don't you think?'

'Yes, but even I know it wouldn't be proper for me
to go myself. I suppose I could ask Murray?'

'You could, I'm sure he'd be delighted to accompany
you, but why not ask your husband instead?'

'Owen!' Phoebe's eyes lit up, but almost immediately her smile faded. 'No, it's too much to ask.'

'Then don't ask. I shall offer. Would you like to accompany me to the fruit and vegetable market at Covent Garden early tomorrow morning?'

'Truly? It will involve a good deal of walking about.'

'I am sure I can manage.'

'It's true, I have noticed…' She covered her mouth, her eyes wide. 'Sorry.'

'You may as well say it now.'

'I have noticed that you seem to be in less pain of late, and you're certainly walking much more freely. I was wondering if you had restarted the exercises your doctor prescribed?'

It was ridiculous to be flattered by this, but he was, and he had been working extremely hard, though he wasn't yet prepared to admit it. 'Not as such,' Owen said, which was true. 'So, tomorrow morning then?'

'Will we take the carriage?'

It was a relatively short walk, no more than twenty minutes, half an hour at a saunter, but Owen wasn't convinced he could manage that quite yet, not if he was going to be trailing around the market stalls too, so he nodded reluctantly.

'Are you sure—that you want to go, I mean? I would much prefer you to accompany me than Murray.'

'From you, that is a very great compliment.'

Phoebe laughed. 'Why would I not prefer the company of my very attractive husband to his bluff and craggy Scots chef? I am not the only one who underestimates themselves.'

'Perhaps not.'

'Then we will make it our business to bolster each other's confidence.' Her hand crept up to his cheek. Her fingers fluttered over it, caressing the line of his jaw, before she blushed and snatched her hand away. 'Talking of Murray, I had better go and discuss the menus for the rest of the week with him. He is overly fond of spices. I'm surprised he has not tried to serve us porridge with chilli pepper.'

The door closed behind her, and Owen sat back down at the table, pouring himself a cup of cold coffee. His muscles ached from his gymnastics this morning, but it was the pleasant ache resulting from hard work, not over-taxed injuries, save for the dragging pain in his hip, and even that was easing. If only he'd thought to return to his own regime earlier in his recuperation. He took a sip of coffee, grimaced and put it to one side. He'd been following doctor's orders not to take risks. Besides, he'd had no incentive to follow such a punishing schedule until Phoebe came back into his life. It was Phoebe who had inspired him, Phoebe who had, metaphorically, given him the much-needed kick up the backside.

And now his body was recovering in more ways than one. Desire had been absent from his life for so long, he had hardly recognised it when it had flared a minute ago. He allowed himself a moment of pure, sweet, unutterable relief, at this evidence that his accident had not wholly unmanned him. But it was short-lived, for there was no way in hell he could do anything about it. It was a sign that he was improving, physically, that was all, and really, he should have been expecting it. Phoebe was a very beautiful, extremely sensual woman. She had been the last woman he had found himself wanting, prior to his accident. It was no coincidence that she should be the first. After.

What's more, she found him attractive. She admitted it freely enough, though that was most likely because she knew—because he'd told her—that nothing could come of it.

And nothing could. Though he couldn't quite bring himself to wish he was still numb, this new development was a poisoned chalice, for the only outcome could be frustration, where before there had been indifference. Owen peeled off his gloves, forcing himself to study the backs of his hands, the fretwork of scarring, the pale pink colour of the tenderest skin, the hard callouses where the worst blisters had been, the permanently swollen middle knuckle. Flexing his fingers, he reminded himself that he'd been lucky that the damage had not been more extensive. They were ugly, they looked to him like the hands of an old man, but it wasn't vanity that kept them covered. It was fear.

He couldn't remember exactly what had happened, but it made a cold sweat break out on his back simply looking at his hands. Something too awful to bear lurked beyond the black wall of his memory, something that made him want to curl up on himself. Something terrible had happened and it had somehow been his fault. He could feel it building now, exactly the same feeling that he awoke with after his night sweats, an agony of grief and guilt.

He was attracted to his wife, but he dare not allow himself even the indulgence of imagining what it would be like to make love to her. Whatever had happened that day of his accident, his every instinct was to keep it walled up behind the emotional dam he had built. To let down his defences, even for the sweet delight of lovemaking, would be to release something that might make an emotional as well as a physical wreck of him.

He would not inflict that creature on Phoebe. Owen pulled his gloves back on. Phoebe was a naturally sensual woman, who probably had no idea of the effect she was having on him. Besides, he reminded himself, she wanted only one thing. Her restaurant. Her dream. He had married her in part to help her realise it. It would be madness to muddy those waters with anything more intimate. And despite his mental turmoil he was not, yet, barking mad.

Chapter Six

At just after five in the morning and in the pitch dark, Phoebe and Owen descended from their town coach on the edge of Covent Garden. Braziers lit up the market and surrounding streets. Housed in a new building, its neo-classical façade of columns and a balustraded second floor facing out on to the piazza, the market was already alive with traders and customers. Dray carts and their horses jostled for space to unload. Wooden crates tossed carelessly down were expertly caught and carted into the market by an endless stream of porters in leather aprons. Horses whinnied, wheels grated on the cobblestones, and men called out greetings, warnings and prices in a cacophony of sound that transported her back to the fresh-produce markets Phoebe had visited in France.

Putting her basket over her arm, she huddled close to Owen, intensely grateful for his presence, quite overwhelmed by the noise and the bustle. 'It's even bigger than I had imagined.'

'There's even more to it than you can see. It extends

into the surrounding streets,' Owen said, 'or it used to. I don't know how much of a difference this new building has made.'

'You are familiar with the market, then?'

'I've never bought so much as a potato, but I've walked home through it in the early hours many times.'

'When one commercial enterprise is shutting up shop and the other opening?' Phoebe said with an arch look. 'I do know, Owen, what other kind of business goes on here. It's like the Palais Royale in Paris.' She swept her gaze around the piazza, imagining a very different type of business being transacted in the cloisters where flower sellers were setting up. 'It even has the look of it, a little. In Paris, you know, courtesans—the more exclusive ones—are very much respected. The most famous of them dined at La Grande Taverne. Their presence was very good for business, for they set the fashion.'

'I hope you're not thinking of trying to attract London's most famous courtesans to your restaurant?'

'I wouldn't know who to invite,' Phoebe said, eyeing him speculatively. 'Would you?'

'It makes no difference, because it would be a sure-fire way of ensuring that you failed.'

'But you said that scandal was good for business.'

'Yes, but customers who don't pay their bills are not and neither London's most notorious courtesans nor their protectors are inclined to do that. They would expect you to be satisfied with the honour of their presence. Now, can we stop discussing Covent Garden ladies and focus on a different sort of fruit which is also ripe for the plucking?'

Phoebe giggled. 'Yes, I think that would be wise.'

The market hall was enormous and brightly lit, with stalls occupying two storeys built around a huge central area. Phoebe was immediately entranced, her senses swimming with the smells, the colours and the bounty, her brain busy concocting ideas for every single ingredient. Boxes of seasonal greens were stacked high, each vendor vying for trade by calling out the quality and price. Everything, they claimed, was freshly picked that morning, though on closer inspection she could see that the freshest produce was on full display and artfully sprinkled with water to resemble dew, while underneath more wilted specimens lurked, ready to be passed off on the less discerning customers, or those with a smaller purse.

'I will have to be careful when it comes to my own purchases,' she said, pointing out this practice to Owen.

'Once they learn that you are a regular customer and a good one, you'll find them easier to deal with,' he replied, frowning. 'Though I'm not sure that it will be such a good idea for you to do the buying. Have you noticed, it's nearly all men here?'

'I expect the housewives come later, as the market winds down, looking for bargains.'

Phoebe pulled out a notebook and pencil, and began to scribble notes as her basket filled up with samples, muttering about prices, dishes, and comparing what she saw with what she knew of Paris. Owen watched her, delighted to see that her enthusiasm had been rekindled, but not quite so delighted at the notion of her transacting business here on a daily basis. No, she couldn't possibly come herself. He already knew her too well to suggest that she delegate what she'd see as a vital task, so he would have to think of a strategy to ensure that she had an escort.

Adding this to the mental list of tasks he'd already assigned to himself, Owen listened with half an ear to his wife's essay on the various merits of one variety of carrot over another, careful to keep an interested look on his face. Until he met Phoebe, he'd had no idea there were different varieties, let alone different colours—and though it was always a pleasure to see her enthuse, he had to admit to himself that there was a limit to his interest in this particular subject, and he had reached his at the mention of the rare Scarlet Horn and Long Orange.

As they reached the fruit market, Phoebe's musings switched to desserts. She was dressed very simply in a long, enveloping cloak over a plain dress, but she had pushed back the hood in her excitement, and she wasn't wearing a hat. As usual, she was utterly oblivious of the effect her beauty was having, bestowing her generous smile on every trader who offered her a sample from his stall, leaving a trail of dazzled vendors in her wake. They'd be vying for her business, he reckoned, charmed into selling her their best wares at their keenest prices.

'I'm not much interested in flowers,' she said, as they reached the end of the fruit market. 'I think I've seen more than enough. My head is brimming with ideas. You've been very patient.'

'It has been a pleasure,' Owen said.

She chuckled. 'Half the time you haven't listened to a word I've said, but it's of no consequence since I'll doubtless repeat myself endlessly over dinner tonight.'

'Then if you've really had enough, we should be able to pick up a hackney cab in Henrietta Street. I didn't ask our coachman to wait, since I didn't know how long we'd be.'

'And how long have we been here?'

Owen consulted his watch. 'Longer than you think. It's after seven. Time for breakfast.'

'I've kept you on your feet for more than two hours. I am so sorry. Are you…?'

'I'm perfectly fine, Phoebe,' he said, surprised to discover that he was. 'Put your notebook away and let's get out of here. I'm hungry.'

'Is Rules nearby?'

'Rules? Oh, you mean the chop house? Yes, it's just down there.'

'May I take a look?'

'It won't be open at this hour.'

'I know. I just want to get a feel for what a London restaurant looks like.'

'You want to peer in the windows? I think you'll find that they are curtained.'

'Please?'

Owen laughed, shrugged and took the slight detour to Maiden Lane. As he had expected, the place was in darkness, with curtains drawn over the windows, the door barred. Phoebe, to his amusement, jumped up to try to peer through a crack in one of the curtains, then put her eye to the door. 'There's no menu,' she said. 'In Paris, all the restaurants and cafés have a chalk menu outside.'

'There's no menu because it never changes. Oysters. Puddings and pies. Game. It'll probably still be the same a hundred years from now.'

'You've eaten there?' she exclaimed. 'Why on earth didn't you tell me?'

'You didn't ask. Inside it's plush and ornate with velvet banquettes. Now can we return home? There's a hackney stand over there.'

'Yes, let us—why is that man staring at you?'

Thinking that he was more likely staring at Phoebe, Owen turned around, only to be confronted with a very old acquaintance.

'Owen Harrington, as I live and breathe. It is you, isn't it?' Hugo Burnes-Smythe crossed the narrow lane towards them, his hand held out in greeting. 'Good lord. I thought I was seeing a ghost.'

'Hugo.' Owen eyed his former friend with some misgiving for he was clearly three sheets to the wind. 'How are you?'

'More approp—approp—question is, how are you?' Hugo took a tottering step back. 'You're on your feet. I heard you'd lost your legs.'

'No, mislaid them temporarily. I have them both back in my possession as you can see.'

'Excellent news, excellent. I've just remembered something else,' Hugo said, peering over Owen's shoulder at Phoebe. 'Heard you'd tied the knot. 'Scuse me, Mrs Harrington—oh, excuse me, *not* Mrs Harrington. Was pretty sure Olivia Braidwood was a blonde.'

'I didn't marry Olivia Braidwood, Hugo.'

'I remember now. Lucky escape for her, that's what they are saying, though you look remarkably well to me.' Hugo shook his head. 'Where was I? I'm a bit befuddled, if you want the truth. The Running Footman race was today—race that you called your own, too, now I come to think of it. Your record time still stands, you'll be pleased to know. Now that you're back in town, maybe you'll show 'em a clean pair of heels next year?'

'I rather think race running is a bachelor's sport. Now, if you'll excuse me, Hugo, my wife and I are heading home for our breakfast.'

'Of course, of course. Could do with a bite to eat myself. I'm off to an Early House.' Hugo pumped his hand again, made an uncertain bow in Phoebe's direction and staggered off.

'What on earth is an Early House?' Phoebe asked.

'A tavern that opens for the market traders and porters. Not a place you'd care to eat, I assure you. Come, let's go before I meet any more ghosts from Owen Harrington's past,' he said, ushering his wife across the road where, to his relief, a cab had just arrived.

'Who was that man?' Phoebe asked, once they were comfortably settled in the hackney.

'Hugo Burnes-Smythe. I didn't think it was a good idea to formally introduce you.'

She chuckled. 'I doubt he will even remember meeting you, never mind me. What on earth is the Running Footman race?'

'There used to be a tradition of hiring a footman to run alongside your coach—I mean a tradition amongst the upper echelons who liked to demonstrate their superiority to mere mortals,' Owen said sardonically. 'The Duke of Marlborough was one such. He raced his own footman from Windsor to London—he was driving a coach and four, the footman was...'

'On foot! Against a coach and four! That is preposterous. I presume the Duke won the race?'

'Only just. The poor footman died from his exertions. The race was set up in his memory,' Owen said, cringing. What had once seemed to him a fitting tribute, now seemed, recounting it to Phoebe, not only insulting but ludicrous.

'Jasper told me that you were a talented runner.'

'I used to be. I loved the sense of freedom it gave me, and I did enter that race and won it several times. But even if I could, I can't imagine doing such a thing now.'

Or any of the things he'd done in the past, Owen though—save his gymnastics. If he had remained in England instead of setting out for the Continent two years ago, he'd probably have been with Hugo tonight, celebrating another win. He'd have been wandering aimlessly through Covent Garden, half-cut, half-awake and half-aware, and when he woke up later, he'd look back on the day as one well spent. Seeing Hugo was a reminder of the sort of man he had been, and he didn't like it one bit. Which was exactly why he'd left London in the first place.

The hackney dropped them at the door, and Phoebe, after checking as usual that he was not in need of assistance while pretending that she wasn't checking at all, bustled off to the kitchen to hand over her basket of fruit and vegetables to Murray. Owen made his way to his own room to take off his hat and coat, deep in thought.

He had so dreaded meeting any of his former friends that he'd closeted himself away. He'd become so accustomed to thinking of himself as an object of pity, yet Hugo had seemed to him the pitiful one, a fossil locked in amber. The life that Owen had lost was a pretty worthless one. Did that mean he'd rather be as he was now, even if it meant his nightmares would continue to haunt him, living with the blank space in his mind and his blank moments? He didn't know the answer, but it wasn't as straightforward as it used to be.

Certainly not since Phoebe had entered his life. He wondered what she would have Murray cook up with her harvest from this morning. Smiling to himself, Owen quit his rooms in search of breakfast and his wife, to find out.

Phoebe had spent the two days following their trip to Covent Garden working on compiling draft menus. This morning, she planned to try cooking some of the dishes and, wanting to have the kitchen to herself, had given the staff the day off. Pulling an apron on over her day gown, she decided to start by making both a beef and a vegetable stock. But as she began to assemble the ingredients on the huge scrubbed pine table which took up the centre of the room, her mind went completely blank, and her heart began to flutter in her chest so fast that she was compelled to sit down.

Stock, she mouthed, beef stock. The most basic thing to make, she'd done it a hundred, a thousand times, but she could not for the life of her think what else went into the pot save the roasted bones. It had been her responsibility to put the various stocks on first thing in the morning at La Grande Taverne. They simmered all day on the big range, and had to be skimmed every fifteen minutes for the first hour, then every half-hour after that. A good stock was the base for so many sauces. She knew how to make a good stock, for heaven's sake.

Though Pascal had claimed she didn't. Pascal had said that her stock was like dishwater and her pastry was like leather. But he'd used the stock every day, and surely if it was like dishwater then he wouldn't have put it anywhere near his precious dishes? And as for her pastry—but Pascal had always been a bit derisory about pastry and patisserie, claiming it was women's work and that was why she hadn't made a complete pig's ear of it.

She could cook. She knew she could cook, and it was time to stop questioning herself—something she hadn't realised she did quite so often, until Owen pointed it out. But since he had, she'd been thinking about it a good deal. She *was* very guilty of running herself down, expecting to fail, and astonished when she succeeded. It wasn't so much that Estelle undermined her as such, she just felt so inferior in every way to her talented, beautiful and charismatic twin. Owen was right, she had fled to Paris to escape the unflattering comparison, but he was also right when he said that it had been easy for Pascal to destroy all the confidence she'd built up over her two years in the city— because she'd never really believed she was worthy of his attention in the first place.

Well, no longer. Phoebe picked up an onion and began to chop furiously. She was a *damned* good cook and she would prove it to everyone, starting with Owen. Who knew nothing of such matters. But who believed in her, which Pascal did not. And who understood that her cooking deserved an audience, which Estelle did not.

Owen believed in her enough to emerge from his self-imposed isolation to go shopping with her. He'd done it for her, and she hadn't told him nearly enough, how grateful she was, or how much she admired him for doing it. When he had proposed, he'd been adamant that he was gaining as much from their marriage as she was, but thinking back over the weeks since they made their vows, Phoebe found that difficult to believe. The confidence he had in her was immense, to say nothing of all the practical help he'd given her. And she'd repaid him so far with doubts and indecision.

He deserved more than that. He wanted her to succeed. He wanted to be part of her success. She owed it to him and to the fates which had brought them together at the Procope, to have a bit more confidence in herself. She was only twenty-three, and she had made a disaster of her first job, and the best chef in all of

France, the culinary capital of the world, said that she couldn't cook, and her twin said that she shouldn't, but she would prove them wrong and she'd prove Owen right!

Phoebe put the lid on the vegetable-stock pot, and looked with surprise at the beef-stock pot beside it, bubbling away. She didn't remember making either, but that was a good sign. Cooking was instinctive, it was in her blood. She might be neither mature and confident like Kate and Eloise, nor talented and entertaining like Estelle, but she was born to be a chef!

Two hours later, with dinner prepared and the kitchen tidied Phoebe, excited and inspired, decided to seek out Owen. After a brief check of the main rooms downstairs, she concluded that he must be working in his study. He had never forbidden her from visiting his suite of rooms, but nor had he ever invited her. Pushing open the door, she found herself in a square hallway, tiled in black and white marble, and the choice of three doors. One would be Owen's bedchamber. One would be his study. She couldn't imagine what the third one would be. A soft thud from behind the nearest door made her jump. Listening carefully, she thought she could hear him moving about, so she knocked. There was no answer, but the noise of movement continued. Opening the door carefully, Phoebe peered in.

The room faced out on to the back gardens of the town house, the curtains not yet drawn against the fading light. The walls were lined with bookshelves overflowing with books. A comfortable sofa faced the fireplace, there were more books stacked on the floor beside it, but here convention ended. The polished floorboards were bare save for a large rush mat, on which lay a set of heavy-looking metal weights. A bar was suspended about four feet high between two supporting poles at the other window. And in the middle of the room, his back to her, was Owen, working on another set of bars.

She knew immediately that she was intruding on a very private space, but Phoebe couldn't move for fear of disturbing him. Positioned in the middle of the bars, he was stripped to the waist, wearing only a pair of loose cotton trousers, his feet bare though he still wore his gloves. As she watched, he took hold of the bars and began a series of lifts and dips, his legs tucked up under him. He moved fluidly, with apparently little effort, the muscles on his shoulders and arms flexing rhythmically. Moving smoothly on from one exercise to the next, he continued to dip while holding his legs straight out in front of him. His skin was damp with sweat, but his breathing remained regular. She could see, from the way he moved, that this was a regular routine. His upper body would delight a sculptor, Phoebe thought, pretending to an artistic appreciation that she was very far from feeling, for she was in thrall to something far more feral, fascinated by the sheer athletic power of him. He'd told her he had resumed his exercises but this was akin to acrobatics.

His arms straining now, he was holding his upper body quite still and working on his legs, straightening them, then lifting them together until they were at right angles to his body. His breathing was becoming laboured, sweat trickling down his back, but still he continued to work, ten, fifteen, twenty repetitions, until he finally let his legs fall, clinging to one of the bars to support himself, and breaking the spell Phoebe had fallen under. She moved, meaning to back out of the room without him seeing her, but he whirled round, and she froze to the spot.

'Phoebe! How long have you been there?'

'I'm so sorry, I didn't mean to spy on you, I did knock, but you clearly didn't hear because you were— you were—and then I started watching because it was so—goodness, I've never seen anything like it, you are so strong, and so graceful, and it was like a dance, and I—' She broke off, flushing. 'I should leave.'

She was backing out of the door. 'Wait,' Owen called. 'I'm finished for the day. Was there something important you wanted to ask me?'

'No, I—yes. Do you do this every day?'

'That was your burning question?'

'No, of course it wasn't. I didn't even know that you did—do these exercises have a name?'

'Gymnastics. From the Greek, meaning to exercise naked. Fortunately for the sake of your modesty,' Owen said, picking up his cotton gown and pulling it on, 'I'm not a purist.'

'But you are most certainly an athlete.' Closing the door behind her, Phoebe smiled at him. 'To be so—so accomplished, you must work very hard.'

'I can't do half of what I used to do. Years ago, when I was fourteen or fifteen, I saw a performance by a Russian brother and sister called the Flying Venga-rovs. They were acrobats, most renowned for their rou-tines on the tightrope. I was utterly entranced by them, and the next day, I sought the brother, Alexandr, out at the theatre where he was practising on equipment just like this. I knew that I *had* to learn to do what he could do. He knew of a place I could get lessons.'

'And you proved an apt pupil?' Phoebe ran her hand over the smooth wood of one of the bars. 'What is this apparatus called?'

'Parallel bars.' Phoebe was flushed. Embarrassed, Owen assumed, though the way she was looking at him, the softness of her smile, the fact that she was looking at him and not at the floor or the ceiling or even the bars made him wonder. 'This is called a pom-mel horse,' he said. 'Unfortunately I have no use any more for the vaulting variety.'

Phoebe followed him across the room. She studied the piece of equipment, smoothing her hands over it as if she were stroking a real horse. 'What do you do with this?'

She could not possibly realise the effect she was having on him. He could not quite believe the effect she was having on him. Contrary to what he had come to believe, that side of his nature was very far from dead. 'It was originally used to help soldiers prac-tise mounting and dismounting from their horses. A skilled practitioner can support himself on these,' Owen said, indicating the pommels, 'and then swing his legs around underneath him.'

Phoebe frowned. 'I can't imagine how you even

mount this thing, never mind swing about like a pendulum.'

'What you do is...' But it was much easier to demonstrate than to explain, and if he focused on demonstrating, he'd be able to ignore Phoebe and the disturbing effect she was having on him. Owen divested himself of his robe. 'Let me show you.'

Holding on to the pommels, he mounted the horse smoothly—something he couldn't have done a month ago—and positioned himself, legs stretched outwards and together, arms braced. The strength, he had learned, came not from the arms but from the centre of his body. He clenched his stomach muscles. Closing his eyes as he concentrated, relishing the new, solid muscles his dedicated training had developed around his abdomen, he began to swing his legs around anti-clockwise, which was marginally easier on his right hip. To move with such freedom was still so new to him, Owen gave himself over to the pleasure of it, barely noticing the pain of his protesting hip as he changed direction, then finished with a forward-balancing handstand before dismounting.

He had forgotten all about Phoebe until he opened his eyes again to see her gazing rapt at his sweating body and it felt so damned good, that raw appreciation, and he'd worked so diligently these last few weeks, he felt he'd earned it.

'I've never seen anything like that,' she said, 'but you are obviously very good.'

'Not bad,' Owen said, 'for a few weeks' work.' His training regime, so radically different from the one his doctor had prescribed, had begun painfully, for he had launched himself into the exercises as if there had not been a gap of more than two years. Forced to go back to basics, progress had been frustratingly slow at first, but as he had started to improve, he had come to enjoy his new regime. 'It's as much about technique as strength,' he said to Phoebe. 'It's easy to achieve a basic level of competence when you have nothing else to do.'

'I think you are being extremely modest. I couldn't even climb on to that thing without a mounting block to boost me.'

He didn't think. He forgot who he was now, and he acted on impulse, just as he would have done if he'd been the man he was before, in the presence of such beguiling beauty, putting his arms around her waist and sitting her up on the horse effortlessly.

Phoebe gasped in surprise, laughing. 'Owen! My goodness, it looks a long way down from up here.'

'Hold on to the pommels.' He let her go as she did so, stepping to the side. 'Straighten your arms and sit back a bit. You won't fall,' he said as she hesitated, 'and if you do I'll catch you.'

'Promise?'

'Promise. Now, hold your tummy in tight.' Phoebe took a deep breath and Owen, his eyes on a level with her bosom, was momentarily distracted. 'Not like that,' he said, dragging his eyes away, 'as if you are trying to press your navel into your back.'

'What a strange thing—oh, yes, I see.' She was frowning in concentration. 'What now?'

What now? He hardly knew where to look, for all the most delectable bits of her body seemed to be straining at her gown, which was wrapped tight around her bottom and riding up her legs. 'Try to lift yourself up,' Owen said, 'not just with your arms, but from your middle, here.'

'I can't—I don't…'

'Stop talking. Save your breath and concentrate. Imagine there's a rope pulling you up from your middle.'

'That is—oh!' Phoebe swung precariously, but there was a tiny gap between her body and the horse. 'Look, Owen, I'm doing it.'

Her delight was infectious. He laughed. 'Stop talking.'

'It's really difficult.'

'Even more difficult when you don't save your breath. Just breathe, and hold everything in.'

'That is easier said than done when you are as fond of food as I am!'

'Phoebe, shut up and breathe.'

She pursed her lips and breathed exaggeratedly, but her eyes were brimming with laughter.

'Now,' Owen said, 'try to lift your legs up just a little.'

She opened her mouth to protest, then closed it again, her expression becoming focused as she tried—and failed—to move her legs. After taking a brief rest at his suggestion, she balanced and tried again with limited success, her face florid with the effort, but shaking her head violently when he told her that was enough. 'One more time.' She took a deep breath and lifted herself up. She screwed her face comically tight, and for a brief second, lifted both legs.

'Well done.'

'I did it!' Her eyes flew open. Her arms and legs collapsed and Phoebe fell straight into Owen's arms. 'I did it,' she said again, triumphantly. 'I did do it, didn't I?'

'You did.' His arms automatically tightened around her. She was flushed, her eyes gleaming, her lips parted as she smiled up at him, her arms twined around his neck. Her body, pressed against his was so lush, sensual and utterly beautiful, that his senses swam, and he dipped his head, feeling her breath on his face, drinking in the sweet scent of her.

Their lips met. He knew it was wrong, but he couldn't resist her. It was a soft, tentative kiss, for he had all but forgotten what kisses were like, but as her mouth yielded to his, as she sighed and kissed him back, he stopped thinking and gave himself over to the pleasure of it. The taste of her. The touch of her tongue. The soft whisper of her breath on his, the little sighing sound she made, and the delight of her body, the sheer otherness of her body, the very definite indent of her waist, the curve of her bottom, her breasts pressed against his naked chest.

Her kisses went to his head. They inflamed him. They made his blood zing in his veins. Her hands were on his shoulders, his back, smoothing down his spine, curling into his behind, making him hard. Their tongues touched again. Their kisses deepened and he was filled with such longing, such an intense yearning to touch her, skin on skin.

Owen broke the kiss, breathing heavily. Phoebe staggered as he released her, leaning against the support of the pommel horse. She was flushed, heavy-lidded and delectable. And he was aroused, confused and—and very aroused! He swore under his breath. 'I'm sorry.'

She gazed at him, looking as dazed as he felt. 'Are you?'

'No.'

'Nor am I.' A laugh escaped her that had an edge of hysteria to it, then her face flooded with colour. 'That will be a lesson to me to come seeking you out in the middle of the day. I should go. Dinner,' she said, backing away from him. 'I'm making dinner. I must see to my pots.'

Owen made no attempt to stop her. Utterly shocked, he stared at the pommel horse, as if it was to blame for his throbbing erection and his wildly beating heart and the sheer elation that was making him grin like a lunatic. He felt as euphoric as if he had made love. His whole body tingled and pulsed. If there was a vaulting horse in the room, he was convinced he'd clear it with several feet to spare. Leaning back against the pommel horse, he closed his eyes, reliving the taste of Phoebe's kisses and the way Phoebe's body had melted into his, and the way his body had responded. The surge of blood to his groin, the throb of arousal, and the unique sense of anticipation that accompanied it, imagining the slow slide into slick heat that felt like nothing else on earth, and then the rhythm building…

He cursed under his breath, sweat sprinkling his back, his heart racing. Another few moments of thinking like that—dear God, if she had stayed, if he had not broken their kiss, would they even now…

Owen picked up his dressing gown, tying the sash in a ruthless knot, striding out of the room across to his bedchamber and into his bathing room. He needed a bath. A cold one! Catching sight of himself in the mirror, his hair dishevelled, his cheeks flushed, his pupils dark and dilated, he was startled into a laugh. He looked almost like himself. Though older.

Wiser? He swore again, sitting down on the rim of the bath, turning the tap which allowed the hot water to fill it, temporarily distracted as he was every time by this innovation. He had lost himself in Phoebe's kisses, but he had not disappeared into himself as he'd feared he might. Was he getting better? Taking a deep breath, he peeled off his gloves and forced himself to stare down at his hands, but all he could think about was how much he wished he'd not been wearing his gloves when he held Phoebe in his arms.

Was he getting better? He still had nightmares, but the moments when he disappeared into himself were much less frequent. Being with Phoebe was easy, no effort at all. And with others too, sometimes, he felt— well, something approaching normal. Did that imply that he was getting better? He was too afraid to hope. A step at a time, he reminded himself, just as he'd cautioned Phoebe.

Bloody hell, Phoebe. Owen turned off the tap and quickly stripped, catching his breath as his body hit the tepid water. It was because he hadn't kissed any woman in over two years, he told himself, that Phoebe's kisses felt to him like no other kisses, like the best, most arousing kisses he'd ever shared. He knew that, but it made no difference. They *were* the best, the most arousing kisses he'd ever shared.

But he had no right to be kissing Phoebe, even if she was his wife. Kissing Phoebe had not been part of their agreement. In fact he'd assured Phoebe that he would never have any interest in kissing her or any woman. And Phoebe had assured him that she had no interest either. Yet she'd kissed him back with—with abandon! Perhaps she felt sorry for him? No, those were not pity kisses. It was the gymnastics, then? He wasn't and would never be as good as he had once been, but there was something mesmerising about the movements, a sensuality, a—a primal connection between muscle and man.

Was he being fanciful? He was procrastinating. He had no idea why Phoebe had responded the way she had to his kisses, but the simple fact was he shouldn't have kissed her. She was his wife in name only. He was her investor, not her husband in any real sense, he had no right to kiss her, and the only reason he was fit to kiss her in the first place was because he'd got himself fit! In order to help her with the restaurant! So he'd better bloody well concentrate on that.

Owen lay back in the bath, putting a wet flannel over his face. He would. He'd concentrate on their business venture. Just as soon as he got out the bath.

* * *

Back in the kitchen, Phoebe tied on her apron and tended to the stock pots before sitting down at the table, staring sightlessly at her notebook where she had written out tonight's menu. Kissing Owen had been—no, she was most certainly not going to compare him to Pascal. There was, she thought with a satisfied smile, no comparison. Kissing Owen had been quite simply delicious. She shivered, remembering the way his mouth felt, the touch of his tongue, the way he'd smoothed his hands over her, clearly relishing her curves. If she had needed proof that Pascal was confined to history—which she didn't—then her response was more than sufficient. Kissing Owen had been like eating an ice, the sharp burst of awareness, the mingling of hot and cold as it melted, then the lingering sweetness, and the craving for the next taste. Kissing Owen was, like watching him exercise, a sheer, sensual delight.

But she didn't have any business kissing Owen, and Owen—goodness, Owen certainly hadn't kissed like a man who had lost all desire. He hadn't been acting, when he kissed her. Or had he? When Pascal told her he'd never loved her, she hadn't believed him. How could he have made love to her with such passion—and so often, right up until the night before he ended their affaire!—if he hadn't loved her. But it was different for men, he'd told her disdainfully, especially a man ruled by passion such as he. And she had been so very eager, he'd said. Had she? She hadn't thought so at the time, she'd thought—but what was the point of going over it, when she'd decided just a few moments ago to confine Pascal to the past.

Had she been too eager with Owen? Seeds of doubt began to sprout in her mind. She was not in love with Owen, but did that make her kissing him worse or better? Would he be angry with her, for awakening feelings he'd thought dead? But he'd said he wasn't sorry. He hadn't looked angry, he'd looked as dazed as she. What was she to think? Perhaps she oughtn't think.

She had kissed her husband, and her husband had kissed her back, and that was the end of it. Save that her husband's kisses were vastly superior to Pascal's kisses, she thought, mentally thumbing her nose at her former lover and making herself smile. Owen was getting better—better enough to want to kiss her—and a *lot* fitter too. Goodness, that physique!

No, she mustn't think about that either. Owen was getting better because he had a purpose in life. She was getting better because she had a purpose in life too, thanks to Owen. So she'd better stop allowing herself to be distracted by kisses, and concentrate on what mattered, and right at this moment, it wasn't superior kisses but superior cooking.

Phoebe scraped her chair back and headed for the pantry to assemble the rest of the ingredients for dinner. Happily turning her mind from one sensual delight to another, she set about constructing what she hoped would be the best dinner Owen had ever tasted.

Chapter Seven

Owen set his napkin down and picked up his wine glass. 'That, I can say without fear of contradiction,' he said, 'was the best meal I've ever eaten.'

Phoebe chuckled, touching her glass to his. 'Well, I was never going to go far wrong by serving venison, was I?'

'How so?'

'Back at the Procope, don't you remember? When we played my game of guessing favourite foods. I guessed that your favourite dish was a hearty breakfast of ham and eggs, and you told me that you preferred a dinner of venison stew.'

'How very ungallant of me. Stew does not adequately describe the fragrant dish you served tonight.'

She rested her chin on her hands. 'You cannot remain a culinary philistine if you are investing in London's newest and most popular restaurant, Owen. I intend to educate your palate, starting now. Tell me what you think was in the dish, besides the venison.'

'Mushrooms.'

'Very good. What else?'

He frowned in exaggerated concentration. 'Chestnuts—yes, there were definitely chestnuts.'

'Think of the flavours, remember how it smelled. What other ingredients spring to mind?'

'I feel like I'm back at school and I'm about to fail a very important exam. I'm sorry Phoebe, I haven't a clue.'

'There was bacon, to give it richness and a little fat because venison is a very lean meat. The warmth comes from cinnamon—though I used a very little of Mr Murray's extensive spice store—cloves and a pinch of nutmeg. The sauce is a reduction of red wine, the good beef stock I made this morning, and the pulped flesh of a tomato for a little bit of tartness. Oh, and bay, onion, salt and pepper of course, those go without saying.'

'Of course they do,' Owen said. 'And what it added up to was the best plate of venison I've ever tasted. I mean that.'

'Thank you. I won't bore you by dissecting the other dishes, I'm just happy that you sampled all of them.'

'I am certainly enjoying my food a great deal more these days—no doubt due to the excellent company provided by my dining companion. I'm also very honoured to be the recipient of the first dinner you've cooked since you returned to England, though it was much more homely fare than I was expecting from a top chef.'

'I reckoned that you're not fond of overly refined and elegant food.'

'Not particularly, to be honest, but isn't that what restaurants like the one you aspire to open serve?'

'I cooked this meal just for you, as a thank you. When I sought you out earlier and interrupted your training—' She broke off, for despite her determination not to think about it, she remembered the kiss and felt the heat stealing over her cheeks. 'I should have knocked more loudly.'

'I'm glad you didn't, but I want to assure you that what transpired was furthest from my thoughts. Or would have been, until very recently.'

'There's really no need...'

'Oh, but there is.' Owen picked up his wine glass, changed his mind and set it down. 'Let me explain, or attempt to. It is a delicate subject. You've inspired me to—to look at life afresh, I suppose. To haul myself out of the doldrums, is another way of putting it. I feel better. I'm fitter. And as a result I discovered today that I—I am no longer without urges,' he said, colouring. 'Our marriage has provided me with an unexpected, but very welcome sense of purpose, thanks to you. But I want you to know that's more than enough for me. Today was a—it happened, but it would be best if we concentrated on the matter in hand, which is the restaurant, don't you agree?'

Phoebe heaved a sigh of relief. 'I was thinking much the same thing. It wouldn't be a good idea at all for us to mix business with pleasure—I mean—oh, goodness, you know what I mean.'

'I do.'

'Good. I haven't told you properly, Owen, how very grateful I am for the help you've been giving me.'

'I said I would, Phoebe, I've simply been keeping my side of the bargain.'

'No, I don't mean the practical help you've given me—or not only that. You've made me see that I've not been helping myself. What you said, about under-estimating myself—I do that, I see that now, and I'm going to try to change.'

'Phoebe, I...'

'No, let me say this. It's very difficult for me to hear any sort of criticism of Estelle because she's my twin, and it was even more difficult for me to accept what you said about her. She doesn't mean to run me down, she's trying to protect me but—well, the effect is that I do have a fairly low opinion of myself.' Phoebe took a reviving sip of wine. 'You know me better than myself or my sisters do, it seems. So thank you, Owen. I've rewarded you with nothing but doubts and worries so far, but that is going to change. I won't let you down—or at least if I do, it won't be for the want of trying. And as to that, I have an idea I'd like to discuss with you.'

'Good, I'm all ears. Shall we take our wine through to the parlour?'

Phoebe jumped to her feet. 'You're in sore need of a more comfortable seat. You should have said. Did you overstretch yourself with your gymnastics today because of me? I'm so sorry.'

'I didn't. No, actually I probably did, but it wasn't your fault. I was showing off for your benefit,' he admitted sheepishly.

And she had appreciated it. Very much. But she must not think about that! 'You go on,' Phoebe said, turning her back on him to look for a tray. 'I'll bring the drinks.'

She took her time putting the decanter and glasses on a tray, and by the time she reached the parlour, she had supplanted thoughts of those kisses with the subject they had agreed must take precedence.

She handed Owen his glass and took her usual seat on the sofa, curling her feet under her. 'Do you know of a place called Crockford's Club?'

'You mean the gambling club in St James's?'

'You do know it then.'

'I don't frequent it, never have. Cards don't interest me.'

'It has a restaurant,' Phoebe said, 'with Eustache Ude, no less, in charge of the kitchen.'

'Another culinary hero of yours, I gather from the gleam in your eyes.'

'His father worked in the kitchens of King Louis the Sixteenth.'

'Who gave his head to Madame Guillotine. There are doubtless a great number of gentlemen who have lost their shirt at Crockford's tables who would wish Monsieur Ude Junior's employer a similar fate.'

'If I had to lose at the tables in order to sample Monsieur Ude's menu, then it would be a price worth paying.'

'A moot point since females are not permitted to cross the threshold. No respectable female, that is. I'm not sure what Crockford's rules are regarding light skirts.'

'I could pass for a light skirt,' Phoebe said.

Owen raised a quizzical brow. 'It conjures an image not without its attractions, but it would be to no avail. I am fairly certain that the dining room is a strictly male-only preserve.'

Phoebe rolled her eyes. 'As I had assumed. Well in that one sense our restaurant is going to be very different, since I am determined it should serve a mixed clientele. But I would dearly like to taste the food.'

'Why is it so important?'

'Aside from the fact that Monsieur Ude is one of the most famous chefs in the world, you mean? We need to understand the competition in London, so that we can then make a judgement on whether we set out to serve the same but better or whether we serve something different altogether. I have always dreamed of a restaurant very much like La Grande Taverne, but what if I'm wrong? What if I discover that the last thing I want to do is serve food that reminds me of Paris and my humiliation.' Phoebe sighed. 'If you were not such a culinary philistine I would ask you to go on a—a tasting mission to discover whether it really is as good as they say, or whether it is a case of style over substance, you know?'

'Clearly you don't consider that I am up to the task.'

'I'm so sorry. I didn't mean to insult you.'

Owen got up, picking up both their glasses to put them on the tray, before sitting down on the sofa beside her. 'I'm teasing, Phoebe,' he said gently.

'Oh. Am I being tediously intense?'

'You are simply being determined.'

'Determinedly tedious, you mean. I am though, determined I mean. To make a success of our venture. To prove that you were right to believe in me.'

He shook his head, smiling softly. 'When I first saw you in Paris, I was dazzled. I've seen more classically beautiful women, but you—you were so bright and so full of life. You can be that person again.'

'You rescued me that night. And now you've rescued me again. No, that's not right. I need to rescue myself. You've taught me that. Not being able to visit Crockford's is a setback but I won't let it defeat me.' She leaned over to kiss him on the cheek. His skin was fresh-shaved, smooth but rough at the same time. She sat back very reluctantly. A lump rose in her throat. 'Thank you for being my inspiration.'

'You give me too much credit, Phoebe.' He touched her cheek, cursed, looked down at his gloves.

'Why do you wear these? Are your hands so very badly damaged?'

He shook his head. 'It's more that they are a constant reminder.'

'I thought you didn't remember what happened?'

'I don't, but when I look at them I feel—that I don't want to remember. That whatever happened—that it's better for me if I don't try. So I prefer not to look at them.'

'I'm so sorry, I won't ask again.'

'But the strange thing is,' Owen said, still staring down at his gloves, 'today, after you left me in the gymnasium…' He looked up. 'After we kissed, and I realised that I wasn't entirely dead inside—I took them off. And it didn't happen, Phoebe. I looked at my hands, and all I felt was—it doesn't matter what I felt, what matters is that I didn't feel what I'd always felt before.'

'So you think you really are getting better?'

'I dare not raise my hopes. But—small steps, yes? So perhaps now's as good a time as any to risk another one.'

Owen began to take off one of his gloves and Phoebe's heart began to pound as she watched him. Slowly, he eased each finger free, until his left hand was exposed. He didn't look at her, his gaze remained concentrated on his hand.

'May I?' Phoebe, bracing herself, gently took his hand to study it. She traced the fretwork of scars delicately. There were patches of pale new skin, hard patches of darker skin where the scarring was deeper. His middle finger was swollen at the knuckle, giving it an odd shape. Aware of him sitting stock still beside her, holding his breath, she lifted his hand to her mouth, pressing the lightest of kisses to the scars before turning it over and kissing his palm. She gingerly removed the other glove. easing the fingers free, no longer apprehensive, only touched to her heart, seeing the history of his suffering mapped out so clearly, and knowing that he had never before revealed it to anyone save presumably his doctors.

His right hand bore the same scarring, the same patches of rough and tender skin. His little finger jutted at an odd angle, having obviously been broken and badly mended. Phoebe kissed these scars too. Then she pressed his hand to her cheek. Owen inhaled sharply. His fingers fluttered on her skin, tracing the line of her jaw, her neck, then releasing her, to clasp her hand between his. He stared, frowning deeply, at their twined fingers for a long time. She couldn't fathom what he was thinking, though she had the oddest impression that he was waiting. Then he released his breath in one long sigh and looked up, meeting her eyes, and smiled.

'Thank you.' He got to his feet, holding out his hand to help her. 'I think we've had more than enough excitement for one day.'

Phoebe nodded, suddenly overwhelmed. 'Goodnight, Husband.'

He touched her cheek again. 'Goodnight, Wife.'

Lying in bed, Phoebe wrapped her arms around herself and snuggled down into the pillow. Something momentous had occurred tonight, much more significant than the kisses they had shared earlier. Owen had changed, had been changing almost every day since their marriage. The moments when he went quite blank were becoming far less frequent, and he seemed more natural and at ease with her, reserving what she had called his acting for conversations with strangers. With her, he was, as far as she could see, himself. His laugh was rarely forced. He teased her. He smiled at her. Today he'd kissed her. And tonight, he had taken off his gloves in her presence. She would not be so foolish as to fall in love—again!—with the man who was pivotal to her achieving her ambition, but the emotions that were now churning up inside her were unsettling.

Owen was not Pascal, he could not be more different. He had married her when he was by his own admission in the slough of despond, when his glittering aura was tarnished, the flame which had burned so brightly in him before his accident, all but extinguished. When they had married, they had been two lost souls hoping to heal one another. But Owen was no longer a lost soul, and he was healing himself. He had promised to support her in her business venture and he was an honourable man, he would honour that commitment. But one day soon, he would want to take up his position in society again, and society would embrace him like a prodigal son. Then, he'd have little use for a tarnished and food-obsessed wife.

What was the phrase they used about racehorses? She wasn't up to his weight. So she'd better make sure that she kept her heart to herself and focus on the reason they'd married, just as he'd said they should earlier. Had that been an oblique warning? When he took off his gloves, had be been trying to tell her that he was ready to go out in the world, ready to leave her behind? It was a deflating thought, but she would do well to bear it in mind.

'Mr Forsythe apologises for calling at such an early hour, but he says the matter is urgent.'

'*Extremely* urgent,' Jasper said, striding into the breakfast parlour.

'Another setting for Mr Forsythe, if you please, Bremner,' Phoebe said, raising an enquiring brow at Owen, but he shook his head, clearly as in the dark as she. 'Won't you sit down, Jasper? May I pour you a cup of coffee?'

'Thank you, Phoebe. Coffee would be very welcome. Owen, apologies again for the intrusion.' Jasper took off his hat and gloves, placing them an a spare chair before taking a seat at the table.

'Do you wish to speak to Owen in private?' Phoebe asked. 'Shall I…'

'No, don't get up. I'm afraid the matter concerns both of you.'

'What matter?' Owen asked, when Bremner arrived with the extra place setting and a fresh pot of coffee.

'Well?' Owen prompted again, when the butler quit the room.

'You're looking very well. Marriage obviously suits you.'

'You didn't come here to compliment me, Jasper. Cut to the chase.'

Jasper took a sip of coffee, looking utterly wretched. 'Truth is, I'm not quite sure how to put this. You're going to be furious with me, but I swear to you, Owen, I had no idea that the man was a journalist. He gave me the impression he was a relative of Phoebe's. In fact I'm almost sure that's what the fellow said, that he knew Lord Fearnoch, though he might not actually have been so specific. I don't recall. I'm so very sorry, Phoebe.'

'What in devil's name are you talking about?'

'Jasper,' Phoebe interrupted, a horrible premonition making her feel sick. 'What did you discuss with this mysterious relative?'

'I'm so sorry. I had no idea…'

'Just spit it out, dammit,' Owen said, his mouth set.

'It was about two weeks ago. I was taking a glass at the Cock Tavern in Holborn as usual, to brace myself for dinner with my Aunt Clementine. Terrifying woman,' Jasper said to Phoebe. 'She must be about a hundred and twenty-five by now, filthy rich, and I'm her heir as well as the only relative she claims to be able to tolerate, so I have dinner with her every Thursday. My uncle, who has long since departed, was a prominent lawyer, and my aunt still lives near Chancery, which is why I drink at the Cock.'

'Get to the point, for the love of God!' Owen exclaimed. 'Phoebe isn't interested in your Aunt Clementine. She would far rather hear, as I would, what it is you've been saying to her relative.'

'I'm nervous. I always talk to much when I'm nervous. The chap wasn't Phoebe's relative, that's the point. Came up to me in the Cock, knew my name, shook my hand and bought me a drink before I had said a word. "You're a good friend of Owen Harrington," he said, "who has married a relative of mine." Or he implied as much, as I said. Mentioned Lord Fearnoch. I had no idea you were so well connected, Phoebe, and I said. It turns out that your sister is a countess.'

'I think you'll find she's aware of that,' Owen said, pouring his friend another cup of coffee.

Phoebe, by now feeling as if she was about to lose her breakfast, picked up her own tea, but her hands were shaking too much. 'My sister Eloise, the Count-

ess of Fearnoch, she is in the country, in Lancashire.
What did this man have to say about her?'

'Nothing at all,' Jasper replied, much to Phoebe's
relief. 'He didn't seem much interested in her. He was
much more interested in how you and Owen had met,
so I told him that it had been in Paris, two years ago.
I didn't think that it mattered—I mean it's the truth,
isn't it?—and I must confess that I found your story—
well, I'm not the romantic type—or not usually—but
anyway…'

'You told him that we'd met in Paris,' Phoebe said,
her relief short-lived. 'What else did you tell him?'

'Nothing, I swear. I didn't know there was anything
else to tell until this morning.' Jasper reached into his
pocket and pulled out a newspaper. 'My man drew my
attention to it. I don't read the scandal sheets, but he
does. I'm so very sorry.'

Owen took the newspaper from him. 'The *Town
Crier*,' he said, eyeing it with disgust. 'Shall I do the
honours?'

Phoebe nodded, feeling rather like an aristocrat
waiting for her turn at the guillotine. She had never
heard of the *Town Crier*, and knew that her sister
wouldn't read such rubbish, but she didn't doubt some
kind thoughtful soul would send a copy to her. At least
it sounded as if they had not actually tracked Eloise
down. Which was a very small consolation.

'"Speculation has been rife,"' Owen read, '"since
the rather restrained announcement in the press informing the world that Mr Owen Harrington has tied
the knot with Miss Phoebe Brannagh. Though we all

know the reclusive Mr Harrington as one of London's most successful investors and speculators, of his new bride, next to nothing was known—save that she was not the bride we all expected him to marry!'" Owen broke off to curse before continuing.

"'As you know, it is our mission at the *Town Crier* to keep you fully informed. When we discovered that Miss Phoebe Brannagh is the sister of the Countess of Fearnoch, what joy we felt on Mr Harrington's behalf that he had made such a well-connected alliance. Alas, our joy was short-lived. Dear reader, if you are of a delicate disposition, we would suggest that you read no further, for what we have to reveal is of a most scurrilous, scandalous and shocking nature.'"

Once again Owen broke off, cursing fluently while Phoebe, horribly conscious of Jasper's presence, wished that the ground would open up and swallow her.

"'Miss Brannagh and Mr Harrington first encountered each other in Paris. It was, we were told by the groom's close friend, love at first sight.'"

Jasper groaned.

Owen continued reading in clipped tones. "'Following our own investigations in Paris, we can reveal that alas, these two hearts who longed to beat as one were denied a happy ending at this point by a prior claim. Not, we hasten to add, the well-known arrangement which Mr Harrington's parent had agreed for him, but a claim of a foreign nature! *Oh, là-là*, Miss Phoebe Brannagh had given her heart to a Frenchman. A common cook, no less, though Monsieur Pascal Solignac does not charge common prices at the restaurant where the former Miss Brannagh peeled potatoes, we hasten to add, lest any of our readers are tempted to sample his wares for themselves." Which means,' Owen said viciously, 'they must actually have talked to Solignac.'

Phoebe, now mute with horror, watched as he turned the scandal sheet over, wondering how much more if it she had to bear.

"'Broken-hearted,'" Owen continued to read, "'Mr Harrington fled Paris and at some point prior to his return to England, as London society is all to well aware, met with a tragic accident which deprived him of the use of his legs. His heart, however, remained true to Miss Brannagh, and she, it seems, finally saw the error of her ways, abandoning her garlic-infused paramour for a slice of English roast beef."

"'How much did Mr Harrington's fat purse have to do with her change of heart? A little bird, with an ear to the ground in the London property market, tells us that despite Miss Brannagh's singular lack of talent in the kitchen—a fact on which Monsieur Solignac was most vociferous—now she is reincarnated as Mrs Harrington, she will be making an assault on London's stomachs at her own restaurant some time in the new year. Yes, dear reader, you heard it here first. Rejected by Paris, the gourmet capital of the world, Mrs Harrington, nothing daunted, is currently looking for premises in which to set herself up as the doyenne of British cooking, right here in London. What dish will she serve? It is to be hoped that it will not contain any trace of garlic."' Owen crumpled up the scandal sheet and threw it in the fire. Phoebe dropped her head into her hands.

'I cannot apologise enough,' Jasper said.

'It's not your fault,' Phoebe said, lifting her head. 'It's mine.'

'If there is anything I can do,' Jasper said, looking helpless. 'Anything.'

'Don't speak to any more journalists.'

'That goes without saying. If I'd had any idea…'

'But you didn't. Stop apologising, man, it's not your fault.' Owen tugged the bell, demanding a fresh pot of tea for Phoebe as soon as possible.

'I don't need…'

'You do.' He pulled his seat closer to her, putting his hand on her knee. 'It's disgusting and slanderous, but it's not a tragedy, Phoebe.'

'But it's not slanderous it's true, Owen—well, aside from the bit where they refer to Pascal as a "common cook". It's all true.'

'Good lord. Beg pardon, but—all of it?'

Jasper looked quite astounded. Mortified, Phoebe could only nod and hang her head.

'I don't know what to say. None of my business of course, but—well, none of anyone's business what you did before you married Owen,' Jasper said, the tips of his ears burning bright red. 'But they must have made up the bit about opening a restaurant, surely?'

'No, it's true enough,' Phoebe said dejectedly. 'That was our intention, but now…'

'That remains our intention,' Owen said firmly.

'How can we, after this? Owen, you must see that this changes everything,' Phoebe said wretchedly.

'I don't see why. You've done nothing to be ashamed of.'

'As I said, nobody's business but yours, what you did before you were married,' Jasper added valiantly before catching Owen's eye, holding his hands up and mouthing, *Sorry.*

'You're very kind, Jasper, but this rag has made it everyone's business,' Phoebe said. 'Now my sister's name and more importantly Owen's, have been dragged through the mud because of me.'

'My name's been dragged through the mud so many times I have lost count and long since stopped caring.'

'Scrapes you got into when you were younger, no doubt. This is very different.'

'Phoebe, I was never anywhere close to being a saint. Was I, Jasper?'

'Nowhere near. But this…'

'We can turn it to our advantage,' Owen said firmly.

'How?' Phoebe asked.

'I don't know, but we will.'

'Owen, you must see…'

'In a moment, Phoebe. Drink your tea, and you'll feel better. Jasper, could I ask a favour of you?'

'Ask away. Anything to make amends, old chap.'

'Would you visit Olivia and let her know about this unfortunate development? That rag doesn't mention her by name, but it's best she is aware of it. Sorry if it is a bit of an imposition.'

'It's the least I can do, in the circumstances. And no

imposition whatsoever. Seeing her later today anyway, as it happens. Drive. Fresh air. That kind of thing.'

'Fine. Good.' Owen got up, pressing Phoebe's shoulder. 'We'll talk, but I'll just see Jasper out.'

'I'm so sorry, Phoebe. If there's anything…'

'I've told you to stop apologising, and I've told you what you can do to help. Now go and do it.'

'You're not limping.'

'No.' Owen held the door open.

'You sound different. And you look well. I meant what I said when I arrived.'

'Thank you. I will be even better after a chat alone with my wife.'

It took Owen another five minutes to finally rid himself of his best friend, whose surprised delight at his much-improved appearance would have amused and pleased him were he not anxious to get back to Phoebe. He found her white-faced, exactly as he had left her, her tea untouched. Sitting down beside her, he clasped her hands between his. 'It's not the end of the world. We'll find a way to turn this to our advantage.'

She slipped free of his grasp, her mouth wobbling, her eyes stricken. 'I'm so very, very sorry.'

'There's no need to apologise. There was nothing in that piece of bilge that you haven't already told me.'

'There is every need. If I chose to behave in a way that the world sees as scandalous, I must expect to be judged accordingly. But to have inflicted the shame and scandal on my sisters and my aunt! And you, worst of all, that is unforgivable.'

Phoebe dropped her face into her hands and burst into tears. Appalled, for he had never seen her cry, Owen pulled her to her feet, wrapping his arms around her. 'What is unforgivable is exposing someone's private life in order to sell newspapers.'

'You've been so kind to me, and this is how I reward you.'

'Phoebe, stop it. Please don't cry.' He tried to tilt her face up, but she buried it in his chest, sobbing as if her heart would break. All he could do was hold her, after tugging off his gloves so that he could smooth her hair, until her sobs became hiccups and then finally stopped.

'I've made your coat all wet.'

Owen pulled out his handkerchief. 'Here, use this instead.'

She caught his hand, rubbing it against her cheek. 'I really am sorry.'

'Stop apologising, you've even less reason to do so than Jasper.'

'Jasper was hoodwinked by a journalist. I have no one to blame for this mess but myself. You shouldn't have married me.'

'Phoebe.' He gave her a little shake. 'That's quite simply nonsense. Come on, let's retire to the parlour,' Owen said, 'and see if we can turn our new-found notoriety to our advantage.'

But to his dismay as they sat down, fresh tears sprung from Phoebe's eyes. 'I have been selfish and thoughtless. Eloise was right after all.'

'Your sister surely didn't accuse you of any of those things.'

'Not me,' Phoebe said, wringing her hands. 'My mother.'

'Your mother! What on earth has she to do with this?'

'I think I told you that Mama was a—a free spirit— or at least that's how I've always thought of her. She was so very beautiful, and so popular and so passionate— that's what she always used to say, "I am a passionate creature."'

Which certainly did sound, Owen thought, like the words of a woman determined to have her own way. He tried to recall what else Phoebe had said of her mother. Not very maternal—yes, he remembered drawing the comparison there with his own mother, but while he had been well cared for by a host of other responsible adults, Phoebe and her twin seemed to have relied on their elder sister. 'I'm sorry,' he said helplessly, 'I can understand why Eloise would think your mother was selfish, thoughtless even, to have preferred a career as the toast of Dublin society to looking after her children, but you don't even like going to parties.'

'I thought she was bold and brave enough to refuse to be bound by convention. I admired her for that. Eloise and Estelle think very differently, so I kept my opinions to myself, but when I went to Paris, I felt as if I'd been brave and bold too.'

'You were.'

'It was a huge step to go, but when I got there, instead of concentrating on working hard to achieve the one thing that I wanted, I was dazzled by the city and seduced by the life I was leading. I knew that it was wrong of me to have an affaire with Pascal, but I wanted it. So I—this is so mortifying—I told myself that *I* was a free spirit like my mother, and was emulating her. I pretended to myself that she'd be proud of me for doing as she did, for bucking convention. Mama had countless affaires. I thought I was finally doing something that would have made her notice me, something that would have met with her approval. You see, that's how pathetic I am. So I blithely carried on, thinking of no one but myself, heedless of the impact my behaviour might have on anyone save myself. And now it's not me who has to pay, it's you and my sisters.'

'So, naturally you have concluded that your sisters were right about your mother. And if you are like her then it follows that you are also selfish and thoughtless.' She had it so wrong, and she looked so woebegone, he wanted to wrap his arms around her, but he'd done that already and it hadn't helped. 'Women like your mother don't care who they hurt, do they, provided they get their own way?'

'She always said that Papa was trying to suppress her true nature.'

'And you felt that your sisters were suppressing yours, in a way, didn't you? Because in their misguided attempts to protect you from what they thought was certain failure, they were trying to stop you from becoming a chef?'

'I don't know. I suppose. But…'

'So you went to Paris, all on your own, and for the first time in your life you were free of them. There was no one to watch over you, no one to advise you.

It's not surprising that you went a little wild, Phoebe. I certainly would have.'

'No one cares if a man has an affaire. It's expected of them.'

'You weren't married to anyone else. You weren't promised to anyone else. And it wasn't just any old affaire, it wasn't a meaningless fling. You thought you were in love. You thought that you and Pascal had a future together.'

'You make it sound as if what I did was perfectly acceptable.'

'It's completely understandable. I won't insult you by pretending that the world won't see it as scandalous, because the world does judge men and women very differently. But you knew, Phoebe, even when you were relishing every moment of your life in Paris, that your sisters would be shocked.'

'And yet it didn't stop me!'

'But you did your best to keep it from them. Not because you were ashamed but to protect them, shield them from what for them would have been an unpalatable truth. Would your mother have done that?'

'No, because she didn't—' Phoebe broke off, looking stricken.

'Go on,' Owen said gently.

'Because she didn't care,' Phoebe whispered.

'But you did, enough to try to keep your sisters in the dark.'

'She guessed anyway. Eloise sees everything. That's why she sent Estelle to Paris. If I had only listened to Estelle…'

'Phoebe, as far as you were concerned at the time, Estelle was asking you to abandon your life-long ambition.'

'If only I had, we wouldn't be at odds as we are just now. Do you think—Owen, do you think Mama simply didn't care for any of us girls?'

'I think,' Owen said carefully, 'that perhaps she cared for herself first and foremost.'

'That's what Eloise believes.'

'If that rag had written a story about your mother, how do you think she'd feel?'

'I don't know. Not like this. She was forever declaring that she wouldn't apologise for her behaviour. I used to think that was brave of her to thumb her nose at convention.' Phoebe winced. 'Poor Papa. And now I'm inflicting the same thing on you. Like mother like daughter!'

'You went to Paris, the culinary capital of the world, because you passionately wanted to learn how to be a chef. Your passion is something you do have in common with your mother—though I suspect it's the only thing. You had the courage of your convictions, you were determined to chase the pot of gold at the end of your rainbow. So tell me, what is there in that to be ashamed of?'

'I failed.'

'There is no shame in failing. Failing to even try would have been a much bigger crime.'

'But I didn't consider the consequences.'

'There would have been no consequences if some

low-life hack hadn't dished up your broken dreams as salacious gossip.'

'And now everyone will know that you're married to a hussy and a failure.'

'Then there is only one thing to be done.'

Phoebe's face fell. 'Oh! Of course you would be well within your rights if…'

'Not that, silly. We must simply prove them all wrong.'

She opened her mouth to speak then closed it again. He waited, watching the emotions flit across her transparent countenance, delighted to see the way she set her shoulders, braced herself as if readying herself for battle. 'Do you think we can?'

'Of course we can, but we're going to ride out this storm first. We are the scandalmonger's dish of the day. I could pull strings, have a denial printed, make them retract it even, but that would simply lend it credence, fuel the fire. They will have other fish to fry soon enough, and then we will be yesterday's news.'

'Leaving you married to a—a fallen woman, as far as the world is concerned!'

'Do not ever say that!' Owen jumped to his feet. 'Do you hear me, Phoebe?' He pulled her to her feet, forcing her to meet his eyes. 'I am proud to call you my wife. In fact I'd go so far as to say that I can't think of any woman I'd rather call my wife than you. You don't have a selfish or thoughtless bone in you're body. You don't trample over your nearest and dearest—or indeed neglect them—just to get what you want. You are not your mother's daughter. Are you listening to me?'

'I'm just terrified I'll let you down.'

'The only way you could let me down would be if you threw in the towel. Stop living in your sisters' shadow, Phoebe and once and for all, put that bas— put Solignac's opinion of you out of your head. If the restaurant fails, it won't be because you haven't put your heart and soul into it.'

'I won't fail. We won't fail.'

Owen smiled. 'That's the spirit.'

'What was it you said, notoriety whets the appetite? If our restaurant was open tonight, we'd be left with a roomful of plates scraped clean! I'll have to write to Eloise.'

'Would it be better if I wrote to her?'

'Prove to her that you're standing by me? No, thank you, then I'd actually be hiding behind you. I'd better do it today, then I may even pre-empt her seeing that article. I can reassure her that it makes no difference to our plans, that you stand foursquare behind me. As to her name being mentioned in the press—there's nothing I can do about that save to apologise to her and to Alexander. At least I don't need to write to Aunt Kate, she's still away.'

'What about Estelle?' Owen asked tentatively.

'The chances of her seeing that story are remote. I have enough on my plate as it is.'

'I think that's wise. Time enough for that when the dust has settled.' A tear trickled down her cheek. He brushed it away, forgetting that he wasn't wearing his gloves. Her skin was warm, soft, damp. His fingers tingled.

'Is my nose red?'

'Yes.' He kissed it.

He felt her inhale sharply. He let her go, taking a step back, but she caught his hand, lifting it to her mouth, pressing a gentle kiss to his swollen knuckle. 'Thank you. I am so proud to be able to call you my husband. In fact,' she said, smiling up at him, 'I'd go so far as to say that I can't think of any man I'd rather call my husband than you.'

A bittersweet compliment if ever there was one, for her kiss, just a silly little kiss, had set his senses alight, and right at this moment, he wanted to be the kind of husband he'd promised he would not be. 'Thank you, but do try for a little originality in your compliments.'

'This, from the man who appropriated Benjamin Franklin's words as his own!'

'*Touché.*' Reluctantly, Owen extracted his hand from her grasp. 'I haven't done my exercises today, and I want to be fighting fit if we're going to brazen this out.'

'If only we could lock ourselves away from the world for a month or so—oh, good heavens, I didn't mean...'

'It's fine. Don't look so horrified, Phoebe, I can't pretend that I didn't do exactly that. But I'm not doing it again. We're going to face this down.'

'How?'

'I've no idea, but we'll find a way. Do you think you are ready to face the world?'

'If you can do it, then I can.'

She was so brave, and so lovely, all he wanted was

to sweep her into his arms and kiss her. God, he really wanted to kiss her. 'Good,' Owen said, stooping to pick up his gloves. 'Go and write to Eloise. We'll talk later.'

'Thank you. For everything. Just one more thing,' she called as he reached the door. She pointed to his discarded gloves which were sitting on the table. 'It's likely to be a bare-knuckle fight, isn't it? I don't think you should wear those any more.'

Chapter Eight

'Are you teasing me?'

Owen shook his head, concentrating on peeling an apple for Phoebe. 'One sure-fire way to stop that rag digging up more dirt from either of our pasts is to give them something new to write about.'

'So we'll give them a new scandal.'

'Of our own making. What do you think of my daring plan?'

'I thought that only men were allowed to dine at Crockford's?'

'They are.' He finished cutting the apple into thin slivers, laying it out like a fan on the plate the way she liked it. 'Would you like some stilton with that?'

'No, thank you. Well, just a smidgen. Do you intend that I dress up as a man? Or do you plan to smuggle me in?'

Owen guffawed. 'I'd very much like to see you in breeches…'

'Owen!'

'You wouldn't fool anyone, Phoebe,' he said, looking quite unabashed. 'You will go as yourself. It will be our first formal appearance in society as Mr and Mrs Harrington.'

'Yes, but how?'

'Before we got married, I told you that I was a bit of a "name" in the city? Well, another man who has an eye for investments is William Crockford—Crocky to those who think he is their friend. In his case, the "investors" are the poor deluded souls who play at the tables. They say he can predict to the pound and to the hour when a man will come into his inheritance, and that's how he times the invitations to grace his tables. He has become one of the wealthiest men in London by knowing how to calculate odds. He also likes to see the money he makes working for him. And I can help him with that.'

Phoebe frowned. 'Didn't you say that you never give investment tips?'

'I'm happy to make an exception if it suits our purpose.'

'You'll bribe him!' She clapped her hands together gleefully. 'Really? And then he'll let me eat in the restaurant?'

'If I also have a word in the ear of the most esteemed member of the club too, I reckon so.'

'And who is that?'

'The Duke of Wellington.'

Phoebe choked on her apple. 'You are acquainted with the Iron Duke?'

'Our paths have crossed.'

'Goodness. I had no idea you moved in such circles.'

'We were never exactly friends, but London is a small village.'

'Did you ever come across the Earl of Fearnoch—not Eloise's husband, but his brother, the previous earl?'

'He was a bit of a loose fish by all accounts. Not my set. I was feckless, Phoebe, but I was never a libertine.'

'I never thought for a moment that you were.' Her eyes widened. 'Do you mean that Alexander's brother was?'

'And his father, too. He has a cousin, Raymond Sinclair, who seems to be trying his best to keep up the family tradition. Rumour has their coat of arms features a codpiece. I've never met your sister's husband though—which is odd.'

'Alexander spent all of his time working abroad until he married Eloise. He was something in the Admiralty.'

'That explains it. The family won't be strangers to scandal though, will they? No, I don't mean that as a consolation,' Owen added hastily, 'just a fact. And I know it's your sister you're more concerned about than her husband. Did you write to her as planned?'

'I hope I said enough to stop her from worrying. As to her name being dragged into that horrible story—well, at least she and Alexander spend hardly any time in London. Now that she is expecting a baby, she'll spend even less time here.'

'When is the child due?'

'Late spring. Goodness, I wonder if she'll have twins! I shall have to take time away from our restaurant to visit her—but I'm not sure if I'd trust anyone to deputise for me, when the business is so new.'

'We haven't even found the perfect premises yet,' Owen chided her, 'and you're already thinking of closing up!'

'I will not rise to your bait,' Phoebe said with a grin. 'Do you honestly think you can get us into Crockford's?'

'Wellington considers himself something of an epicure. Combine that with the fact that he has an eye for a beautiful woman, and I reckon his curiosity should see us gain entry.'

'I can't believe it. I'm going to taste Louis Eustache Ude's food.'

'Phoebe, you're going to have to do so with the eyes of everyone else in the room fixed on you, you do know that?'

Her excitement fizzled out. 'Can't we request a private room? In fact, if you are so influential—couldn't you simply ask Monsieur Ude to come here to cook for us?'

'But the point of this exercise isn't only to allow you to see what our competition may be.'

Phoebe pushed her plate of untouched cheese and half-finished apple aside. 'We'll be giving them exactly what they want, you mean—playing up to what they expect of us—a scandalous couple, daring to thumb our noses at society's conventions.'

His eyes gleamed. His smile was mischievous and quite irresistible. 'I have to admit, it's an enticing idea,' Phoebe said. 'Monsieur Ude will know from the recent revelations in the press that I am contemplating setting up in competition.'

'That will only serve to put him even more on his mettle. How dare an English person presume that they can cook as well as a Frenchman,' Owen said in a preposterous accent, 'It is an outrage. That a woman think such a thing is a sacrilege. It is unnatural.'

Phoebe collapsed in a fit of giggles. 'You are mocking one of my heroes.'

'He certainly has an inflated opinion of himself. I've heard that if his diners fail to be appreciative enough, he emerges from the kitchens to chastise them.'

Just as Pascal had, Phoebe thought. Though he would never admit it, Pascal had revered Monsieur Ude and been extremely envious of his success, but she'd had no idea he took his admiration to the point of emulation. It made Pascal seem rather pathetic, but she decided not to mention the fact. She did not want him, even as a subject of derision, to pollute the conversation. 'When will we go?'

'You think it's a good idea then?'

'I think it's outrageous. Will it work, do you think?'

'At the very least, you'll get to eat dinner prepared by your food hero.'

'A dinner made by my food hero, eaten with my husband hero. I hope I won't be too nervous to enjoy it.'

'In all seriousness, Phoebe, if it's too much…'

'Don't forget that this will be a big step for you too, Owen.'

'I'll have you by my side to prop me up.'

'And I'll have you, to prop me up.'

'It will probably take a week, perhaps ten days to make the necessary arrangements with Crockford and Wellington. You'll need to order a new gown. Expensive. Chic. Something that treads the line between *à la mode* and *oh, là-là*. You know the kind of thing.'

'I don't. Pray tell me.'

'For a start, nothing pale. It should be bright, vibrant, emerald or sapphire or ruby, the colour of a jewel, drawing attention to the jewel wearing it.'

'Mama always said that redheads should never wear red,' Phoebe said, entranced by this new, charming, flirtatious version of Owen. 'That's why it is Eloise's favourite colour. A scarlet woman. Why not give them exactly what they expect?'

'Tempting, but a bit too obvious, don't you think?'

'Which is why I've not to dress demurely in white, yes?'

'And why you should make the most of your quite delightful figure, but by hints and allusions rather than brazen display.'

'Can a dress hint and allude? How do you know such things—no, don't answer that I don't want to know. I know there have been other woman. I didn't mean I wanted to pretend there haven't been, I meant that I really don't want to know. Or to think about— any more than I wish to think about my own past, to be perfectly frank.'

'Do you wish it undone?'

'No, but I'm not that Phoebe any more.'

'I like the new Phoebe.'

'Do you? There's certainly more of me! I've been eating too much.'

'No. When you left Paris, you'd been eating too little.'

'Mama always said that Estelle and I would run to fat.'

Owen rolled his eyes. 'You once told me that your mother was the kind of person who drew every eye in the room when she walked into it. That's what you do. It's not just the way you look—you are undoubtedly a very beautiful woman—it's something in you. You are captivating. I suspect that your mother recognised that and I'm sorry to say that a woman as vain as she was, would not have wanted her daughters to outshine her.'

'Oh, we didn't.'

'Perhaps not then, you were too young. But if she could see you now—' He broke off, shaking his head. 'She's not here to defend herself, and she's your mother. It's not for me to tarnish your memories of her.'

'I'm beginning to think that my memories of her were—oh, never mind. We were talking about my gown for Crockford's.'

'You could walk in wearing a flour sack tied around the waist and every man in the room would still know the moment they clapped eyes on you why I married you. I've embarrassed you,' he added, seeing her blush. 'I'm sorry. I enjoy your company, I just sometimes forget that I shouldn't be enjoying it quite so much.'

'Don't be sorry. I feel exactly the same.'

'What are you saying?'

'I don't know. Would it be so wrong for us to enjoy each other's company a little bit more?'

Owen set down his wine glass. 'Not if you don't think it's wrong. And not if you're absolutely sure. I don't expect…'

'That's why I'm sure,' Phoebe said. 'Because you don't expect. That's why I'm sure.'

He laughed, pushed back his chair and pulled her into his arms. 'I've never met anyone like you.'

'That's the other reason.' She smiled shyly up at him. 'I've never met anyone like you either.'

Owen fluttered his fingers over the nape of her neck. 'You've no idea how good it feels, just to touch your skin. Lovely Phoebe.' He dipped his head to kiss the hollow of her collar bone. 'Delightful Phoebe.' He trailed kisses up the column of her neck. 'Delicious Phoebe.'

Their lips met. Heart thudding, she closed her eyes and surrendered to the sweet, drugging pleasure of their kisses, twining her arms around his neck, opening her mouth to him, melting, slowly melting. They kissed, and kissed, and kissed some more, breaking off to breathe, to stare wide-eyed with wonder, and then falling back into each other's arms to kiss and kiss and kiss again. They kissed as if they had only just discovered kissing, finding new ways for their mouths to taste and to tease, small fluttering kisses and long, deep kisses. He ran his fingers through her hair, smoothed his hands over the exposed skin at the back of her evening gown, and all the time they kissed. She felt as if she could float away on a cloud of delight, as if she would melt, as if she had turned into something molten and hot and sweet.

And then there came a point when their kisses could have changed. When they hovered on the brink of delight and desire. And they stopped of one accord, silently agreeing that it was enough. For now it was more than enough. And that's when Phoebe knew she'd been right to trust him. That he really was different.

'Goodnight,' Owen said, kissing her gently one more time.

'Goodnight,' Phoebe said, pulling his face down for one last kiss. 'Sleep well, husband of mine.'

For Mr and Mrs Harrington's somewhat unconventional London debut, Phoebe wore an evening gown of bronze silk with a black-net overdress, and a black-velvet bodice edged with bronze-satin ribbon. The sleeves were full but not so full as to require the newly fashionable plumpers, and the décolleté was low enough to accentuate the curve of her bosom but not nearly low enough to show off her cleavage. The hem of the overdress was edged with black-satin leaves embroidered with bugle beads to weight it down, the skirts were full, tightly pleated, and swished alluringly when she walked. It was not a dress Phoebe would ever have chosen for herself, but it was, she thought, exactly what Owen had requested, treading the line between *à la mode* and *oh, là-là*. Talking of which! She unfurled the fan of black ostrich feathers and after peeping over the top of it coquettishly at her reflection, burst into a fit of giggles.

'I think this might be a step too far,' she muttered to herself.

'Oh, no, madam, it works beautifully with the gown.'

She still wasn't used to having a maid, and often dispensed with Jennifer's services altogether, but the undergarments that had been delivered with this gown were impossible to deal with single-handed. 'If you're sure,' Phoebe said, a little dubiously.

'Let me fasten your gloves.'

They were long, white, very tight and brand new, Phoebe was already worried about spilling her dinner on them. Owen had insisted that she didn't ask the price of anything when shopping, but she could guess, and the number made her eyes water. A velvet stole completed the outfit. She gave herself a little curtsy in the mirror and made her way down the stairs, her heart fluttering with anticipation.

Owen was waiting for her in parlour, dressed in black evening clothes with an embroidered silver waistcoat. His hair had been cut short, and looked fairer against the high black collar of his coat. He had filled out in the two months of their marriage, and no longer looked gaunt, but it was the way he held himself that had changed the most. He was confident, comfortable in himself, and though he still walked with a slight limp, which was more pronounced when he was tired, there was an agility in his movement and a supple strength that could only be attributed to his gymnastics. Beneath the stylish evening clothes, his body was hard-packed muscle.

'You look absolutely divine,' Owen said, breaking into Phoebe's reverie to kiss her softly. 'I'm glad you decided not to be a scarlet woman. This suits you perfectly—you are a bronzed goddess.'

She giggled, opening out her fan and fluttering her eyelashes. 'A scandalous, bronzed goddess.'

'A seductive one. I beg you not to look at me like that in Crockford's or we'll cause an even bigger scandal than the one we've already planned, because I won't be able to resist kissing you in public.'

Phoebe waved her fan slowly in front of her face. 'We're not at Crockford's yet.'

Owen pulled her into his arms and the fan fell to the floor as he kissed her swiftly. 'If we don't leave now, we'll miss dinner. It is served strictly from half past four until six, and it's already after four.' He picked up the fan and handed it to her. 'Ready?'

She was immediately serious. 'As ready as I'll ever be. What about you, Owen—this is a very big step for you?' She scanned his face. 'Are you sure you'll be able to cope?'

He visibly braced himself. 'I'm about to find out.'

It was already dark when the town coach deposited them outside Crockford's. The impressive red-sandstone building with its portico frontage dubbed Fishmonger's Hall by those whose fortune was insufficient to gain them entrance, was opposite White's Club and right in the heart of St James's. Phoebe was creating a scandal by her simple presence in this male enclave, though Owen refrained from reminding her.

In the carriage, she had been unusually silent, but her hand had trembled in his.

Two months ago, even a few weeks ago, he'd have considered this an ordeal—or more likely he wouldn't have contemplated being here at all! Would it trigger one of his episodes? Was he asking too much of himself? Though he'd been out of the house regularly of late, traipsing around London's markets, exploring commercial properties or taking Phoebe on sightseeing drives was very different from mingling with society. He was about to walk into the lion's den now. If something went wrong, then the gossip in tomorrow's rags would be very different from what Phoebe and he had planned.

He had a moment's panic, but taking several covert, deep breaths, he reminded himself of how well he'd been over the last few weeks, without a single nightmare for more than two. Thanks to the woman sitting beside him, who was depending on him now, to support her through this ordeal.

'Remember,' she said, as the coachman let down the steps, 'I'll be right by your side.'

He preceded her out of the carriage and helped her down. 'And I'll be right by yours,' Owen said. 'Every small step of the way.'

A blaze of light emanated from the beacons in the club's entranceway. Crockford's thugs stood aside to allow them to pass into the massive entrance hall which was randomly peppered, it seemed to Owen, with Doric and Ionic columns. It was quiet at this time of day, the real business of the club would not get underway until much later, but beneath the smell of burning oil from the huge chandeliers Crockford was so proud of, the lingering smell of sweat, stale perfume and defeat could be detected. 'Crockford has spared no expense on his decor,' he said to Phoebe, who was gazing up at the domed ceiling.

'It is like a palace,' she whispered, 'though a rather tawdry one. Versailles on a budget.'

Owen bit back a laugh as a servant approached them, informing him that they were expected. Which explained the deserted entrance hall, he thought. Everyone else was already seated and awaiting their arrival. He took Phoebe's arm as they ascended the stairs to the dining room, smiling down at her in what he hoped was a reassuring manner. The steps were shallow and wide, an easy climb, but none the less one he'd have struggled with a few short weeks ago.

'Brace yourself for a baptism of fire,' he said, keeping a firm hold of her arm as the double doors were thrown open and Phoebe obediently took a deep breath.

The dining room was long and rather narrow, with the look of a ballroom. The ornately corniced ceiling was painted in muted tones, as were the walls, which were panelled well above head height, then decorated with rows of yet more interspersed Doric and Ionic columns rising to meet the ceiling. There were no windows but the room was very brightly lit, with a central chandelier and any number of sconces burning, making it stiflingly hot. Tables were set in three regimented rows, far too close together. There was only one free, in the very centre of the room.

Phoebe's fingers were digging into his arm. The eyes of every single person in the room was upon them. What on earth had he done! But it was too late to back out now, and Phoebe, bold Phoebe, was rising to the occasion, her head held high, a faint smile curving her lips which only he could tell was rigidly held in place.

'This way, Mr Harrington,' the major-domo said, leading them needlessly to the table. The silence was dagger-sharp. He could hear the rustle of Phoebe's dress as she sat down, but when his own chair was pulled out, Owen stood his ground, taking his time to survey the other diners. He recognised many but none were among his friends, most from an older generation— presumably Wellington's cronies. Some looked away from his gaze, some met it. A very few nodded. Owen made a flourishing bow, then took his seat.

'That's the worst part over,' he said softly to Phoebe, 'forget the audience, and let's see what Monsieur Ude has to offer us.'

'Every one is watching.'

'That was rather the point, but it won't last. If they don't turn their attention to their food, Monsieur Ude will have something to say. Try to forget they are here. I'll order the wine, you concentrate on memorising the menu. Order whatever takes your fancy and as many dishes as you want to sample.'

'It is eye-wateringly expensive, even compared to La Taverne.'

'As is the wine,' Owen said, scanning the huge leather-bound tome he had been handed. '"Our cellars boast more than three hundred thousand bottles of the best that France has to offer,'" he read. 'Presumably so that Crockford's diners are well lubricated before they try their luck at the tables later. We should start with champagne, I feel our audience expects it of us.'

A bottle appeared with impressive speed, with two glasses. As soon as they were poured, Owen raised his glass, first to the room, and then, theatrically, to his wife. 'Well done,' he said as she copied him. 'Now, why don't you try really hard to forget our audience, and try to make the most of this unique, never-to-be-repeated experience.'

'We did it!' Phoebe danced into the parlour, casting off her wrap. 'We braved the lion's den and lived to tell the tale. Owen, you were magnificent.'

He laughed, following in her wake and closing the door. 'Thank you, though I'm not sure what I did to merit such fulsome praise.'

'You mean aside from gaining us unprecedented access to London's most exclusive restaurant.'

'Yes, apart from that,' he said, pulling off his gloves and pulling her into his arms.

'I know that can't have been easy for you,' Phoebe said, 'though no one would have guessed since you looked so perfectly at home, as if you had never been away. And the way you raised your glass to everyone at the start of the meal with such—such panache! While I took one look into that dining room and would happily have turned tail.'

'You carried it off every bit as well as I did.'

'I didn't want to let you down.'

'More importantly, you didn't let yourself down. Was it worth it?'

'Yes. It was invaluable. Though it's not an experience I'd ever want to repeat.'

'The main thing is we've achieved what we set out to do. You have run the rule over the competition and we have given the *ton* something new to tittle-tattle about other than your Parisian past. And here we are, unscathed.'

'Are you? Really?'

'I am. You gave me a reason to get better, Phoebe. Tonight—I really think that tonight was proof that I can.'

'Owen! I can't believe it.' With a muffled cry, she threw her arms around his neck, covering his face with kisses.

Laughing, he pulled her tighter, and their lips met. And then they kissed, as they had kissed every night since the night they had planned this Crockford's coup, slow kisses, deepening until they were verging on the frantic, before they forced themselves to stop. This was where Owen would say goodnight. This was the point where they always stopped, because if they didn't it would change everything.

Their eyes met, and suddenly Phoebe couldn't breathe. She wanted everything to change, and she could see in his eyes that Owen wanted it too. Though he would not ask. So she pulled his face back towards her and kissed him again, a long, languorous kiss whose meaning could not be mistaken.

Owen was panting when this kiss finished, his eyes dark with desire. 'Phoebe?'

She nodded.

'Are you sure?'

She didn't hesitate. 'I'm sure.'

The fire in Phoebe's room was burning brightly. She hastily pulled the screen over it, confirming, as he had suspected, that she knew it was his orders which kept the other fires in the town house burning low, though she had never once commented on the fact. Owen pretended not to notice, locking the door, and as she turned back to face him, he forgot everything else.

Wrapping his arms around her, he could feel her trembling. 'It's not too late to change your mind,' he said.

'I'm nervous. I don't want to dis...' She bit her lip. 'I won't say it.'

Owen laughed softly. 'If one of us should be worrying about disappointing the other, don't you think it should be me?'

'I didn't think! Perhaps we shouldn't...'

'Phoebe, I'm teasing you.' Though he wasn't, not completely. He was nervous. He kissed her softly. 'You are so lovely.' He kissed her again. Kisses were definitely an excellent remedy for nerves. 'I want you so much.'

This kiss was deeper. Blood rushed back to his groin. He needed to be patient, there was no rush. He had waited more than two years for this, he could wait a few minutes longer. He dragged his mouth away from hers, scattering kisses down her neck, across the swell of her breasts. Turning her around he tugged at the laces of her gown, kissing the nape of her neck, her shoulders, the knot of her spine, as he eased the dress down her body and she shivered.

The laces of her corsets were tightly tied, but his fingers were much more nimble these days, from practising—ironically—tying knots. Dropping the stays to the ground, he pulled her back against him, his erection pressed against the plump curve of her bottom, cupping her breasts. She moaned, a guttural sound that made him harder. Her nipples were erect. He circled them through her chemise, and she wriggled against him. This time it was he who moaned.

As Phoebe twisted around in his arms, her mouth sought his, and he surrendered to the clamouring need to kiss her again, shrugging out of his coat. More kisses, while her hands tugged at the buttons of his waistcoat, and he pulled the pins from her hair, until it rippled down her back, over her shoulders in a glorious wave of burnished gold.

He ran his hands down her back to cup her bottom, then back up again. Her hands were yanking his shirt free of his trousers, smoothing over his back, making his muscles clench, the sensations she was arousing in him making him shudder. His waistcoat fell to the floor. She pulled his shirt over his head, but when he would have kissed her again, she shook her head. A sensual smile curved her delicious mouth as she touched him, stroking his chest, his shoulders, back to his chest down to his belly, her eyes widening as his muscles flexed, her delight in his muscled body so patently obvious.

'You are so lovely,' she said, sounding awed, and his engorged shaft throbbed in response.

Not yet, he cautioned himself, not yet. He kissed her again—he could kiss her for ever and never tire of her—and undid the ties of her petticoat, leaving her in her chemise, drawers and stockings, a sight that temporarily deprived him of the ability to breathe. The chemise went next. He lost long, delightful minutes kissing her breasts, taking her nipples into his mouth in turn, becoming ever more aroused by her response, the way she moaned, clutched at his shoulders, shuddered against him. His self-control was pushed to the limits.

One more kiss, and Owen scooped her up, making her cry out in surprise, making for the bed, setting her down on it before he'd had time to consider whether or not he was even capable of such a feat. Tearing off the rest of his clothes, he lay beside her on the bed, pulling her tight against him, skin melded to skin. Their kisses were feverish now. He rolled between her legs and she arched under him. He eased himself into her. She was slick, hot, and dear God in heaven he was hard. He pushed higher, feeling her clench around him, and he thrust. Pain seared through his hip, drawing a hoarse cry from him.

'Owen.'

'Wait.' He breathed deeply, shaking his head when she made to move, kissing her again, deeply, until it eased. 'This way,' he said, rolling on to his back, still inside her, the surprise on her face telling him that this was a novel experience for her.

She moved, carefully, tentatively at first, but the

way she clenched around him, the visible shivers that ran through her as he pushed higher, made her bolder. She needed no urging to go faster, to rock backwards and forward, crying out as she reached a juddering climax, sending him over the edge so quickly that he only just managed to free himself, before his own release ripped through him.

'Phoebe?' Owen shuffled over in the bed, wrapping his arms around her, burying his face in her hair, heaving a deep sigh that was unmistakably satisfied 'Oh, Phoebe.'

She curled into him, pressing her cheek to his chest. 'Oh, Owen.'

She felt the rumble of his laughter, and thought that her cup might brim over with happiness. Everything about what had just happened felt so new and so perfect. The kissing. The delicious, delightful kissing that went on and on, as if they were starving and couldn't get enough of each other. And the way Owen had looked at her, devouring her with his eyes, leaving her in no doubt about what he thought of her, how much he wanted her. And even right at the end, the way he had thought of her, of protecting her—when it was her responsibility to take care of such details. Or so Pascal said.

No, she wouldn't think of him. She had not once thought of him, she realised now with quiet satisfaction, pressing a kiss to Owen's chest, breathing in the scent of him, clean sweat and soap. Nothing that Owen had done had reminded her. Nor anything she'd felt either. It wasn't like the first time—now that was something she really didn't want to think of—but it felt new. Delightfully new.

Owen trailed his hand down her back, to rest on her bottom. She wriggled closer, resting her hand on his flank, encountered a hard ridge of scarring and his hand, which had been drawing little circles on her bottom, froze. 'Is it painful?'

'Not the scar.'

Phoebe lifted her head. 'May I look?'

He shrugged, which was what he often did when he was embarrassed, and rolled on to his stomach. She sat up, pushing back the sheet he had pulled over them. The scar ran in a jagged line from halfway up his thigh, all the way up his flank to end at the top of his hip. 'How did you get this?'

'Not in the accident. It was afterwards. An operation to piece together the shattered bone.'

'Dear heavens, Owen, that must have been an agony.'

'I barely remember. I think they poured a bottle of cognac down my throat.'

'Did it make it better or worse?'

He laughed grimly. 'The big question. I will never know.'

Phoebe traced the line of the scar with her fingers. 'Can you feel that?'

'Not really.'

She leaned over, pressing a line of little kisses along it. 'Can you feel that?'

'A little. Perhaps if you tried again.'

She did, this time with more lingering kisses, using

her tongue and her lips. Owen gave a muffled groan. 'Did you feel that?'

'I definitely felt that.'

There was laughter in his voice. Something else that was entirely new. Phoebe kissed her way along his scar again, then carried on, kissing up his back, sliding down the bed to lie by his side again, pressing a last kiss to his ear. 'Did you feel that?' she whispered.

He rolled over, wrapping his arms around her, his eyes alight with laughter and desire. 'What do you think?'

His erection was pressing into her stomach. Her breasts were pressed against his chest. Her body was already starting to clamour for more in a way that astonished her. Another novel development, she thought, answering him with a kiss.

They made love for the second time that night, more slowly this time, savouring each other. Their kisses were languorous. Owen devoted long, exquisite minutes to her breasts, licking, kissing, sucking, so that she thought she might have fainted with the bliss of it. And he wanted her to touch him, to wrap her fingers around the thick, silky length of his erection, to stroke him, his pleasure at what she was doing written so clearly on his face that she gained confidence. And then he touched her too, slow strokes, without urgency, aiming not for completion but only to draw out the pleasure—dear heavens, such pleasure. And all the time, their eyes locked, between kisses, communicating silently.

Their lips met again, and of one accord their kiss

deepened, and with a speed that left her breathless, Phoebe went from floating on a cloud of delight to a swooping, shuddering climax, and Owen pushed inside her, hitching her leg over his, and his slow, deep thrusts stretched the pleasure out further, making her cry out with each one, clutching at him to pull him deeper inside her, murmuring his name over and over, until he pulled free with a hoarse cry.

And afterwards, once more wrapped tightly together, her back to his chest, he nuzzled her ear. 'I have never felt like this, Phoebe. Never.'

Owen left for his own room, leaving her alone in the dishevelled bed. She would have preferred him to stay with her, but had not said so. In this new world order, she had no idea what the rules were. Tonight had been perfect beyond her wildest dreams already, she didn't want to spoil it. She wanted to wake in Owen's arms, but he was accustomed to sleeping on his own, so she must not read anything into his leaving her. And besides, she told herself sternly, she had always preferred to have her bed to herself too. She liked to stretch out, didn't she?

She normally did, but not tonight. Instead, she curled up into the warm space that Owen had left, and nestled her cheek on the pillow where he had lain. She could not compare tonight with any other night, because there was simply no comparison. She hadn't realised until tonight that Pascal was a selfish lover. She hadn't known that making love was a conversation as well as an act. She certainly hadn't known that desire could be rekindled so easily by shared laughter. She hadn't had to think, when she was making love with Owen, about whether she was pleasing him, because she could see it writ large in his face, in his reactions.

Had she been too bold? She had been so carried away, entranced by the effortlessness of it, and the depth of the pleasure, and the sheer delight of it, but what if Owen thought differently? What if he thought her confidence came from her experience? The idea was like a dousing of cold water. Ought she to have pretended ignorance? But tonight had shown her she *was* much more ignorant than she'd realised. And she was in danger of spoiling it, with her insecure doubts.

So she would cast her doubts away, confine those to the past, and enjoy the present. Well, she might just think about the most recent past again, just until she fell asleep. *'I have never felt like this, Phoebe. Never.'* Owen's words. Phoebe could only echo them.

Chapter Nine

Phoebe gazed around the vast space that was earmarked for the main dining room of her new restaurant. The ceilings were picked out in white and gold to match the wall panelling. The windows were tall, French-style. The basement kitchen needed a lot of work, but it had running water and more importantly, the passageway to the dining room was wide and short. There were even a number of small rooms which could be converted for private dining. 'It's perfect,' she said, 'if I want to compete with Monsieur Ude. We could easily seat fifty people in here—double that if we put the tables closer together.'

'I never did go to La Grande Taverne,' Owen said, 'but I'm assuming it looked something like this?'

'Yes.'

He watched her, pacing out the floor, and when she departed to take another look at the basement space, Owen occupied himself with rereading the lease. There was a great deal of leeway, he reckoned, for renegotiating the terms, but the many clauses and sub-clauses failed to hold his attention. It was over a week since that night at Crockford's changed everything for him. And, he hoped, for Phoebe too.

It had borne fruit in a different way too. The *Town Crier* had stopped digging into Phoebe's past and was now breathlessly speculating about the unconventional couple's possible assault on London's gourmands. All excellent advance publicity as far as Owen was concerned.

They hadn't discussed their feelings, but every time they made love, their bodies spoke for them. He had never felt like this before. It might be a cliché, to say that the two of them became one, but it was also true. He shook his head wryly. Who would have thought it!

He was in love with Phoebe. Bloody hell! Owen stuffed the documents back into the leather portfolio, and headed for the window. The glass was icy on his forehead as he leaned against it. Outside, the leaden sky looked ominous, heralding a dusting of snow. Was he really in love? His foolish smile was answer enough, but he still couldn't quite believe it. He wasn't only in love, he was well. Love had cured him, Owen thought, mocking his own mawkishness, but once again, the cliché seemed to be true. He hadn't lost a second to those peculiar lapses for some time. He was still haunted by the asylum nightmare, as he now referred to it in his head, but each time it occurred, the dream moved further on. He had now located the source of the high-pitched wailing, when he opened a door and found himself not in the usual empty room but some sort of crèche. Though as far as he knew, the asylum where he had first come to his senses after his accident had not been a lying-in hospital, his memory of those ago-nising days was hazy to say the least. He had decided that this nightmare was in fact based on some vague memory. Though he still couldn't understand why he awoke feeling so racked with guilt and sorrow, he be-lieved he was making progress and hoped that one day he'd have progressed far enough to be able to spend the night sleeping in Phoebe's arms. Not yet, but soon. What mattered is that he wanted it, that it was an am-bition he believed he could one day realise. His appe-tite for life had returned, thanks to her.

And here she was, his lovely, funny, brave wife, with dust on her nose and a worried frown. Now was not the time for a declaration. She knew, she couldn't doubt the depth of his feelings, but he wanted the first time he told her to be special. And though he was pretty certain she was in love with him, he wasn't sure that she realised it quite yet. It was too fragile and too new for them to talk about. And besides, she was dis-tracted by her restaurant. So he'd wait until after the opening night—however long away that might be. It would be worth it. There was no rush. They had the rest of their lives to spend together.

Owen had been staring out of the window, but as she came back into the dining room, he turned and smiled, and Phoebe forgot her worries for a moment, stepping into his embrace, resting her cheek against the rough wool of his greatcoat. Every day, she came to care more for him. Every time she saw him, her heart did a little leap and she felt as if the sun came out inside her. She had never been so happy, but she was determined to look no further ahead than today, and then tomorrow and the next day, to enjoy and relish every moment. She was terrified it might end, and so she would not tempt fate by putting a name to her feelings. She wrapped her arms around her husband's waist, reassured by his now familiar shape, then let him go.

'You've got dust on your nose,' he said, wiping it with his kerchief.

'The kitchens haven't been used for some months.'

'It was a town house. When the last lease expired, it was parcelled up into smaller premises. I think this must have been the drawing room. What do you think?'

She took a deep breath. 'I'm sorry. If you'd asked me back in October, when we were first married, I'd probably have said it was perfect. But now…'

'What has changed?'

She smiled at him, suddenly quite sure. 'Everything.'

Owen laughed. 'I think you need to explain.'

'That visit to Crockford's, it was the turning point for me. The food was superlative, exactly what I expected. Even the mackerel roe dish that he is most famous for lived up to my high expectations, and as for the *boudin de cerises a là Bentinck*—who would have thought that cherry pudding could taste so heavenly.'

'You don't think you can compete with that? I can't say I share your enthusiasm for the mackerel concoction, there was so much butter and cream it gave me indigestion just looking at it, but I am not a gourmand.'

'No, but you do like to eat, don't you, Owen?'

'I like to have dinner with you, but the company is far more important than the food—forgive me, I know that's tantamount to heresy for you.'

'But it's not!' Phoebe clapped her hands together, beaming at him. 'You have hit the nail exactly on the head.'

'If I have, it was an accident. What nail?'

'I don't want people to come to our restaurant to worship the food—I want them to enjoy it, but I don't want it to dominate. I can see from your expression that I'm still not explaining it very well. Bear with me.' Phoebe wrapped her cloak more tightly around her, shivering. 'Do you remember the first meal I cooked for you?'

'Of course I do. Venison stew.'

'And when I asked you what was in it, you didn't much care, did you? As far as you were concerned, it was delicious, and that was all that mattered. At La Grande Taverne each ingredient would have been dissected and discussed endlessly. The diners would not have commented on how delicious it was, but how extraordinary or unusual it was, whether it was the *amuse-bouche*, the *entrée* or the dessert. Honestly, Owen, when they were presented with Pascal's *rôti sans pareil*, they were expected to swoon.'

'I know I'm going to regret asking, but what is a *rôti sans pareil*?'

'It is when a series of birds are stuffed inside each other, smallest to largest. The culinary term for it is *engastration* which doesn't sound particularly appetising.'

'It sounds more like a surgical procedure.'

Phoebe chuckled. 'It *is* a surgical procedure. You have to debone each of the birds, and tie them together, as if you were wrapping it up like a present, with a layer of stuffing in between. Most chefs are content with four or five birds, but Pascal insisted on serving twelve.'

'I am not remotely surprised to hear that.'

'The customers loved it. Pascal always came out of the kitchen to carve. If he had not been a chef I think he would have been on the stage.'

'By the sounds of it, he treated the restaurant as his stage, and his customers were his adoring audience. What happened if they didn't adore him?'

'He would have them summarily ejected. How dare they question his cooking! His notoriously temperamental nature added to the sense of theatre, much as like Monsieur Ude.'

'Do you intend to be equally volatile?'

Phoebe rolled her eyes. 'You know that I am not a performer, I want my food to speak for me. Now I've completely lost the thread of what I was trying to explain to you.'

'*Engastration.*'

'Oh, that was just an example. In fact, it was not Pascal's invention, though he claimed it was. The recipe was published in the *Almanach des Gourmands*, which is a sort of gastronomist's periodical, about ten or fifteen years ago. Pascal had a complete collection of them, and I read them. I didn't tell him that I knew he'd purloined the idea for his own though.' She waved her hands dismissively. 'What I'm trying to explain, Owen, is that I don't want to cook that kind of food. I don't want to prove Pascal wrong by imitating him—though Crockford's demonstrated very clearly to me, that in fact Pascal has been imitating Monsieur Ude. But I don't want to give London another Crockford's either. I want our restaurant to be the very opposite of both of those establishments. It will be a place where people will feel comfortable, as if they were sitting down to a meal in their own dining room. The food will be excellent…'

'Of course!'

'But it won't be like a piece of art to be admired. I would like us to have restaurant more like a Parisian café, you know, with a real mix of people. What do you think?'

'Well for a start, we'll have to look at rather different premises.'

'I know, I'm so sorry I've wasted your time.'

'No, don't be sorry, my little revolutionary.'

'Is it so radical? Too radical?'

He laughed. 'I have no idea, but my eye for a business opportunity is telling me that London is ready for something new and different.'

'I thought you only had eyes for me.' Owen smiled down at her, and her heart skipped a beat. 'So, we are decided then,' Phoebe added, feeling not a single twinge of doubt.

'It seems we are,' Owen said, kissing the tip of her nose.

'Such a huge decision merits a proper kiss, don't you think?' she said, laughing.

He swept her into his arms, and her laughter faded immediately as their lips met, to be replaced with desire. 'As ever, my lovely wife, you are absolutely right.'

Christmas Day

The house was unnaturally quiet, since all the servants were enjoying a rare official holiday, leaving Owen and Phoebe to their own devices. Which suited them very well indeed. The festivities began with Owen bringing Phoebe breakfast in bed, before snuggling in beside her to share the simple repast. The tea had grown quite cold by the time they were ready to drink it.

It had been very tempting to remain in bed all day, but the snow which had been threatening for the last week finally started falling so they had ventured out, walking through St James's park then round Hyde Park and on to Regent's Park, following Owen's old running route. Their footsteps were muffled on the snow-covered footpaths, the vast expanses of grass a smooth carpet of white, the trees decorated with clumps of snow clinging to branches.

On their return, they had drunk mulled wine in the kitchen, Owen sitting at the table inexpertly but happily carrying out the more menial tasks, Phoebe bustling about happily in her element, preparing Christmas dinner. Now, with the feast over, they had decamped from the dining room to the parlour, curled up together at either end of the sofa like bookends, Phoebe's stockinged feet resting on Owen's lap.

'My parents always spent Christmas in Dublin when we were growing up,' she said. 'So we never exchanged gifts or made much of a fuss. It was different at Elmswood Manor, Aunt Kate held a big party for all the tenants, and there was a village fayre too. Last year in Paris, Christmas was a working day, cooking other people's dinner. Now this year, I'm here with you.'

'Still cooking dinner, too! My compliments to the chef.'

'My compliments to the *sous-chef.*'

Owen laughed. 'You re-chopped every diced onion I handed you, and you had to dig the eyes out of the potatoes.'

'I hoped you hadn't noticed.'

'I notice everything about you. It really was a delicious dinner, Phoebe, thank you.'

'It was a pleasure. If all our customers are as easily satisfied as you, then I shall have a very straightforward time of it in the kitchen.'

'You think me easily satisfied?'

Her eyes had drifted shut, for he had been playing with her toes, but now they flew open. He was smiling at her, one brow slightly raised, that smile of his that instantly made her pulse race. She wriggled her foot free, to rest it on the top of his thigh. 'On the contrary, I think you might be insatiable.'

He ran his fingers up her calf, stroking circles at the backs of her knees, something which he had discovered made her giddy with delight. 'I don't think I'll ever be able to get enough of you. Not even if I live to be a hundred.'

She was stroking him with her foot, the ridge of his arousal clear through the material of his trousers. He gently pulled her towards him, sliding his hand up her thigh, finding the gap in her drawers, to cup her. She pressed against his hand.

'I'm not the only one who's insatiable,' Owen said, teasing her, lightly stroking her.

Phoebe bit her lip, trying not to moan, and he slid his fingers inside her. Sometimes she enjoyed making love slowly. Sometimes, like now, there was an urgency in her that took her breath away. Always, Owen seemed to know exactly what to do, to read her body as if she had given him a recipe for every occasion. She rushed towards a climax, and it was barely over when he helped her upright, where she was more help than hindrance tugging at his clothes, smoothing the sheath which he had procured over his throbbing arousal, then taking him inside her quickly, deeply, with a harsh groan of satisfaction. Though she was on top, once again he sensed her needs, taking charge, encouraging her to thrust, fast and hard, sending her spiralling out of control, as he came, pulling her tight against his heaving chest, saying her name over and over.

Later, making the most of their deserted home, they returned to the kitchen, where Phoebe warmed the last of the mulled wine and Owen sat at the table watching her. She was wrapped in one of his dressing gowns, a dark green velvet quilted affair which was far too big for her, and made her impossibly endearing. He turned the little box over in the pocket of his own dressing gown, unaccountably nervous about giving her his gift, for it was such an obvious token of love. He had kept his promise to himself not to declare himself, but there were moments every day when he was tempted.

It was never in the aftermath of lovemaking, there was no need for words then. It was when she handed him his breakfast plate, a dainty montage of choice morsels set out with such care and precision, for she knew he had to be tempted to eat in the morning. Or when she was perusing one of the regular letters she received from Eloise, her face an ever-changing picture of emotions, so that he could guess almost every line of it without her reading it out. Or when she was sitting with her precious book of recipes, staring into space, tapping the end of her pencil on her nose, then she would suddenly smile to herself with such glee, and begin to write furiously. Or sometimes it was simply seeing her face light up when he walked into a room, so transparent with love that he thought his heart might burst.

He knew she loved him, but he sensed that she was still fragile. She might not have loved Solignac as she had thought, but she had still been hurt, damaged by the experience. She needed time to become confident in his love for her, and he was still determined to give her as much time as she needed.

But his love token was like a hot coal burning in his pocket. As he took the glass of wine from Phoebe, chinking it to hers, he decided. This had been such a perfect day, he wanted it to end perfectly. 'Close your eyes,' Owen said, 'and hold out your hands.'

'Why?'

'It's a surprise. That's why I told you to close your eyes.'

'A nice surprise?' Phoebe asked, sounding suspicious, though she did as he asked her.

'I'll let you be the judge of that.' He placed the small box in her outstretched hands. 'You can look now.'

She looked at him first, her mouth trembling, though he wasn't sure if she was on the brink of smiling or crying. His stomach cramped with nerves, anticipation making him feel as if he might actually be sick. Had he done the wrong thing? Phoebe opened the box and stared at the ring. She took it out, tracing the heart shape of the rubies which surrounded the central diamond, holding it up to the light to admire the delicate pierce work on the gold band.

'Do you like it?' he demanded, unable to contain himself any longer.

'Oh, Owen.' To his dismay, she burst into tears. Then she threw her arms around his neck. 'Oh, Owen, I've never seen anything so utterly beautiful. Thank you so much.'

'Here, let me put it on.' Weak with relief, he slipped the ring on to her finger above her wedding band. 'Does it fit?'

She splayed her fingers out, gazing rapt at his gift. 'It might have been made for me.'

The truth was, it had been, and at great expense. Now was the perfect moment to tell her he loved her. He was sure of it. There was no point in waiting. She had his heart, that's all he needed to say, and this was a token.

'Phoebe, I…'

There was a rushing in his ears and the stone floor seemed to swoop up to meet him. His knees gave way. As he pitched forward, he saw her face, stricken with horror. And then there was nothing.

'Owen?' Fighting back her rising panic, Phoebe dropped to her knees, easing him down with her, placing his head on her lap. How she had managed to catch him as he fell she had no idea. 'Owen', she said again, leaning over him, listening with her heart pounding for a breath, holding her own, until she heard him, shallow and faint, but he was definitely breathing. She laid her hand on his forehead. His skin was cold, clammy. Feeling helpless and foolish, she placed her hand over his heart under his dressing gown, trying to time her own breathing with his heartbeat. Just when she was beginning to wonder if she should try to rouse him, he opened his eyes, staring blankly at her.

'You fainted,' Phoebe said.

Owen heaved himself to his feet, staring around him as if he had no idea where he was.

'Sit down for a moment. I'll get you some water.'

But he was already pushing past her, heading out of the kitchen.

'Owen?' She ran after him, grabbing his arm.

He shook her off with a snarl. 'For pity's sake just let me be!'

* * *

'Is there something wrong with your tea?'

'What?'

Owen smiled at her, indicating her full cup. 'You've normally emptied the pot by now.'

Phoebe picked up her cup, taking a quick swallow of the cold tea. 'How are you feeling?'

'That's the second time you've asked me that. I'm fine.' She was not fine, she was at a complete loss. After Owen had stormed off last night, she had crept with the stealth of a thief to his rooms. Unable to summon the courage to face him, she had listened intently, until she heard him moving about. After that, she'd sat for over an hour in the kitchen, waiting in vain for him to return.

A sleepless night had brought her early to the breakfast parlour, waiting on tenterhooks for him to join her. Which he had, acting as if nothing untoward had happened. If she hadn't caught him as he fell, she'd have been worried that he'd hit his head. But she had caught him. Had he suffered some sort of apoplexy that had affected his brain? But aside from the fact he was quite oblivious of how the night had ended, he seemed perfectly sane.

Was he *pretending* that he didn't remember because he was embarrassed? 'Did you sleep well?' she asked helplessly.

'I don't know what you put in that mulled wine, but it knocked me out.'

But he hadn't actually touched the mulled wine before he fainted. He wasn't pretending, he really didn't remember, she was certain of that much. Could this be some new phase of his illness? Her blood ran cold at that thought. But, no, why should it be, when there had been no other signs whatsoever? Whatever had happened was an aberration of some kind.

Could one have a surfeit of lovemaking? They had been making love at least once a day, often more, almost every day. And Owen had been celibate for over two years, after all. Was it possible to have an excess? Did it deplete some vital bodily humour? She had no idea. What she did know was that she was clutching at straws.

'Phoebe?'

She blinked.

'Do you like it? The ring?'

So he had noticed she was wearing it, and he did remember giving it to her. 'Oh, Owen, it's beautiful. I've never seen a design like it. The heart, I mean.' Just before he fainted, she had been so sure he was going to tell her that it represented *his* heart. She waited, hoping, longing for him to take the opportunity now. But he was staring at the ring as if he had never seen it before.

'I'm glad it fits.'

'Yes,' she said, struggling to hide her disappointment. 'It's a perfect fit.'

'I'll get you a fresh pot of tea. If you're up to it, I have a new list of premises for us to explore, but if not…'

'I'm fine, Owen. I'm keen to find the right place, now that we have settled on a café-style restaurant.'

* * *

'I think this might be the one,' Phoebe said, gazing around the room, her eyes shining.

Owen smiled at her enthusiasm. 'You've only just walked in the door.'

'I know, but I have a good feeling about it.'

The premises was low-ceilinged, and had clearly been some sort of shop, with panelled walls and wooden floors, and two bow windows facing on to the street. Phoebe was right, there was something very reminiscent of Parisian cafés about it. It was certainly not grand, but it could be made to feel extremely comfortable.

'I can already see it,' Phoebe was saying. 'We'll put seating all around the walls, and rows of little tables— though not crammed as close together as they are in Paris. Then over here, we'll have some more private seating, tables for four or six. And here, the front desk— see, it's an excellent position for the waiters to view the whole room. Come on, let's look upstairs.'

He followed her up the rather narrow staircase.

'Owen! I think the fates must be telling us something.'

The room was built into the eaves and stretched the full length of the café. The floor was bare boards, rather than black and white tiles, the walls painted an unappealing brown rather than red, but the resemblance to the top-floor room at the Procope was nevertheless striking. 'We'd better work out where we might locate the kitchens first,' he cautioned.

Phoebe caught his hand, pulling him down the room. 'Do you remember?'

'Of course I do. Our table was about here, I think.'

'I think you're right. Oh, Owen, this is it. This is our restaurant.' She whirled around, her arms spread, her skirts flying out. 'This really is it.'

He watched her, rooted to the spot, as she danced around the room, opening cupboards, brushing the dust from the window panes to peer out. She was so lovely, and he loved her so much. Seeing the ring on her finger the morning after Christmas had been a shock. He had no recollection of giving her the present. Phoebe had behaved oddly over breakfast, she'd seemed unsettled, though when he asked her, she said there was nothing wrong. The loss of memory panicked him, but six days had passed without further incident. If he'd had a relapse, it was a minor one. He had been premature, he'd concluded, in giving Phoebe such an obvious token. He should have waited, as he'd planned, until after the restaurant was open. Time to make sure too, that he really was cured.

'Kitchens,' Phoebe said, taking his hand again, leading him back down the stairs and then down again, to the basement, where she exclaimed at once, 'This will do nicely.'

Owen, unconvinced, gazed around the empty room.

'Trust me, it's the perfect space,' Phoebe said earnestly. 'You just have to use your imagination.'

'That's your job.' He took out his notebook and pencil. 'You imagine away, and I will make a list.'

'You do like it as much as me, don't you?' she asked, her expression becoming troubled. 'You aren't having second thoughts?'

'Of course not, why would you think that?'

'No reason. You've been a little distracted, that's all.'

Owen had, once again, underestimated his wife's powers of observation. 'I'm not having second thoughts, Phoebe. I've not been sleeping very well, that's all.' Which was true. 'There's so much to think about, if we are to be up and running for the new Season,' he added. Which was also true, but it was not what kept him awake. Or more accurately, prevented him from going back to sleep. Resolutely, he put the latest development in his asylum nightmare to the back of his mind, and smiled down reassuringly at his wife. 'If you are happy with this place, then I am delighted.'

She wrapped her arms around his waist. 'We'll remember this moment in the future, when we are the toast of London, won't we? We'll remember the day when we first walked into this place and we just knew. Don't you think?'

'I don't think, I know we will.'

'Tomorrow is the first day of the new year. It's an omen, isn't it? Everything is falling into place. It's going to be perfect.'

He couldn't bear to disappoint her. He so desperately wanted her to be right. 'Perfect,' Owen said. And kissed her.

'Good morning.' Phoebe forced herself to remain seated as Owen walked into the room. It was better, she had learned these last three weeks, to gauge his mood before rushing into his arms for their first kiss of the day. Today, his smile was forced. Today, he kissed her cheek as he pulled out his chair. So instead of an embrace, the day began with her putting together a small plate of breakfast which she knew, with a sinking heart, that he would only pretend to eat.

She poured him a cup of coffee, trying to assess his mood. There were dark shadows under his eyes, but he hated her to ask him how he had slept and she hated this constant reminder that though they made love as frequently as ever and if anything even more passionately, they had never actually spent the night in the same bed.

'There you are,' she said, putting the plate of food down in front of him.

'What is that?'

'Smoked haddock and a poached egg.'

'No, that noise.'

'I can't hear anything.'

Pushing his chair back, he threw open the door to the breakfast parlour, standing stock still in the doorway for several painful seconds before returning to his seat.

'What did you hear?' Phoebe asked.

'Nothing.' Owen picked up his fork, stared at his plate, then put his fork down again. 'Has the kitchen cat had kittens?'

'No. Did you think you heard…?'

'Nothing!' He sighed heavily, then reached over the table to cover her hand. 'Sorry. I'm a little tired, that's all. This looks lovely. Tell me what your plans are for the day while I eat it.'

She did so, pretending to concentrate on her own breakfast as Owen forced his down with grim determination, finishing with an equally grim smile. 'So, what are your plans?'

They had not changed in the last ten minutes, but he clearly hadn't heard a word she'd said. 'The usual,' Phoebe said brightly. 'Check on progress at the café. Listen to our foreman's reasons for why progress has once again failed to be as expected and as he predicted. Extract yet another promise that he will make up the time.'

Owen threw back the last of his coffee. When he smiled this time, the stranger who had been sitting beside her vanished, and she was once again breakfasting with her husband. 'I'd offer to sort him out for you,' he said, 'but I don't think the threat of a kick up the backside from me will be nearly as effective as one of those little smiles of yours. "Oh, Mr Gilligan, if you can see your way to making up time, it would make me so happy,"' he teased, clasping his hands and assuming a saintly look.

Phoebe giggled. 'I do not sound so pathetic.'

'Tragic, not pathetic. And it works too, so I won't interfere.'

'Wouldn't you like to come with me all the same? The new stoves are arriving.'

'It's a tempting offer, but I've a ton of paperwork to catch up on. I'll see you at dinner.'

As he got to his feet, Phoebe with difficulty refrained from asking him yet again if he was worried about something or if she had offended him, knowing that he would either tell her to stop being foolish, or to have a little faith in herself. And if she asked him if he had a headache, he'd snap at her, though she was sure that his head had been paining him. He was drinking more. Could that be the cause? Could he be drinking because he'd taken on too much? But when she'd asked him that the other day, he'd barked at her. *'I'm not an invalid,'* he'd said.

He leaned down to kiss her cheek, and she turned her face so that their lips met. He stilled and her heart skipped a beat as she silently pleaded with him to kiss her. Which he did, but only fleetingly, patting her shoulder as if she were a child needing reassurance.

It had taken another three weeks for the stoves to be delivered. Finally, they had arrived, and Phoebe had come to inspect them. It was Sunday, so she had the place to herself and was intent on assessing the true state of progress as opposed to the foreman's version of it. Her first impression was that Mr Gilligan had indeed made up for lost time. Stepping inside, she was assailed by the smell of fresh paint. The sconces had been fitted in the freshly varnished wood panelling, the floor had received another coating of wax, and the shelves which would hold glasses, decanters and jugs fixed to the wall where the waiters' station would be. The banquettes had been built and were awaiting the upholsterer.

Upstairs, the decor was also done, the walls painted red, the floor tiled black and white, just like the Procope, and the carpenters had begun work on the seating. But it was in the kitchen where the main transformation was taking place. The two huge stoves were in position waiting to be fitted. The scullery now had sinks, and the building work required for the various pantries, larders and storage cupboards was completed.

Phoebe tested the pump, giving a squeak of delight when water gurgled out of the tap. Perching on a stack of planks, she took off her soaking gloves, intending to check the list in her notebook, but the heart-shaped ring distracted her. She had been so sure it was the prelude to a declaration, but it was almost six weeks since Owen had placed it on her finger, and as her hopes faded, fear took their place.

Frowning down at the ruby-encrusted diamond, she tried to persuade herself that her fears were unfounded, the product of her own insecurities, but her instincts told her otherwise. Christmas day had not been the start of something between them but the beginning of the end. A slow, painful end, but she was coming to believe it was nevertheless an end.

Owen had changed that night. Whether he had had some sort of recurrence of his previous condition was the obvious question, but so far she hadn't had the courage or the conviction to ask. His accident had made him morose and numb. He was neither of those things. They made love ever more frequently. She had only to touch him, hand him his plate at breakfast, press his shoulder when he was poring over papers, for him to pull her into his arms and kiss her—not gentle, teasing kisses, not affectionate kisses, but always kisses with intent. Sometimes she felt as if he were trying to devour her, his need was so insatiable. But then so was her own. She craved him, just as much as he craved her. As if a clock was counting down their time together.

Why would she think that? Owen was not Pascal. Owen admired her. He encouraged her. He understood her so well that he'd been able to make her see herself in a whole new light. He hadn't told her he loved her, but he showed her he did, not only when they made love, but in a hundred different ways. He knew how to make her tea just the way she liked it. He knew that she never added milk save to the first cup. He knew just how to rub her feet without tickling them. She had lost count of the number of excursions they had taken to London's markets, all of them initiated by Owen, and though he claimed still to be a culinary philistine, though she knew he would happily have gone the rest of his life without being able to tell a chanterelle mushroom from a cep, he knew the difference now. He even had a book, *Forest Flora and Fungi*. Recalling the day he'd brought it home, flourishing it under her nose, Phoebe smiled. He had promised to take her foraging for mushrooms, but only when he could be sure that he wouldn't inadvertently poison the pair of them.

He had not told her that he loved her, but he did love her. For all her flaws and her insecurities and her scandalous behaviour and her unconventional ambitions, he loved her. Why would he have given her this ring in the shape of a heart, save as a token of that love? He had married her partly to find a purpose in life, and he had found it. He was no longer a recluse. He had not returned to his old life, but that was because he didn't want his old life. Or so he said. She had given him a purpose. He said that too. But he hadn't told her he loved her. And she loved him so very, very much.

There, it was out in the open, no taking it back now. Not that she wanted to. She loved him. She pressed the diamond to her lips. She loved Owen in a way that made her feelings for Pascal seem utterly trite. She hadn't loved Pascal, she'd loved what he represented, and the life she thought she was leading with him. But Owen—oh, for Owen she would live any kind of life, provided she could be with him. Though the sure and certain knowledge that he would never ask her to lead any kind of life other than the one she wanted, was one of the many reasons she loved him so very much. He had changed her—no, not changed, he'd made her a better version of herself. She hoped that was what she had done for him. She had almost come to believe it.

She must not get things out of proportion. This was an anxious time for both of them—and this place, this café-in-the-making, was the reason for it. That was why he was tired, had the headache, was short-tempered. Owen hadn't told her he loved her simply because the time wasn't right. And she hadn't told him because—because she was just a little bit afraid. Quite a big bit, truth be told. Scared that she might be rejected. That Owen's headaches and tiredness and short temper were caused by his not loving her, and he was feeling guilty about it. He could be regretting the change in their marriage, from platonic to passionate, and because he was such an honourable man, he was trying to steel himself to tell her.

No! Phoebe jumped to her feet, catching the notebook which had been sitting on her lap just before it fell on to the dusty floor. She was making a mountain out of a molehill. Owen loved her. She loved Owen. When the café was launched, the time would be right for them both to admit it. Until then, she would have to guard against these pointless and debilitating and destructive musings, and focus on making a success, first of this place, and then of her marriage.

Chapter Ten

'No need to ask you where you've been,' Owen said. 'Your boots are dusty, there's red paint on your cloak, you have soot on your nose and I'm pretty sure that's a cobweb in your hair.'

'I wouldn't have disturbed you here, only Bremner told me you'd been asking for me. I'll go and get cleaned up. I only wanted to let you know that I was back.'

'Don't go yet. Jasper called while you were out. That's why I've only just finished my exercises. I was catching up on some reading while I cooled down before I take a bath. Come in, Phoebe, stop hovering at the door.'

She came in hesitantly, casting him sidelong glances before seating herself nearest the fire, clearly trying to assess his mood. It pained him to see her do this, for he'd half-convinced himself that she hadn't noticed his erratic moods. Just thinking about his other new symptom made his heart begin to race. So the trick was *not* to dwell on it, Owen told himself, taking a couple of deep breaths.

'There's a new piece in the *Town Crier* this week,' he told Phoebe, handing her the copy of the rag. 'Jasper brought it, though apparently it was Olivia who spotted it in the first place.'

'Miss Braidwood reads this!'

'Everyone reads it, Phoebe. They dread finding their name in it, and are disappointed when they don't.'

'I would be delighted if our name never featured again.'

'Nonsense. Read what it says and tell your clever husband that he was right.'

She smiled at that, no longer wary but simply amused. He could not resist that smile of hers—no one could, male or female—and the most charming thing of all about it was that Phoebe was blissfully unaware of the fact. He'd watched her with the tradesmen at the café. She didn't flirt, she didn't play the simpering miss though he teased her about it. In fact she had no airs and graces at all, she simply told them what she wanted done. And smiled. And then gave him the credit when what she wanted was done in double-quick time!

'Well, what do you think?' he asked, seeing that she had finished reading.

'My husband is a genius. "Mixed dining comes to London for the first time. London is set to loosen its stays and mimic the Continental way, with the opening of Mrs Harrington's exciting new venture. Following their landmark appearance in Crockford's dining room, the Harringtons are enhancing their ground-breaking reputation by opening a restaurant whose exclusivity will be determined by the limited number of dining tables rather than the cost, or the gender of the diners,"' Phoebe read. 'I bet I know where they got that from. I told Mr Gilligan that he and his wife could command a table any time. He said they wouldn't be able to afford it and I said that my intention was to serve a menu that any tradesman could afford.'

'By the sounds of it, your Mr Gilligan will have his dinner paid for him by the *Town Crier*. Jasper has asked me to make sure he has a table at the opening night.'

'Of course. I wonder if he'll bring Miss Braidwood as a guest. He seems to be seeing rather a lot of her.'

Owen shrugged. 'Their mothers are school friends.'

'You don't think that it could be more a case of Jasper and Miss Braidwood becoming friends?'

'They are friends—at least they've known each other all their lives. You know, as children, their mothers visiting each other, that kind of thing.'

'I didn't mean that kind of thing,' Phoebe said drily. 'Never mind.'

'Good grief, you don't mean Jasper and Olivia are becoming an item?'

'Would you be upset?'

'Why on earth would I be upset?'

'No reason,' Phoebe said, in a way that meant there was every reason but she didn't want to tell him.

'You can't possibly imagine that I'd be jealous?'

She shook her head, but she wouldn't look at him, pretending to flick through the scandal sheet.

Appalled that his moods had caused her even a moment's doubt, Owen leaned over to pull the newspaper from her grasp, forcing her to look up. 'I'm married to you,' he said firmly. 'Provided it makes Olivia happy, I don't give a damn who she marries.'

'Do I—are you happy, being married to me, Owen? Only these last few weeks—since the start of this year, you've been—'

'I've been like a bear with a sore head,' he interrupted hastily. 'I know, and I'm sorry for it. After two years of inaction, I may have been overdoing it somewhat.'

It was the only believable lie he could think of, but he regretted it the moment he saw Phoebe's face fall, guessing before she spoke that she was about to blame herself.

'It's my fault,' she said, and Owen groaned inwardly.

'No, it's mine. After two years of wrapping myself in cotton wool, I've allowed my new-found enthusiasm to get the better of me. I've overstretched myself, it's as simple as that.'

'So if you rein back a bit, you'll be perfectly well again, won't you?'

He hated lying to her. But was it really a lie, to say what he fervently hoped? 'It's what I intend to do.'

'In that case I won't burden you by reporting the latest progress.'

'I didn't mean I wanted to return to doing nothing.'

'It's Sunday. It should be a day of rest. I'll go…'

'Stay. Please. We should both have a day of rest, you've been working all hours.'

'I'm enjoying it so much, it doesn't feel like work.'

If nothing else, Owen thought, he had given her this. 'Have you given any thought to a name for your exclusive establishment?'

'What about Café Phoebe? Simple and to the point.'

'And a bit too obvious, if you don't mind me saying.'

'The London Procope Café, then?'

'We could have a little brass plaque put on our up-stairs table: *Here, in this exact seat, in the Procope Café Paris in August 1828, Owen met Phoebe.*'

'The *Town Crier* would love that.'

'I'm rather fond of it myself.'

'Who would have thought that meeting would turn out to be so momentous?'

'I always had a sense that it might. I would have turned up for our planned reunion if it had been humanly possible,' Owen said.

'I went. And I waited. And you didn't come. But eventually I came to you.'

'And that was the second-best day of my life. The best being our wedding day, in case you were wondering, though it's pretty obvious to me.'

'It was the best day of my life too, Owen. I—I've been worried that you were regret—'

'Don't even say it. I haven't. Not once. And I won't. Not ever. I promise.'

She blinked away a tear, and Owen cursed himself again. He would get over what was currently tormenting him. And if he didn't, he'd make a better job of keeping it hidden. 'So, if not Café Phoebe, or the London Procope Café, what is it to be then?'

'I don't know. I want it to mean something, have sig-

nificance. A Leap in the Dark! The Fresh Start Café!
New Beginnings! No, I know what it should be. Small
Steps. Because that's what we've both taken on our
journey to reach this point.'

'I like that,' Owen said touched, 'but shouldn't it
have a French name, since it's a Parisian-style café
and not just a coffee shop?'

'*Petites etapes,*' Phoebe said, screwing up her nose.
'Aux Petites Etapes doesn't really sound right. Oh, I
know! *Pas à pas*—that means quite literally step by
step. One step at a time. Le Pas à Pas! What do you
think? Will people understand what we mean?'

'As long as we do, who cares? It's unusual and there-
fore memorable. I love it!'

'Le Pas à Pas! It's silly, but it feels much more real,
now it has a name. Only a few more weeks and we'll
be ready to open for business. Once the kitchen is complete, I'll be able to start cooking.'

She was glowing again, his lovely Phoebe. He'd forgotten himself, talking to her. Looking at her, he was
filled with hope. He could conquer this thing that was
trying to take possession of him. He'd done it before.
He could do it again, with Phoebe by his side. 'We'll
toast the name tonight, before dinner.'

'I look forward to it.' She got to her feet, picking up
her paint-stained cloak. 'Le Pas à Pas is going to need a
thorough clean-up before any cooking gets done there.
I'd better go and get changed out of these things now.
And you will be wanting to bathe after your exertions
on the apparatus.'

'Stay and bathe with me,' he said impulsively.

'What!'

'I have a bathing chamber containing a bath, with hot running water. A very large bath.'

'Owen, you're surely not suggesting we share it?'

'It would save water. And it would save your maid all the effort of carrying your bath water up the stairs.'

'So it would be economical and thoughtful?'

'It would be both economical and thoughtful,' he agreed. A thick curl of her glorious hair had escaped its pins. Owen tucked it behind her ear, letting his fingers trail down the column of her neck, feathering over the skin at her nape, something that always made her shiver with pleasure. 'But I think it might also be fun.'

'Fun?' She smiled at him. *That* smile. She hadn't smiled that particular smile for weeks. 'What kind of fun?'

'Whatever kind we like.' He kissed her gently, at the same time cupping her breast, his thumb slowly circling her nipple. He felt it bud, through her corsets and her gown. He kissed her again, feeling himself stiffen.

'Owen, I have never—I can't imagine…'

'Phoebe, I have never and I can't imagine, but I'd like to try, wouldn't you?'

'Yes.' She placed her hand over his heart, a new and strange little habit of hers. Then she smiled up at him again. 'Oh, yes.'

Owen was different. No, not different. He wasn't different, he was the man she had fallen in love with, the smiling, teasing, irresistible Owen. Not that she'd been able to resist the darker version of him either, but Phoebe was immensely relieved to see that the real one was still there. She followed him, intrigued and excited, across the small hallway to his bedchamber. It was a very masculine room, the furniture dark, solid, the bed much lower to the ground than hers and without posts or curtains. There were books and papers everywhere, but nothing else by way of decoration, no pictures on the walls, only a set of silver-backed brushes on the dressing table.

He locked the door behind them. Needlessly, she knew. None of the servants came to these rooms unless summoned. Casting her cloak on to the bed, he led her towards another door. A huge bath dominated the square room, set into the corner and taking up most of one wall. The bath was enclosed in white-painted wood. Fascinated, she watched as Owen fitted a stopper to what was presumably the draining hole, and turned on the brass tap. Air clanked out, followed by a thin stream of piping hot water, which became a gush when he made some complicated adjustments.

'Don't imagine that it's always this co-operative,' he said, smiling at her astonished expression. 'Half of the time, the water is no more than tepid.'

'It's wonderful. I've never seen anything like it.'

A porcelain sink was built into a marble-topped table which held Owen's shaving soap, razor and strop, and this too had brass taps attached to it. A mirror hung on this wall, already beginning to mist over due to the steam rising from the bath water. The floor of the bathing chamber was covered with large black and white tiles, smaller tiles in the same monochrome design covering the walls. A selection of towels were laid out ready on a wooden rack. There was a dish of soaps set on a wash stand beside the bath, a large loofah, a scrubbing brush and several sponges sat in another dish.

'Are we really going to get into that together?' Phoebe asked, unable to decide whether the prospect was enticing or simply odd.

'I won't drown you, if that's what you're worried about.'

She giggled. 'It does look almost big enough to swim in. Not that I can swim.'

'I can. I used to swim around the Serpentine, in Hyde Park in the summer. In the early hours, obviously,' Owen added, 'lest my semi-naked state cause offence. Fortunately there's no one here for us to offend, so we can bathe completely naked. If you want to, that is? I don't want you to do anything...'

'I want to,' she said, because she didn't really care whether they were in a bed or a bath or the back of a carriage, for that matter, as long as they were together. 'I really do want to,' she said, reaching up to kiss him.

It was a long, slow kiss, the kind of kiss that had been missing for weeks from their lovemaking. This kiss went on and on, breaking only when Owen cursed, and hurriedly switched off the tap to prevent the bath from overflowing. Then the kiss started again, and it carried on as they undressed each other, dropping their clothes heedlessly on to the damp tiles. She watched her own pleasure reflected in his eyes as he touched her, caressed her, stroked her, and she echoed every one of his movements. When they were naked, he helped her step into the bath, joining her with a fluidity that still astonished her, when she looked at the scarring at his hip.

He took one of the sponges from the dish and soaped it. And then he soaped her, slow sweeping strokes, first her back, down to her bottom, then her front, using the sponge to tease her nipples, until she was only just clinging to the edge of self-control. She lost it very quickly when he gently rubbed between her legs, the soft soapy sponge, the warm water, and Owen, watching her so intently, wrenching her climax from her. She clung to him, panting, conscious first of his erection pressing into her belly, then of the delicious sliding sensation of soapy skin on skin. Taking the sponge from him, she set out to tease him as he had done her, watching him, the sinful smile fading to sensual pleasure, his eyes darkening, his breath becoming shallow.

'Phoebe, you have to stop or I'll…'

'I want you to.'

'Inside you,' he said. 'Please, I want to be inside you.'

She dropped the sponge, bracing herself against the wall tiles. They felt cool on her hot skin. He entered her slowly, pushing higher inch by inch, his eyes on hers, and she instinctively angled herself to take him higher. And then he thrust. Slowly, so she wouldn't over-balance. Slowly, because it was what they both wanted. She had never felt so close to him before as this, their bodies slick and sliding, their eyes locked. It seemed to go on for ever. She never wanted it to end. But then she tipped over to the point where she was desperate for it to end, to rush to the ending, and he sensed it, thrusting harder, faster, until she cried out, and he cried out only seconds later, pulling himself free of her, but holding her, their mouths clinging in one last utterly sated panting kiss.

Phoebe woke with a start, completely disoriented. She was in Owen's room, lying on the very edge of the bed, with her husband splayed out beside her naked, the sheets a tangle around his legs. She shivered and was about to claim a share of the bedcoverings back when Owen muttered. He was dreaming. Tentatively, she put a hand on his shoulder to try to wake him, but he shuddered, cowering away from her.

Phoebe edged out of the bed, putting on his dressing gown. His breathing was fast and shallow, as if he had been running hard. There was a sudden stillness to him, then his arms shot out in front of him and he strained, as if he was trying to push away some invisible obstacle.

'Owen.'

She touched his shoulder. He heaved again, then with a cry sat up, his eyes wide open, a blank look of abject horror on his face. 'I can't stop them.'

'What can't you stop?' she whispered.

'If I could get the door open, they would stop crying. I can't get the door open. I can't get them out. I can't get them out.'

He dropped his head on to his hands and broke into wild sobs. Appalled and helpless, Phoebe tried to wrap her arms around him, but as soon as she touched him he pushed her away. 'What are you doing here?'

'Owen, I...'

'Get out.'

'Owen, you were dreaming, I...'

'Get out! Get out! Why can't you leave me alone.'

March 1831

She had put it off long enough. It was almost a month since she had witnessed Owen's nightmare, a month in which his behaviour had become more and more erratic, his moods more and more volatile. Phoebe was treading on eggshells all of the time, never knowing from one morning to the next how he would be, or if he would even remember how he had been the day before.

There were periods of calm, when she persuaded herself that he was improving, but they were getting further and further apart. She couldn't pretend any more, but as she waited, sipping her tea in the breakfast parlour, she would have given almost anything to persuade herself that she could.

It was no use. She had to find the strength to confront him, no matter how painful, because they were already perilously close to the point of no return, a living nightmare where they both pretended that Owen was behaving perfectly normally, and that his 'perfectly normal' behaviour wasn't breaking her heart.

She had tried, a week ago, to talk to him, tried to tell him how upsetting she found his behaviour, but it had only made him worse—not angry, but stricken. Since then, he had retreated into himself, though his efforts to control his emotions at times made him shake visibly. She felt so utterly helpless, watching him suffering, so determined to deny that he was suffering. He had gone from being a man who felt nothing, to someone so full of conflicting emotions he could barely contain them all.

She had shied away from forcing a confrontation because she didn't want to face the truth. If he no longer loved her—but she must not think that. She had to be strong. She had to be positive. If he loved her, then they could conquer whatever ailed him. She loved him so much, she would do anything she could to save their marriage. If he loved her.

'I'm sorry, I've kept you waiting.'

Phoebe forced a smile. 'I was up early,' she said, though Owen was almost an hour later than usual. 'Shall I pour your coffee?'

'Please.'

He sat down without touching her, and her heart sank as he forced a smile.

'Shall I get you some breakfast?'

'I'll get my own. I don't want to keep you back. I know you're eager to try out your new kitchen for the first time.'

'I'm not in such a hurry that I can't stay and have breakfast with my husband.'

'I'm not hungry, Phoebe.'

'Just an egg and some of this—'

'I said I'm not hungry!' Owen swore viciously. 'Look, I'm sorry, but despite what you believe, food is not the cure for all ills. Forgive me, I didn't sleep well. I have the headache.'

She could walk away. He clearly wanted to be left alone. Perhaps he did have a headache. But what if she was the cause? 'Owen.' She angled herself in her chair to reach for his hand. 'Owen, won't you please tell me what it is that ails you?'

'I have the headache, I've just told you that.'

'Is it—didn't you sleep?'

He edged his hand away from her clasp. 'I told you that too.'

'Did you—did you have a nightmare again?'

He stilled. 'What makes you think that?'

'I saw you—don't you remember?' But judging from his blank look, he did not. Though she felt as if she was standing on the edge of an abyss, Phoebe forced herself to continue. 'Last month—after we— it was the last time we made love. In your bathing room—we fell asleep in your bedchamber.' He paled, but said nothing. 'I woke—you woke me up, shouting,' Phoebe said. 'Something about crying. You wanted me to make them stop. I thought…'

He pushed his chair back, stumbling to his feet. 'I don't want to talk about it.'

'But you do remember?' Phoebe persisted. 'The dream, I mean? And when you woke up, sending me away?'

'No. Yes. I don't want to talk about it, Phoebe.'

'Owen, we have to talk about it. Something is wrong, and I can't help you if I don't know what it is.'

'You can't help me.'

He threw himself across the room to look out of the window. She could see his shoulders rising and falling in his effort to control himself. She knew he wanted her to leave, but she had come this far, she couldn't back down now. 'Owen, whatever it is, can't you please tell me?'

'I don't know what the hell it is! I just need you to leave me alone.'

She went to him, wrapping her arms around his waist. 'My love, please won't you tell me? There's nothing you can say that...'

'Don't, Phoebe.' His voice broke. He turned around, pulling her into his arms. 'I beg you, don't say any more. There is nothing to be said. Nothing to be done.'

'But, Owen...'

'No!' Tears tracked down his cheeks. 'I'm sorry,' he said, 'I'm so sorry, but it's simply not possible.'

'What? Owen, please...'

'I can't be with you like this. You have to understand...'

'But I want...'

'Phoebe,' he said, 'sometimes we simply can't have what we want.'

It was the gentleness in his tone that told her all hope was lost. The way he put her from him, so carefully, as if he was afraid she would break. And indeed, her heart was breaking, had been breaking a little bit every day, for the worse he had become, the more desperately she loved him. But it was abundantly clear now that he didn't love her. And it was destroying him, his not loving her. Though she couldn't imagine life without him, for even this Owen was better than no Owen at all, she was going to have to let him go, for his sake.

She ought to have known it wouldn't last. She *had* known. She recalled thinking here in this very room, that she wasn't up to his weight. Why would a man like Owen want to be tied to a woman like her, whose only talent was cooking! But he had tied himself to her, and he was far too honourable a man to admit that he regretted it. Even when he so obviously did.

'Go to the café,' Owen said. 'Go and cook. You're so close to that pot of gold at the end of the rainbow, Phoebe, don't let me ruin it for you.'

She wanted to tell him she didn't give a damn about the café, not compared to him. But the café was what had brought them together. The café had given him a purpose. If she told him she didn't care, she'd only be adding to his guilt.

'Will you still come—tonight, I mean?' she asked, knowing she sounded pitiful, unable to stop herself. It was to be a private dinner for herself and Owen. He had suggested it weeks ago. It was supposed to be a final treat before they both threw themselves headlong into the launch of the café, which was planned for next month. A celebratory meal to toast their future success. Now it was going to be a wake to mark the death of their marriage.

'Of course,' Owen said eventually, forcing another of his rigid smiles. 'The first meal cooked in the kitchen at Le Pas à Pas. Of course I'll come.' He kissed the air a few inches from her lips. 'Go on. I'll see you there later.'

Owen spent the day trying to forget what had happened this morning, trying to eradicate the memory of his brave Phoebe's misguided and doomed attempt to help him. He knew he was beyond help. It was simply a question of holding himself together as best he could until the launch of Le Pas à Pas was complete, and Phoebe's future assured. By the time he arrived several hours later he had himself under control. Or as near as he ever came to that, these days, veering between the feeling that he was no longer part of this world, and the feeling that he could not bear to be part of it. Guilt for some undisclosed crime weighed him down. The wailing was never far away. But the vivid fragments of memory, the latest development in his illness, were the worst. Sudden blazes of light like the limelight they used in the theatre, and then the images would start to flash through his mind. Different each time, nothing seemingly connected, like pieces of a puzzle. They came to him in the night and in the day. He had tried to clutch at the images, to make sense of them, it was like trying to grasp smoke. There was only his palpitating heart, his gasping breath, and the tears streaming down his face. He would not allow them to happen tonight. He would not allow anything to interfere with tonight, for Phoebe's sake.

The café was virtually complete. The tables and chairs were set up, the red-velvet curtains hung in the

window, the banquettes upholstered. Phoebe had lit all
the sconces and the central chandeliers for his arrival,
and laid some of the tables, presumably to give him
a sense of how it would look when they were open,
simple settings with white crockery, plain glasses and
one set of cutlery.

'Well, what do you think?' she asked, smiling nervously as she locked the door behind him.

He took his time answering, knowing how much it
would matter to her, wanting to do at least this small
thing to please her. He was determined to do everything in his power to make tonight a success, but he
was already so terrified of betraying himself, it was
like a self-fulfilling prophecy.

'Owen?'

He started, swore viciously, then was immediately
awash with guilt as he saw Phoebe flinch. 'It's lovely,'
he said, the first anodyne expression he could think
of. Take deep breaths! Turning away from her sad,
tragic gaze, he forced himself to look. 'Cosy, welcoming. The dark panelling you chose was perfect, it will
feel warm, even in the depths of winter. And the banquettes. Very Parisian. It's the sort of place where you
could easily picture your builder and his wife at that
table, Wellington and a few of his cronies there, perhaps your sister and her husband, the Earl of Fearnoch,
tête-à-tête there.'

He was wittering, but Phoebe was either fooled or
pretending to be fooled. 'And upstairs?' she asked,
leading the way.

'The Procope,' Owen said, a lump rising in his throat as he stood at the top of the stairs.

'And here,' Phoebe said, taking his hand and urging him gently towards the only table which had been set, where a jug of wine stood waiting with two glasses, 'where Owen met Phoebe. There is no plaque, but I didn't think we'd need reminding.'

The lighting up here was dim. Owen swiped at his eyes while Phoebe sat down. 'I won't ever forget,' he said, taking his chair, pouring them both a glass of wine, spilling some of it on to the crisp starched linen which his wife, his precious lovely beloved wife, pretended not to notice. 'To brief encounters that change lives,' he said, raising his glass. 'And to you, Phoebe. For being unique.'

'To Owen, who has made all of this possible. The best and only husband,' she said, touching his glass, her voice husky.

'You've done this, Phoebe.'

'I couldn't have even begun without you.' She clutched at his hand. 'You know that, don't you? In a few weeks, Le Pas à Pas will open, my dream come true, thanks to you. I won't ever forget that.' She jumped to her feet. 'Now, if you will excuse me, tonight I am the chef and the *sous-chef* and the waitress all in one. Sit here, enjoy this lovely wine which, I hope you don't mind, I purloined from your cellar, for our own supply has not been delivered yet.'

'What is mine is yours. Purloin the whole lot if you want.'

'Don't be silly.' She leaned over, as if she would kiss

him, then changed her mind. 'The first course will be served in fifteen minutes.'

She bustled away, disappearing down the stairs, her boots clattering on the polished wood. Then he heard her descend the next flight to the kitchen. Alone, Owen felt bereft. He poured himself another glass of wine, though he knew he'd drunk the first far too quickly.

I won't ever forget that.

Her words sounded portentous. He knew he was hurting her. He was shielding her from his torment for her own good as well as his. But to be confronted with the evidence, to see her face, to witness her trying so hard to act as if he was behaving rationally, as if everything between them was normal—it was agony. She knew. She knew their marriage was over in all but name. That's what she'd been telling him.

He downed the rest of his wine and pushed back his chair. If it must be over, let him please, please, please find the strength to get through tonight. He'd join her in the kitchen, watch her at the stove. It was something he'd done many times before at home, something he'd come to enjoy, seeing her skills with the knife, watching her face as she tasted something, that little frown she gave when the seasoning wasn't quite right, the small smile of satisfaction when it was.

Making his way down the second flight of stairs, he was assailed with a medley of delicious smells. Phoebe, a huge apron enveloping her, was at the stove, using a wire brush on one of the burners on one of the two cast-iron, gas-fuelled stoves. Owen had been wary of this very recent innovation from the start, but she insisted they would prove much more efficient.

'What's wrong with it?' he asked.

'The pipe is blocked, I think. There, that's it done.'

She put the brush down and lit the supply. A ball of flame exploded out of the pipe with a whoosh and a searing blast of heat. Owen was dimly aware of Phoebe leaping out of the way. He could hear her saying something. He could see she was unscathed. But he wasn't. In that split second everything fell into place. Everything that had happened. Everything. The full horror of it all.

'No!' he cried out, tearing at his hair, squeezing his eyes tight shut. 'Dear God, no!' But it wouldn't go away. He dropped to his knees, covering his face with his hands. He couldn't breathe, his heart was pounding so fast.

'Owen.'

'Phoebe.' She was kneeling on the floor beside him. 'Phoebe.' He clutched at her shoulders, begging her silently to save him, but the images were playing out again in his head, the whole dreadful scene from start to finish.

He struggled to his feet.

'Where are you going?'

He made for the stairs.

'Owen, you are not fit…'

'You're right. I'm not fit.'

'Owen!'

He had to get away. He had to get out of this place, into the open air and he had to run, as fast as he could, run for his life. And never look back.

He heard her shouting his name from the door of the café, but he was already off. Not running the way he once had, he would never be able to do that again. But running, through the searing pain that now tore at his hip, he ran out into the fading light and into the streets of London, where he prayed he might lose himself. For ever.

Chapter Eleven

Phoebe waited for more than two hours at the café, at a loss to know what else to do, but Owen didn't return. Stripping the table upstairs, putting what was salvageable of the dinner, which she hadn't even finished cooking, away in the larder, she extinguished all the lights and locked up. She had sent the carriage home, expecting Owen to escort her back. Thinking to pick up a hackney nearby, she made her way out into the dark London streets, clutching her cloak around her, the hood covering her face. There were no hackney cabs at the stop. She knew her way to Covent Garden from here, but at this time of night, she didn't think being on her own in Covent Garden was a good idea. So she walked, trying to keep a steady pace, resisting the urge to look over her shoulder, far more concerned about Owen than herself.

The front door of the town house was not locked. A sconce burned in the hall, but the servants had all retired as usual. Heart thumping, the acrid taste of fear in her mouth, Phoebe lit a candle and made for the door to Owen's apartments. Thick silence greeted her. The main room was in complete darkness. Holding her candle high, she could see that the gymnastic equipment had been recently used, the polished bars covered in the chalk Owen rubbed into his hands to give him grip, now that he no longer wore gloves. But the room was desolate. So too was his study. And his bedchamber.

She perched on the edge of his bed, wondering if she dared wait here for him. Where was he? Though her instincts were to search the streets for him, she knew that was about the most foolish and dangerous thing she could do. If anything happened to her, Owen would add that to the burden of guilt that was already crushing him. She could have a note sent round to Jasper. Jasper knew Owen's old haunts, but Owen didn't look like a man in search of company. He had looked like a man in search of oblivion.

Where was he? He wouldn't have harmed himself, surely? He must know how worried she would be. But when he'd run off, he was beyond reason.

Where *was* he? Phoebe, who never prayed, sent up a silent prayer to keep him safe. And then another. If he had not returned by daylight, she'd have no option but to send for Jasper. Her isolation struck her for the first time since she'd left Paris. She didn't have any friends. She had kept herself apart from her family. Without Owen…

She was going to have to live the rest of her life without Owen. Dear heavens though, it was one thing to live apart from him, but for him not to be in this world—no. She would not allow herself to go down that path. She must not linger here either, waiting for him, ready to confront him in whatever state he came home, when he would prefer her not to see him in his distressed state. And she mustn't cry either. There was no point in feeling sorry for herself. Whatever help Owen needed, whatever he wanted or didn't want from her, she had to be prepared to do it.

Phoebe was asleep, still fully dressed save for her boots, on top of the bedcovers, when Owen finally returned, but the creaking of her bedchamber door woke her. She leapt up, saw him, and threw herself at him.

'You're back.' She pressed herself against him as if she was trying to burrow into his body. 'I've been so worried.'

He wrapped his arms around her, resting his chin on her tousled hair, closing his eyes for just a moment to drink in the familiar scent of her, to enjoy the familiar shape of her. And then he let her go.

She stepped away from him, her eyes huge, her face pale and ghostly, determinedly set. 'Before you say anything, I want to tell you that I understand. I won't make a fuss.'

'Phoebe, I don't think you can possibly understand.'

'You're such an honourable man, and I—I've made it pretty obvious what I feel for you, but you can't make yourself feel something you don't, Owen. You can't pretend that you—that you still care for me. I think I've known for a while that you don't, but I didn't want to face it. Today has proved to me that I can't hide my head in the sand any longer. I have to set you free. I'm so sorry I didn't act sooner. I was—well, it doesn't matter what I was. You're free now.'

Her words made him want to sob. They made him want to pull her back into his arms and tell her, finally, once and for all how much he loved her. 'You think that I don't love you,' he said, feeling as if his heart was tearing apart inside his chest.

'I know you don't. Perhaps you thought you did for a while, perhaps you were trying to persuade yourself that you did…'

'Phoebe! Oh, Phoebe, why on earth would I do that?'

'Because you knew it was what I wanted. When you gave me this.' She thrust out her left hand. 'When you gave me this ring, I thought that—I hoped that it was because—that you were giving me your heart. For the next few days, after Christmas, I kept hoping that you'd say the words I was so sure you were about to say before you fainted.'

'I fainted,' he said fatalistically, as his fears were confirmed.

'You simply couldn't bring yourself to lie.'

'I don't remember.' But he did, now. He remembered being so full of joy, so sure that the time was right to tell her. And then the joy turning to blackness.

Phoebe took the ring from her finger and held it out. 'You can have it back, Owen. You're free.'

He hesitated. Wouldn't it be easier for both of them, to let her believe he didn't love her? He could make up some story about tonight's debacle, some sanitised version of the truth, spare himself the agony of recounting the harsh reality. And leave Phoebe imagining she wasn't good enough for him, when it was he who was so unworthy of her.

'No,' Owen said, to himself and to Phoebe. 'You've got it all wrong.' His hip was burning from the amount of walking he'd done. And running. All to no avail. He couldn't run from himself. He waved vaguely at the hearth where the fire smouldered and the chair Phoebe liked to sit in to read was pulled close. 'Sit there. I'll…'

He staggered, lurching like a drunk towards the hearth. 'I'll sit on a cushion.'

'You'll sit there. I'll sit on a cushion.' Phoebe pushed him on to the chair. He was too tired to resist. 'Shall I order some coffee?' she asked, stacking several pillows on the floor. 'Brandy?' she queried, when he shook his head.

'Nothing. Just sit and hear me out, please.'

To his utter relief she did, sensing that he didn't want her to touch him, tucking her legs under her out of reach of his. 'Tonight, in the kitchen, when the stove exploded, I finally remembered,' he began, launching quickly into the story before he could have second thoughts. 'My accident, I mean, everything about it.' He curled his fingers around the arms of the chair to stop himself shaking. 'It's been coming back to me in fits and starts but until tonight, I couldn't—it made no sense.'

'When did you start remembering?'

'After Christmas.'

'After you fainted, when you gave me the ring.'

'Yes. Not straight after. It started with random episodes—that's what I've been calling them, episodes.'

'When you lose your temper?'

'Or pass out. I've lost consciousness a few times.'

'Oh, Owen! I had no idea. I'm so sorry…'

He held up his hand to silence her. 'You had no idea because I didn't want you to know. It was bad enough, pushing you away, seeing you so hurt when my temper snapped, seeing you trying so hard not to upset me. And besides, I didn't remember after—when I fainted, I mean. If I'm honest—and after today, I have no option but to be honest—I was trying to fool myself.'

'Oh, Owen, so was I. If only I'd spoken sooner, perhaps…'

'No,' he said firmly. 'You have to stop thinking like that. This is not your fault. It's mine. Mine completely. I thought for a while I was going mad. The nightmares, and the memories, they jump out at me when I least expect it. I feel possessed. By grief. And by guilt. The guilt has been the worst. I didn't understand until tonight. And now…'

He began to shake again, so hard that he had to dig his heels into the rug, clench his belly tight, just to hold himself steady on the chair. Deep breaths, remember. Stay still and take deep breaths.

Finally it passed. Phoebe hadn't moved towards him, though he could see she was braced to leap into action at the least sign from him. 'Thank you,' Owen said gruffly. Another deep breath, and he was as ready as he'd ever be. Get it over with, he told himself. As quickly as possible.

'There was a fire,' he said. 'You already know that. In Marseilles. In the Panier district, which is the oldest part of the city. The buildings there are tall, tightly packed, tiny windows, narrow alleyways, steep staircases, divided up into homes for heaven knows how many families. I was walking there. Just walking. Thinking. Then I saw the flames. The whole building was in flames, and there was a chain of people passing buckets of water which snaked around the side of the building. They were tackling it from the back. But it was futile. Anyone could see the fire had taken too strong a hold.'

He spoke quickly, urgently, desperate to get the words out, to reach the end. 'I went to help regardless. I was about to join the chain when I saw her. A screaming woman, trying to get into the building. Another woman—her sister, a friend, a neighbour, it doesn't matter—was trying to pull her back. But the first woman was frantic, and all the men were distracted, concentrating on trying to contain the fire. She got free, and she launched herself into the doorway and into the stairwell. I didn't think. I simply acted instinctively. I went in after her.'

'Owen! Oh, dear heavens, Owen.'

'I got to her halfway up the first flight of stairs.'

'You saved her!'

'She was trying to get to her baby. The child was trapped in their second-floor apartment, left behind in the panic and confusion.'

Phoebe had her hand over her mouth. Her eyes were wide with horror. 'You told her you would rescue it.'

'I couldn't let *her* attempt to.'

'No. No, you wouldn't. Of course you wouldn't.'

'The baby—I still don't know if it was a boy or a girl—the baby was in the room at the front of the second floor. I wrapped my kerchief around my face. My one solitary act of self-preservation. I'm surprised I did that much. I got as far as the door. I could hear it crying. The fire had taken hold of the rafters. The ceiling was about to come down, there was plaster crumbling, smoke, flames—but I could hear the baby crying.'

'The crying. "Make it stop", that's what you said in your nightmare. "Make it stop." Was that what you were dreaming?'

'Not exactly. In my dream there wasn't a fire. It was a crèche. A hospital. I couldn't get out, in my dream. What really happened is that I couldn't get in. I could hear voices behind me, pleading with me to turn back. But I was so sure I could reach the child.'

The shaking possessed him again, but he ignored it. 'I thought myself invincible, you see. I could run faster than anyone. I could perform acrobatics to a standard that would allow me to make a living on stage if I had chosen to. I had never been bested in the boxing ring or any sort of race or any sort of competition. I'd never even suffered more than the most superficial injury despite my many hair-raising escapades. It wasn't that I was unaware of the risks, more that I thought myself impervious.' He held up his hands. 'I wasn't. The lintel from the doorframe fell on me, trapping me under it when I was feet away from reaching the child.'

* * *

Owen was trembling violently. Phoebe watched him, numb with shock, his suffering unimaginable, unable to offer any comfort save to listen, to hear him out until the tragic end.

'I could hear the poor little mite crying while I was lying there under the beam,' he continued, 'half in and half out of the apartment. I could hear it crying and I could see the fire creeping towards me.' Tears were streaming down his face. His eyes were wide open, but he wasn't seeing her, he was lost in the unfolding horror. 'Before, before I could remember, before we were married, I had a nightmare. My reaching dream, I'd call it. I'd wake up knowing something terrible had happened, that it was my fault, but I didn't know what or why. Now I know and I'll never be able to forget it.

'When it stopped, when the crying stopped, it was worse. All I could hear then was the fire roaring, see it licking its way towards me. I couldn't move. I didn't feel anything, I didn't know that my hip had been crushed, all I wanted—all I wanted was to crawl forward, even though I knew it was too late.' Owen lifted his head to look straight at her. 'You have no idea how that felt. Knowing how close I was and that I'd never get any closer.'

'Owen...'

He shook his head violently to silence her. 'They pulled me out just in time. Two men took their lives in their hands to rescue me. They should have left me.'

This was too much for her. Phoebe closed the space between them, kneeling in front of him to wrap her arms around him. He let her hold him, but she had the impression it was for her benefit, not his. He had stopped shaking, stopped sobbing, sat rigid in her arms, silent. 'You tried, Owen,' she said. 'That's so much more than most would have done.'

'I failed. That's all that matters.'

'No! You spared that poor woman the agony of heaven knows what.'

'I delayed her. Time was of the essence. If I'd let her go, she might have…'

'You can't think like that. She might well have perished herself, as well as her child. You probably saved her life.'

He disengaged himself from her hold, getting up from the chair. 'We'll never know. All I know is that I failed to save the baby and my recklessness cost me dearly. Don't tell me what I can and can't think, Phoebe, you weren't there.'

'No, I wasn't. I'm sorry, I…'

'I told you so that you'd understand—not what happened then but the impact it's having on me now.'

She stared up at him, dazed. 'But now you have remembered…'

'It makes no difference.' He helped her to her feet, putting his arms around her, but the gesture was wooden, forced. 'Now I have remembered, it will never leave me. What you have seen these last few weeks is who I am now.' He took a step back from her, holding her at arm's reach. 'I've had time to think tonight, you haven't, but when you have, you'll see.'

'See what?'

'I thought I was getting better.'

'You were,' she said fiercely.

'No, Phoebe. I was getting worse.' He was focusing on her now, and the expression on his face filled her with a sense of dread for what she saw there was a firm resolve. 'I wanted to believe I was getting better. I wanted so very much to believe that, because I love you.'

'Oh, Owen.'

'No, don't cry. Please, don't cry. You have to be brave, Phoebe.'

'I didn't understand. I thought you didn't love me. But if you do...'

'I do. Please don't look like that.' He shuddered, pulling her close once more, holding her tightly, smoothing her hair. 'I love you with all my heart, but it's no good, my darling.'

'You got better once, you can get better again.'

'No. I didn't get better, that's what you don't understand. I blocked it all out for a while, that's all. But I think that loving you, being so happy, I think it—' He broke off, swearing. 'This is so difficult to say. I got by before by blocking out the truth, by somehow hiding it from myself because I wasn't able to deal with it. Then you came along, and I fell in love with you, and thanks to you, thanks to the hope you gave me, the reason for living you gave me, I grew stronger. Strong enough to let my defences down. Strong enough to remember.'

'But then if it hadn't been for me, you wouldn't have remembered and...'

'No,' he said firmly, giving her a tiny shake. 'What

I'm trying to say is that you helped me. The dam had to be breached, Phoebe, sooner or later. Tonight it burst completely, and the genie is well and truly out of the bottle. I can't put it back. I don't want to. In a way, it's a relief, don't you see, understanding the grief and the guilt, knowing why I've had all those other symptoms— the tears, the fainting, the nightmares, the temper. At least I know I'm not mad, even though I also know I'm no fit husband for you.'

There was a sense of inevitability in his words, a horrible logic, but she didn't want to hear it. 'You're the only husband I want.'

'Please don't say that,' he said, looking quite wretched. 'Please, I beg you, try to understand. It's going to be hard enough coming to terms with what I've done, trying to find a way to live with myself, without inflicting all my suffering on you.'

'I don't care, Owen, I'd gladly suffer with you.'

'I know, but I couldn't bear that.' He smoothed her hair back from her face. 'Look at you, so lovely and so brave and so defiant. Look at how much you've changed these last five months.'

'Because of you.'

'No. I gave you the means, that's all.'

'You didn't just give me money, Owen. You've made me believe in myself.'

'Then that's one good thing to come of our marriage. I want you to succeed, Phoebe. Do you remember, back in October when you first came to me, I told you that if you succeeded, if I could help you realise your dream, then it would make up for having lost mine?' He let her go. 'I need you to see it through for both our sakes. I deserve to suffer, that's the price I have to pay for having failed. But I cannot—I will not—make you suffer too.'

'You don't *deserve* to suffer. You tried everything humanly possible...'

'And still failed. As I said, I've had time to think about this, you have not. I told you because I didn't want you to think I didn't love you. But it's not good enough. I don't deserve you. You said you were willing to release me...'

'Because I thought you didn't love me, but you do, and I love you—I'm sorry, I know you don't want me to say it, but I love you so much.'

But he simply shook his head, his lips set. 'I will do my best to support you until the launch, but after that— it's over. I will have my lawyer sort out an agreement.'

'I don't want an agreement! I want you, Owen.'

'When you've had time to think it over, to reflect, you'll realise that is impossible. We would both be miserable.' His mouth quivered. His shoulders shook. 'Let me go, Phoebe. If you love me that much, do as I ask. I beg you.'

There was nothing more to be said. She loved him too much to care about her own suffering. 'You don't need to beg,' Phoebe said. 'You're free.'

April 1831

The special celebration menu for the grand opening of Le Pas à Pas was displayed at the entrance on a lectern, with a copy on printed cards placed on each of the tables. The crisp table linen gleamed white in the soft candlelight. The glasses had been polished to a spotless sparkle. Accompanied by her head waiter, Phoebe made a final tour of both the upstairs and the downstairs dining rooms before returning to the kitchens for a last-minute check that all was ready for their first proper service. They had practised endlessly, she and her small team, over the last few weeks, so there was no reason for her to be anxious, but she was sick with nerves. Not that anyone would know, from her demeanour. One of the many skills she had perfected since she had agreed to put an end to their marriage, was the ability to hide her feelings. She hoped that in time practice would make perfect to the point where she fooled herself, but she was a very long way from reaching that goal.

She had been unable to prevent herself from begging Owen to change his mind, trying to persuade him that time would heal his illness. To no avail. Very quickly she realised that the only outcome of her outburst was to increase his suffering. And his suffering continued. He grew hollow-eyed, thinner and paler as the weeks passed. Dinner became an endurance test, with her talking bright inanities, and Owen sitting silently, closed in on himself. He drank too much. He ate too little. She came upon him once, glassy-eyed, muttering, wandering in the garden in the early hours of the morning, when she had been unable to sleep, and smelled opium on his breath. She recognised the drug at once, for there had been a kitchen porter in La

Grande Taverne, a veteran of Napoleon's army, who took it on the days, he used to say, when the past overwhelmed him. It was a turning point for her, seeing that her presence had reduced Owen to seeking oblivion in such a manner. She extracted a promise from him that he wouldn't use it again, and in return, she promised not to try to change his mind again. So tonight, she would launch her restaurant. And tomorrow, she and her husband would part for ever.

She left the heat of the kitchen to snatch a brief moment of solitude in her tiny office, with the door ajar so that she would be able to hear the head waiter greet the first of their invited guests. Owen wouldn't be here for the launch. He didn't want to risk suffering an episode in front of her diners. She understood, but understanding wasn't the same as accepting. This should have been their night. Le Pas à Pas wouldn't exist if it wasn't for him. The guest list had been compiled by him, a carefully constructed mixture of friends with influence and friends who enjoyed food, all friends he had long ago abandoned and had no plans to see again either, cultivated and cajoled into sampling a taste of Paris in London for her sake. Jasper would be here with Miss Braidwood, to whom he had recently become betrothed, and so too would the reporter from the *Town Crier*, for it was better to keep your enemies close, Owen had said. But the guest list was not confined to the upper classes, for Phoebe was determined that Le Pas à Pas would not be the province of the rich, but open to all. So Mr Gilligan, the foreman, and his wife would have pride of place. She wouldn't be meeting any of the diners, distinguished or otherwise, for she would be confining herself to the kitchens. If any of them actually showed up, that is.

Above her, she heard the door open and her head waiter's dulcet tones wishing the new arrivals a very good evening. It was starting. Hearing the sound of footsteps on the stairs, thinking it would be one of the waiting staff, she was about to return to the kitchen when a voice halted her in her tracks.

'Phoebe.'

'Owen!'

He was in evening dress, freshly shaved, and trying to smile. 'Your first night. I couldn't let you endure it on your own.'

'Owen!' Without thinking, she threw her arms around his neck. 'Thank you.'

'You'll have London at your feet, trust me.' He held her briefly, all too briefly, before disentangling himself. 'I know you wanted to wait until you'd made a success of this place before telling them, but I also know how much their support means to you, so I took the liberty of writing to your sisters,' he said, handing her two letters. 'It was presumptuous of me, I have no right—but I hope I did the right thing.'

Both letters were short, loving and full of exclamations marks. Eloise and Estelle were unreservedly delighted and proud. Neither thought she needed luck, but they wished it anyway, and hoped that they'd be privileged enough to dine at what was certain to be the top restaurant in London very soon.

Tears smarted in Phoebe's eyes. 'Oh, Owen, what a

lovely surprise. Thank you. For these. For all this. And most especially for our time together.' She caught his hand, rubbing her cheek against it, the longing to tell him how much she loved him almost overwhelming. But it would hurt him, and he'd been so brave coming here, and she loved him so very much. 'Thank you,' she said instead, turning his hand around to kiss his palm.

The café door opened again, and this time there was the unmistakable clump of several pairs of feet. 'Your first diners,' Owen said. 'Go on, get into that kitchen and work your magic.'

'You're not staying?'

'Le Pas à Pas is your creation. Your very own establishment, with your very own menus, your own dishes. A place where men and women can dine together, as they can in Paris. Just imagine!'

'Did I say that?'

'Your very own words. I've never forgotten them. Enjoy it.'

'Won't you stay, just for a short while?'

His smile faded. 'Not a good idea. You want the *Town Crier* to report on your delicious food, not your lunatic husband.'

The front door opened. Owen heard Phoebe call goodnight to the coachman, heard the clatter of hooves as the town coach headed round to the mews, and the door closed. He had been in two minds all night as to whether to wait up for her, but aside from the sick, jittery feeling in his gut which was his personal countdown to his wife's departure, he could detect no signs of any imminent episode. Not that there were always signs.

He opened the parlour door just as she was putting her foot on the first stair, and called her name. 'If you're not too tired, I'm desperate to hear about your triumphant debut.'

'You seem very confident that it was a triumph.'

'And?'

She edged past him to her usual sofa. 'I am pleased to tell you that your confidence was not misplaced.'

'I knew it!' He resisted the urge to hug her, and resisted the desire to share the sofa with her as he used to do. Phoebe, in the process of taking off her boots, noticed his hesitation before he took the chair, but made no comment. There should be champagne to celebrate a night like this, but champagne was too reminiscent of the halcyon days of their marriage. Besides, he was trying to cut down on his drinking. 'Tell me all about it.'

'Everyone turned up. Every table was filled. The food went out on time. The plates came back empty,' she answered, sounding deflated.

'You're tired. And I've no right—I should have been there. I'm sorry.'

'No, Owen, I'm sorry. I'm not tired, I'm weary, that's all. My head hurts and my feet hurt.' She tucked them up under her.

Owen moved to the other end of the sofa. 'Let me see if I can help.'

She stretched out cautiously, putting her stockinged feet in his lap, but as soon as he began to knead her toes he felt her relax.

'That is so good. Those stone floors are the one thing I'd change about Le Pas à Pas. That, and the staircase from the kitchens. Our waiters had a couple of narrow escapes with the soup tureens.'

'How did they cope? You were worried about one of them.'

'John. I spoke to him yesterday. He was fine. The terrine was very popular. And the confit egg with the smoked fish—that went down very well too. I'm thinking I might try it with asparagus when it comes into season next month, and a little toast.'

'How was the venison received?'

'I think they might have loved it almost as much as you do, judging by the empty plates.'

'Not possible.' Owen kissed the tip of her big toe, the usual sign that she should swap feet. Phoebe's eyes flew open, but he simply continued with the massage, pretending the intimacy hadn't happened. 'Did you speak to Jasper? What did you think of Olivia?'

'I didn't venture out of the kitchens. There were any number of compliments sent down, but I—well, you know I've always believed my food should speak for itself.'

And he'd been adamant that it would be good publicity if people could see the beauty who presided over the pots, but he had no right to say so now. Le Pas à Pas was in Phoebe's very capable hands.

'I know you don't agree,' she said, reading his thoughts.

'I can be wrong. It's not unknown.'

'But you don't think you're wrong about us?'

There was a break in her voice that pierced his heart. 'Nor do you, Phoebe.'

'No, I don't. I don't want you to suffer any more than you have to.'

'I've decided to go abroad. It will be easier for both of us, to resist the temptation to see one another, and I think it will be good for me, to travel.'

'To experience what you missed out on, two years ago?'

'Not exactly. A little. To try to discover if a change of scene will change how I feel, too.'

'You mean you think you might get better? That distance will—'

'I don't know, Phoebe,' Owen interrupted hastily. 'I dare not hope, but I have to act. I won't let myself become what I was when you walked back into my life. I won't undo all the good you've done for me.'

'I could come with you?' But before he could answer, Phoebe was already shaking her head. 'You don't want me to. You don't need to say it.'

'It's not that I don't want you to, it's that I need to do this myself.'

'Will you come back, Owen?'

He wanted to say yes, more than anything else in the world. 'Eventually. But I don't want you to wait. Don't wait. Don't hope. Don't do what I did, and live in limbo. It's such a cliché, but it's true, my darling. Life's too short. Promise me you'll make the most of it.'

Her eyes were bright with tears, but she held them back. 'You ask so much of me.'

'Never anything I know you can't do.'

She closed her eyes, laying her head back. He had ceased kneading, but now she wiggled her toes. 'Don't stop.'

He closed his eyes too, working his way up to her calf, giving himself over to the familiar sensation of her silk stocking sliding over her skin, his fingers working into the muscle until the tension was relieved, and then the sweeping, soothing strokes she liked when he finished. He changed his attention to the other leg, and she rested her foot at the top of his thigh. He started kneading, and she began to stroke his groin with her toe.

Owen groaned. His hands slid up her leg, to the top of her thigh, to cup the heat between her legs. He ached for her. He already missed her, as if a part of him had been severed. If they could just make love one last time—he was trying to close the thought down when she reached for him.

'One last time, Owen. So we can remember it this way.'

It was impossible to resist. He pulled her on to his lap and their lips met in the sweetest, most delicious of bittersweet kisses. She murmured his name over and over as they kissed, as they stroked each other in that familiar way, and he said her name too, over and over, because he couldn't tell her that he loved her, but he could demonstrate that he did. When he entered her, tears leaked from her eyes and he licked them away, and then the sheer delight of being inside her, of having her arms wrapped around him, their partially clad bodies entwined, took over, and the knowledge that it would be the last time, which should have made their lovemaking slow, instead made it frantic. It was over far too soon.

'Phoebe.'

She shook her head, putting her finger over his mouth. 'Don't say it. Don't look for me in the morning.' She kissed him lingeringly one last time. She quickly gathered up her clothes. Then she was gone.

He sat up all night, wide awake in his work room, counting down the hours until she left. She had taken a suite at a hotel in the short term. Now that he had decided to go abroad, there was no reason for her to leave the town house, save that he didn't want her to wait for him. And she had promised him not to.

Was he truly without hope? It was after six and the servants were stirring when Owen finally accepted that he was not. Hopelessness would keep him here, retiring back into solitude, giving up on the world, making a recluse of him again. It was hope that was taking him out into the world, though he dreaded all that entailed, for he would be exposed, raw, and able to rely on no one but himself. He hoped that somewhere in his travels he would find a way to live with himself. Because then, and only then, could he hope that he'd be able to find a way also to live with Phoebe.

Chapter Twelve

One year later, April 1832

Owen stood at the foot of the steps outside Fearnoch House, the London residence of Phoebe's sister, Eloise. Phoebe had moved there shortly after he had left England, according to his lawyer, who also acted for her in matters of business. The man had been astounded when Owen arrived at his office an hour ago demanding to know the whereabouts of his own wife. He'd have been even more astounded if he'd known that the only thing that prevented Owen tracking him down as soon as he arrived back in London last night, was the fact that he had no idea where his lawyer lived.

He had not slept in the hotel where he'd been forced to stay, his own house being locked up, but he had bathed and changed. Now here he stood on the steps outside a London town house he'd never been in before, his stomach churning with nerves. Almost exactly a year and a half ago, Phoebe had stood outside his town house, uncertain of her own reception. Only now did he realise just how brave she had been, simply to knock on the door and beg an audience. How close he'd come to refusing her. Please to all the gods in heaven, she did not refuse him now.

She would be perfectly with her rights to do so. He had asked her not to wait. He had refused to give her any hope. His lawyer had told him enough to assure him that she had made a resounding success of Le Pas à Pas, enough to fill Owen's heart with pride. And now with doubt. Would she want to make room in her life for him? He thought she'd understood his reasons for leaving, but a year was a very long time. What if Phoebe had found someone else to fill the hole he'd torn in her heart?

The very notion of it made him feel dizzy. He told himself staunchly that he would endure such a blow with dignity, that he would understand, that he would be happy that she was happy. That's what he told himself. He didn't believe a word of it as he rang the bell, for the one solid truth he had known all along was that he loved her, and that he wanted to spend the rest of his life loving her. 'Let her see me. Let her listen. Let her give me a chance,' is what he said to himself. 'Let her still love me.'

Phoebe picked up the copy of the *Town Crier*, which had been sent to her courtesy of the publication's editor.

The first anniversary of Le Pas à Pas, our favourite London eatery, was celebrated last night with the usual muted panache we have come to associate with Mrs Harrington, the chef patroness.

Regular diners will be relieved to know that the renowned venison ragout still features on the new menu, though it is now served with an Italian concoction called macaroni served with cheese, rather than the potato gratin that is a particular favourite of Yours Truly.

Is this innovation, which Mrs Harrington credits to Signora Sarti, her Italian sous-chef, an improvement? It is certainly different!

In other words, he hated it, Phoebe thought, setting the rag aside. Which was a pity, because Gina was an excellent chef who deserved a reward for her loyalty. Having her name in print and her first dish on the menu was only the start. Phoebe intended to introduce several more in the coming months, and to delegate more too, with her plans to open a sister café to Le Pas à Pas well in train. There was another pasta dish Gina made, with asparagus and fresh peas, that would eat beautifully paired with pork.

It was Sunday, her day off from the stoves, and a lovely spring day, perfect for a walk in the park. She checked her little enamel watch. Work first. She'd had no idea there was so much paperwork involved in renting and fitting out a new premises. Owen had taken care of that side of the business the first time around. The familiar pain made her heart clench, but she was used to it now. She had promised him not to hope. She had promised him not to wait for him, to make the most of her life. She had been true to both vows, but she loved him every bit as much now as she had done the day she had forced herself to walk away from him.

The distant clang of the doorbell a few moments later made her frown. It was only just after eight in the morning. 'You know I don't like to be disturbed on a Sunday,' she said, frowning at Wiggins, Eloise's butler.

'Indeed, Mrs Harrington, but I think you may wish to make an exception for this caller.'

'I hope you will,' came a voice from behind the butler's back.

'Owen?' The room began to spin. Phoebe clutched the edge of the dining table.

'May I come in?'

'Owen? What are you doing here? You're supposed to be abroad.'

'I came back.'

Wiggins had tactfully disappeared, but Owen was still hovering at the door. He was tanned. His hair had been bleached gold. He looked older, but younger. Different, but the same. And just looking at him, she felt the same too—the tug of attraction, the ache of unspoken love in her heart. Which must remain unspoken, she cautioned herself. It had been a year. She would embarrass the pair of them by throwing herself at a husband who had come seeking a formal separation.

'Come in. Would you like some coffee?'

'No, thank you.' He stepped warily into the room, as if unsure of his welcome. 'I'm sorry to surprise you like this. I only got back last night. I'd have called then, if I'd known where you were.'

'You look very well, Owen.'

'Do I? I feel—I wasn't sure you'd see me. You look lovely, as ever.'

'I've been working hard. The café…'

'Phoebe, I don't care about the café. No, that's not true, of course I care, but not right at this moment.' Owen finally crossed the room to her side. 'I've had nearly a month to rehearse this, the whole journey home, and now I can't think of a thing to say, except that I love you with all my heart and I've missed you with all my heart, and I'm not cured and I may never be, but I don't want to spend another minute of my life without you.'

She stared at him, open mouthed, her heart leaping ahead of her brain, fluttering wildly with joy while she tried to assimilate what he had said.

Owen made to take her hand then changed his mind. 'I know this is a shock. When I left England, I had no idea how long I would be gone. I was lost, I was scared, I didn't know who I was. I thought the worst thing that could happen to me had happened that night, when I remembered my accident, but I knew even then that the worst thing that could happen was losing you. I know I told you not to hope, but I hoped, I never stopped hoping, that I'd find a way to come back to you.'

'Why didn't you tell me?'

'Because I've lived a life in limbo, Phoebe. Before you came into my life, that's what I was doing. Yes, I was working away on my investments, but that was never anything other than a way to kill time. You gave me a purpose, but I've never forgotten what it was like *not* to have one—or rather, what it was like when my only purpose was waiting for something to happen—

waiting to remember, is what I was doing. Instead, you happened. And you changed everything for me.'

She wanted so much to have his arms around her, but she wanted even more to hear him out, because the hope that she hadn't ever fully repressed either, was blooming so quickly inside her. 'Go on,' Phoebe said, indicating a chair.

'Are you sure? I have no right to expect you even to listen to me.'

'Owen, almost exactly eighteen months ago, I called on you. You saw no one, but you saw me, and you listened to me. At the very least, don't you think I owe you this?'

'Is that the only reason? If you would rather not hear what I have to say, if you've made a new life for yourself…'

'Would you leave?'

He laughed shortly. 'I asked myself the same question while I was on the doorstep a few moments ago. I told myself I would, but I know I wouldn't. I love you with all my heart, Phoebe. That's the one constant that's been with me for the last year, and I'm going to do my damnedest to persuade you to give me another chance.' He swallowed, took a visible breath. 'But you found the strength to let me go when I needed you to. Hear me out, that's all I ask. If you decide, after that, that I won't make you happy then I promise I'll find the strength to leave you.'

Once again, the urge to throw herself into his arms and tell him that nothing mattered save that he was here was overpowering. She loved him, she didn't doubt that he loved her, but the last year had proved to her that he'd been right to go, that if he'd stayed, they would have torn each other apart. So Phoebe didn't throw herself into Owen's arms, instead she ordered him a pot of coffee and herself a fresh pot of tea. And when she had poured their drinks, she nodded to him, permitting herself a very small smile. 'I'm listening.'

Owen took a sip of coffee, trying to collect his thoughts. Phoebe had changed. She was still his beautiful, desirable wife, but there was an inner strength about her that hadn't been there before. The old Phoebe would have either thrown herself into his arms or shown him the door. This Phoebe was determined to make a more rational decision, and by the sun and moon and stars, he admired her for it. He loved her so much, but he had a lot to prove. He finished his coffee in one gulp. He was determined to do just that.

'You know why I left,' he said. 'First of all, I thought if I got away from England, it might help my condition, but it didn't. I still had episodes, and I had the additional misery of missing you. Which I came to realise very quickly, was making me much more miserable than the episodes.'

'But you didn't come back, because you were determined not to make me miserable too?'

'That was a big part of it, you know that, but the other part of it was…'

'You needed to be alone.'

'Yes,' Owen said gratefully. 'I knew you understood that.'

'I did, eventually. It hurt, Owen, because at first I thought you didn't want my help. Then I realised that I simply couldn't help.' Phoebe smiled sadly. 'And that hurt too, but in a different way.'

'I didn't know who I was any more, but I knew I wasn't the person I thought I was. When you're alone and no one knows you and no one knows where you are, it does clear your mind. Remembering what happened the day of the fire—' Owen broke off, shuddering. 'The horror and the tragedy of that won't change. But I did start to question how I viewed my part in it.'

'You saw that it wasn't your fault that the poor little baby died?'

He sighed heavily. 'I truly don't think anyone could have saved him.'

'Him?'

'It was a little boy. I know, because I went to Marseille and I tracked down his mother.'

'You did!' Phoebe caught his hand, lifting it to her cheek, pressing a kiss to his palm, a familiar, tender little gesture that was one of the things he'd missed the most about her. 'That was very brave.'

'I almost didn't go through with it,' he admitted. 'But I'm glad I did. I wasn't even sure Madame Le-Brun would want to meet with me. It was her husband, in fact, who came to the café where I was waiting. I thought he was going to attack me, but he took my hand and he...' Tears sprang unbidden. But he was used to tears now, and no longer ashamed of them, so he didn't apologise. 'He embraced me and said he had waited a long time to thank me for saving his wife.'

Phoebe smudged the tear which tracked down his cheek with her thumb. 'I always knew you were a hero.'

'I'm not. I was a fool. I don't think anyone could have saved that child. I may have saved Madame Le-Brun, but I risked my own life doing so. It was mine to risk, but the two men who saved me—their lives were not mine to risk. I was lucky, very lucky, that they were so brave.'

'Did you meet them too, in Marseille?'

'I did. And invested a little money in their fishing boats—I now know a great deal more than I will ever need to about the fish of the Mediterranean. Perhaps even more than you.'

'You're a good man, Owen Harrington. You knew they wouldn't accept money.'

'It's a good investment. More importantly, meeting them, all of them, returning to Marseille as I did, it made me finally see things differently.'

Owen poured himself another cup of coffee, forcing himself not to rush. Phoebe, his lovely, patient, strong Phoebe, was such a distracting presence, but he had to get this right. 'I saw that I'd been looking at my accident the wrong way round, you see. I thought it had deprived me of my second chance. Before you came along, I was wallowing in self-pity, I was miserable.'

'In limbo.'

'Exactly. You dragged me out of the pit of despair. No, don't tell me that I did it myself. I did, in the practical sense, but if it hadn't been for you, for wanting to be better for you, then I wouldn't have done anything. Then I fell in love with you. I was happy, I thought I couldn't be happier, but I was wrong about that. It was still there, the guilt and the grief, waiting until I was well enough to deal with it. You made me well enough.'

'And have you dealt with it?'

'I'm not better,' Owen said. 'I won't lie to you, Phoebe. I may never completely recover. I still have episodes. But I understand them. There's less of them, much less. And because I understand what happened, I can bear them.' He took a last sip of coffee. 'I hope that they are symptoms of progress. Like lancing a boil, the poison has to come out, do you see?'

'I think so.'

'But I could be wrong, Phoebe. I know—don't ask me how, I simply do—that they won't get worse, but I may never be clear of them. I'm asking a lot of you. I'm asking you to take what I say on trust until you have the evidence that I'm right. If that means you want me to wait until you are reassured, then I'll wait for however long it takes. But I can promise you two things, hand on heart. The first is that I won't be going away again. And the second is that I love you. Always.'

He dropped to his knees beside her, finally allowing himself to take her hand. 'That fire didn't deprive me of a second chance, it gave me one. I could have died. I didn't. I have a life to live, and I want to live it with you. Every single second of it. I have made my peace with the tragedy that I was part of, but I want more than that. I want happiness. And the only true happiness for me is with you. But if you don't feel the same…'

'I do.' Phoebe fell on to the floor beside him and

threw her arms around him. 'I love you so much, Owen, so very much.'

'It won't be plain sailing.'

She laughed. 'No, it certainly won't. For a start I'm about to open a second café.'

'Why stop at a second! Why stop at London! You are magnificent. I love you so much.'

'And I love you. I haven't stopped loving you but, Owen—are you absolutely sure?'

'Completely and utterly sure. The whole time I was away, I carried you here.' He touched his heart. 'This is yours, if you want it, my darling. Will you take it?'

He drew the ring from the inner pocket of his waist-coat and held it out to her.

'I left that behind,' Phoebe said.

'And I took it with me. Will you take it?'

'For ever.'

He put the ring on her wedding finger above the wedding band. He kissed the ring. Then he turned her hand over to kiss her palm. Then finally, he pulled her into his arms. Their lips met. Their kiss was awkward, tentative at first, but it deepened quickly and they clung together, kissing until they had to stop for breath.

'Are you really here?' Phoebe asked, touching his tanned face, the rough stubble on his chin.

'For ever.' He kissed her again, and knew without a shadow of a doubt that he had finally found the place where he belonged. 'For ever,' he repeated, then he kissed her again. 'I promise.'

* * * * *

*If you enjoyed this story
be sure to read the first book in the
Penniless Brides of Convenience miniseries*
The Earl's Countess of Convenience

*And whilst you're waiting for the next book
check out Marguerite Kaye's
Matches Made in Scandal miniseries*

From Governess to Countess
From Courtesan to Convenient Wife
His Rags-to-Riches Contessa
A Scandalous Winter Wedding

Historical Note

The Procope, where Phoebe and Owen first meet, is one of Paris's oldest cafés. Situated in St Germain on the Left Bank, it's a fabulously atmospheric place where everyone who was anyone—or more accurately every *man*, in the early days—met to talk, drink and eat. Benjamin Franklin, whose 'I eat to live, not live to eat' quote I purloined, was one of many famous Enlightenment regulars there.

Antoine Beauvilliers was a pioneering chef whose restaurant, La Grande Taverne de Londres, which I've borrowed for Pascal—who *isn't* real—was located in the Palais Royale. His style of cooking went out of fashion in the eighteen-twenties, when his restaurant closed, but his recipe book, *L'Art du Cuisinier*, became a French classic and was translated into English around about the time that Phoebe's sister Eloise bought her a copy as a present.

Two other chefs feature in this book. Monsieur Salois, whose recommendation got Phoebe the job with Pascal, is an invention of my friend and fellow writer

Bronwyn Scott, who introduced him in the first of our joint Brockmore stories, *Scandal at the Midsummer Ball*. Eustache Ude, on the other hand, was very real. I couldn't do justice to the man who really did make a theatre of cooking and dining, threatening customers with a cleaver who failed to appreciate his food as much as he thought they should, so I most reluctantly kept him off the page. Imagine a combination of Gordon Ramsay and Marco Pierre White, multiply it by ten, and you'll be close.

Ude was employed at Crockford's club for the phenomenal salary of one thousand, two hundred pounds a year, when a top-class chef would normally be paid about fifty pounds. I first read about him in Nicholas Foulkes's excellent *Gentlemen and Blackguards*, when I was researching gambling clubs for another book, *Rumours that Ruined a Lady*, where another of my heroines breached that all-male bastion for a very different reason.

Alexis Soyer, another renowned chef who worked at the Reform Club and who doesn't appear in this book, was responsible for making gas stoves popular. This was about ten years after Phoebe's time, but the stoves were patented in 1828, so my heroine is in this, as in so many things, an innovator.

I read about the tradition of running footmen in Karl Shaw's *Mad, Bad and Dangerous to Know*. The Fourth Duke of Marlborough really did race his footman from Brighton to London, the servant on foot, the Duke in a carriage and four. And the poor servant really did come close to winning before expiring.

Regular readers will know that I'm fond of re-using my characters. Jean-Luc Bauduin, Duc de Montendre, who supplies Owen's wine, is the hero of *From Courtesan to Convenient Wife*. The Flying Vengarovs make a cameo appearance in that same book, but they originated in *Scandal at the Midsummer Ball*, along with Monsieur Salois.

Rules restaurant is still going strong to this day. Serving pretty much the same fayre too, so you can enjoy a taste—quite literally—of Regency life if you go there.

And last but certainly not least, I'd like to say a huge *merci* to my lovely French neighbour Hélène, for helping me to name Phoebe's restaurant. *C'est parfait!*